FIREWING

Kenneth Oppel

Hodder
Children's
Books

A division of Hachette Children's Books

A Catalogue record for this book is available from
the British Library

ISBN-13: 978 0 340 91796 1

Typeset by Avon Dataset Ltd, Bidford-on-Avon, Warwickshire

Printed in Great Britain by
Clays Ltd, St Ives plc

The paper and board used in this paperback by
Hodder Children's Books are natural recyclable products
made from wood grown in sustainable forests.
The manufacturing processes conform to the
environmental regulations of the country of origin.

Hodder Children's Books
A division of Hachette Children's Books
338 Euston Road
London NW1 3BH

For my three muses:
Philippa, Sophia and Nathaniel

PART ONE

GRIFFIN

It had rained during the day and now, under a three-quarter moon, the forest was silver with mist. Things always smelled better after the rain, Griffin thought as he sailed through the humid summer air. From the forest floor rose the loamy fragrance of the soil, and the rich stink of rotting leaves and animal droppings. The resinous tang of pitch wafted up from the firs and pines as he grazed their topmost boughs.

A new smell suddenly twined its way through all the others – one that didn't belong to the forest. Griffin felt his fur spike up. Nostrils flared, he sniffed again, but the smell was gone now, evaporated. Maybe just the dying traces of a faraway skunk. It was pungent but . . . somehow hotter and more dangerous. He stored the smell away in his memory so he could describe it to his mother back at Tree Haven at sunrise. Then he angled his wings and set course for his favourite hunting ground.

The giant sugar maple occupied a small rise on the valley floor, and its canopy spread wider and higher than any tree nearby. After Tree Haven, this was Griffin's favourite place in the forest. He loved the way the moonlight washed the leaves a translucent silver, and when a strong wind blew, the leaves looked and sounded like a thousand bats, all taking flight at once.

Circling low overhead, Griffin cast out sound and the returning echoes painted the tree's canopy in his head with more detail than his eyes could ever achieve. He saw each branch and twig, each bud, even the veins of the leaves.

And, of course, the caterpillars.

They were everywhere. The maple, like plenty of other trees in the forest, was infested. Gypsy moth caterpillars, that's what they were, and they'd already stripped the tree of half its leaves. Every night for the past week Griffin had come here and fed, but the next night, it seemed there were just as many caterpillars as before. Just look at them! There must be hundreds of them! His stomach made a hungry popping sound.

He trimmed his wings, and tipped himself into a steep dive, spraying sound ahead of him. The first caterpillar he scooped right off a twig with his tail, flicked it into his wing and then straight into his open mouth. Ducking under a branch, he wheeled and snapped up two more dangling from threads. Curled on a nearby leaf was yet another caterpillar. Griffin streaked in close and with a swat of his wingtip bounced it right off the leaf, gobbling it in mid-air. They were a bit fuzzy going down, and had a slightly sour aftertaste, but you got used to them.

"Doesn't it get boring?"

Griffin looked up to see Luna, one of the other Silverwing newborns, swooping down alongside him.

"They're not so bad," he said.

The truth was, it made him feel useful. The caterpillars were voracious eaters, and his mother said they could gobble up half the forest if they weren't controlled. The thought had filled Griffin with panic. He didn't want to see his forest stripped bare, especially not his favourite sugar maple. A horrible vision had played itself before his eyes. Without any trees the soil would wash away and without soil nothing could grow and there'd be nowhere to roost and nothing to eat and all the Silverwings would probably starve to death or have to leave and find a new home!

So Griffin ate caterpillars.

And every time he swallowed, he was helping stave off total catastrophe. That's how he saw it anyway. But he didn't tell Luna this. She already thought he was crazy.

A nice fat tiger moth fluttered past, no more than a few wingbeats from his nose. Griffin let it go.

"You don't want that?" Luna asked in amazement.

"It's all yours," he told her, and she was already gone, plunging down into the trees after her prey.

Griffin watched, admiring the expert way she swerved and tilted through the tight tangle of branches. He'd tried to catch tiger moths once or twice, but he was no good at it. They sprayed out their own sounds and scrambled up your echo vision, so it seemed like there were a whole bunch of moths, all darting in different directions, and you could end up chasing a mirage and getting *splatted* against a tree. Wasn't worth it. Also, he wasn't the greatest flier. His wings were too long, and he felt clumsy in the forest, couldn't manoeuvre fast enough. And there were beasts down on the forest floor: bear and lynx and fox. He preferred to stay up high, where he could see what was what. He didn't mind eating mosquitoes and midges and caterpillars.

The *boring* bugs, Luna would say. Griffin looked and caught one last glimpse of her before she disappeared into the foliage. He hoped she'd come back afterwards.

Below him, a maple leaf glittered with dew and he carefully checked out the nearby branches before roosting. Further down was a nest of warblers, but they were all asleep, and anyway, birds didn't attack bats any more, so it seemed safe enough. He braked, spun upside down, and gripped the branch with his rear claws. Thirstily he lapped up the bright beads of water on the leaf.

"Why don't you just drink from the creek?" Luna asked as she flipped down beside him.

"You never know what's under the surface," Griffin replied darkly.

"Sure you do. Fish!"

"Right. But from what I've heard, some of them can get pretty big, and what's to stop them from just leaping—"

"*Leaping?*"

"Leaping, yes, right up out of the water and taking us down with them."

"A *fish*?"

"Well, a big one, why not?"

"Fish don't eat bats, Griffin."

"So they say."

"It must be tiring, being you," Luna said, but she was chuckling. Griffin had noticed this about her. She *liked* hearing him worry. She seemed to think it was funny. That must be why she hung around with him sometimes. It certainly wasn't because he was brave or adventurous like her. But she still seemed to consider him a friend, and he was intensely grateful. She had a hundred friends, though, and it was rare he had her all to himself. Normally there were half a dozen other newborns flapping all around her.

Luna's tall ears pricked up, and with a nimble forward lunge, she snatched an earwig off the twig above her.

Griffin cocked his head, studying the insect as she cracked its shell.

"You know," he said thoughtfully, "when you look at most of what we eat, it's not altogether appetizing. If you really stopped and *looked* at it, I mean. All those legs going, and the antenna tickling your throat on the way down . . ."

"Stop it," Luna said, giggling. "You're gonna make me choke."

With a flurry of wings, three other newborns came in to land, calling out hellos. There was Skye and Rowan and Falstaff, who was so stuffed that the branch bowed over and bounced up and down a few times after he roosted. Griffin knew they'd come because of Luna. If it had been just him hanging here alone, forget it. It wasn't that they disliked him – he doubted they even thought about him enough for that. They just didn't see the *point* of him.

Boring, Griffin thought. That's what he was to them. And they were right. There was nothing special about him. He wasn't a particularly good flier or hunter. He hardly ever joined in with their games. And why should he? They only ever seemed to want to do ridiculously dangerous things. Now the little hairballs were shoving their way in and all chittering to Luna at once – Skye about the moose she'd seen earlier in the night, Rowan about how fast he'd flown with the wind at his tail, and Falstaff about all the bugs he'd eaten, what kind, where he'd found them, and what they each tasted like. Luna seemed to be able to listen to everyone, and talk back, all at the same time.

When he was off by himself, Griffin hardly ever felt lonely. But now, amongst the other newborns, he did. He wasn't much like them. He didn't even *look* like them. Sometimes he thought he was barely a Silverwing at all.

Their fur was sleek and black, shot through with silver. He had stupid fur. Most of it was black, but all across his back and chest were jagged bands of dazzling bright hair. The bright stuff came from his mother, a Brightwing. His father was a Silverwing, but it seemed he took after his mother more. Like her, his fur grew longer and thicker than the Silverwings, and his ears were a different shape, round, small and close to the head. His wings were longer and narrower than the other newborns, but that wasn't really a consolation, because they still felt too big on him, made his flight all loose and jerky in the forest.

"Hey, Luna," Rowan whispered. "Look."

Griffin looked too and saw, roosting several trees away, an owl perched on a thick branch. Even though they were at peace with the owls now, the sight of them still sent a tremor of fear through Griffin. They were just so big, easily four times his size, with sharp talons and a hooked beak that was designed for slashing and crushing its prey. Griffin's mother still said they should avoid the owls. They were at peace, but that didn't automatically make them friends. All the mothers said so. Now the owl's huge head swivelled, and fixed them with its moonlike eyes.

"You want to play?" Skye asked Luna.

The owl game was Luna's invention, and it terrified Griffin. The idea was to see who could roost closest to an owl on the same branch, and stay there for ten whole seconds before taking flight. Several weeks ago, Luna came within two wingspans. No one had done better than that.

"Sure," said Luna. "I'm always ready."

"Me too," said Rowan.

"I'm in," Skye said.

"All right," Falstaff agreed, "but only if it doesn't take too long. I'm starving."

Griffin was hoping they'd just forget he was there, but Luna turned to him. "Griffin?"

He knew she meant it kindly; she wasn't trying to make fun of him, was just wanting to include him. He shook his head and caught Skye flashing Rowan a smirk that said, So what else is new?

"Well, that old owl looks pretty fat and dopey," said Luna jauntily. "I figure I can do one wingspan. What d'you think, Griff. Can I do it?"

"I'm sure you can," he said, "but—"

"But what?" she asked. Griffin could hear the other newborns sigh impatiently, but there was definitely a gleeful spark in Luna's eyes. "What's the *worst* that can happen?" she wanted to know.

Griffin almost smiled. *This*, he was good at. "The worst? Well, the way I see it, you fly in, you roost, you're only one wingbeat away. And maybe this owl hates bats, or maybe he's in a really bad mood tonight, or maybe he's so hungry he figures no one'll notice one less Silverwing newborn in the forest. You're so close he can just snatch you up before you even blink. And in one swallow you're down his throat and then you get hacked back up as a little packet of bones and teeth."

"That's *disgusting!*" said Skye.

"Yeah, well, that's how they eat," Griffin said, with considerable satisfaction. "And until a couple of years ago, that's what they did to bats."

Luna nodded, grinning. "Yep, that's pretty much the worst that could happen. Wish me luck!"

She flexed her knees and prepared to take flight, but to Griffin's huge relief, the owl beat her to it. Spreading its huge wings, it lifted from the branch, and swept silently off into the forest.

Rowan looked accusingly at Griffin. Sourly he said, "You talk too much."

"Griffin's good at talking," Luna told the other newborns. "He's hilarious." Skye, Rowan and Falstaff all looked at Griffin, puzzled, considering this for a second. Then they turned back to Luna and started talking about what they should do next. Griffin gave her a grateful smile.

Suddenly, his nostrils twitched. "Do you smell that?" he asked.

Only Luna heard him. "What?"

"I smelled it earlier..." Sniffing, Griffin swooped off the branch, trying to follow the scent. It wasn't hard. The smell was stronger now, definitely not skunk. He climbed above the tree line, and was pleased to see Luna flying after him. Climbing higher still, he turned his face into the wind, breathed again and then saw it.

Far away to the west, a line of dark vapour slithered above the forest canopy, dispersing as the wind blew it towards him. Griffin's eyes traced it back down to the treetops, then into the forest. Through the sifting fog, past a stand of pines, he saw a bright flickering.

"Fire," he whispered to Luna. He'd never seen it before, but he'd heard plenty about it. Fire didn't come out of nowhere. It was made. By Humans. By lightning. But there hadn't been any lightning for weeks.

By this time, the other three newborns were flapping towards them, Falstaff lumbering through the air, complaining about how hungry he was. Then they all saw the light dancing deep in the forest.

"Maybe it's one of those secret places where the owls keep their fire," Skye said to Luna.

Long ago, as they all knew, owls had stolen fire

from the Humans, and kept it burning in hidden nests throughout the northern forests.

"Not very secret if we can all see it," Luna said.

"Must be Humans," said Griffin, and felt a shudder even as he uttered the word.

"Let's go and take a look," said Luna.

"Yeah," agreed Skye. "Come on."

"Shouldn't we tell our mothers first?" Griffin said worriedly. Humans were dangerous. Everyone knew about the things they'd done to bats.

"We'll tell them when we get back," said Luna. "It's just a few hundred wingbeats." Impatiently this time, she said, "Come *on*, Griffin."

"Oh, let him stay if he wants," said Rowan, and the words sounded more dismissive than considerate. As usual he was ruining their fun. Griffin turned east to pick out the summit of Tree Haven. It already looked a long way away, and they would be going even further now.

He wished he were more like Luna. Fearless. He tried sometimes to be brave, but it never worked. He just started thinking and then worrying, and all he could ever see was how things might, could, *would* go terribly wrong. His mother shouldn't have named him Griffin. When he'd asked what it meant, she said it was a creature who was half eagle, half lion – both brave, powerful creatures. It seemed like a cruel joke now, he thought glumly. Should've been called Weed, or Twig, or something.

He glanced at Luna. She looked genuinely disappointed. He gritted his teeth. He'd already said no once tonight. He couldn't face two humiliations in a row.

"All right," he said. "Just a peek, though, OK?"

* * *

Below in the clearing, a small fire burned within a ring of stones. Beside it sat two enormous creatures Griffin knew must be Humans. His mother had described them to him, but he'd never seen them himself before now. Luna made for a high branch overlooking the clearing and Griffin followed, roosting with the others.

"So that's what they look like," said Luna.

Griffin knew they shouldn't be here. His mother had always told him that if he ever saw Humans in the forest, he should tell someone right away. He fought the trembling in his knees as he watched the Humans move things in and out of the fire. Strangely, it was the fire he found most fascinating, and his eyes kept getting drawn back to it, watching its hypnotic upward lapping, little bits of itself shooting off like comets.

"They don't look so scary," said Rowan.

"We should tell them back at Tree Haven," Griffin said.

"There's just two of them," said Skye disdainfully.

"Yeah, well, it only took two to catch my mother," Griffin retorted. "They spread a web across a stream, and caught her and banded her."

He noticed they were all listening to him. About the only time they ever did was when he talked about his parents.

"But they didn't hurt her, right?" Luna said.

"Not those ones, no."

"Yeah," said Rowan excitedly, turning back to Skye and Falstaff and Luna. "But there were those other ones who trapped all the bats in the indoor forest and put explosive discs on their bellies and dumped them out of their flying machines!"

"Remember how Shade saved Chinook by chewing off

the disc?" said Falstaff, talking so vigorously the branch shook.

"And then they had to hide out in the jungle where all those cannibal bats lived," added Skye and then all three were talking at once, retelling Shade's amazing adventures – as if they'd forgotten Griffin was Shade's son, and he knew all about this anyway, and better than them. Griffin scowled, feeling they were somehow stealing his stories, treating them like something that belonged to everyone equally. But he supposed they did, in a way. Within the colony's echo chamber, his father's stories reverberated for ever, as part of the history of the Silverwings. Maybe he didn't have any special claim to those stories.

Especially since he was nothing like his father, anyway. He'd known that almost from the moment he was born. His mother was a hero, but his father was practically a legend. Defeating Goth and the other cannibal bats, making peace with the owls, getting the sun back for the Silverwings. If his father did any more amazing things, the whole echo chamber would explode. When he'd first heard all these stories, from his mother, from the elders, from other newborns sometimes, he'd pictured his father as a giant, with wings that would blot out the moon. Then he'd learned his father was born a runt.

That made everything much, much worse.

A runt, and *still* brave and daring. When he was not much older than Griffin, his father had peeked at the sun, outflown owls, visited the echo chamber, tried to save Tree Haven from burning down, been blasted out to sea in a storm and survived. Griffin had had no adventures, performed no valiant acts. About the most exciting thing he'd experienced was having a squirrel throw a nut at him, and miss.

In just four more weeks, they'd start their migration south to Hibernaculum, and rendezvous with the males at Stonehold. He would meet his father for the first time. And what would his father see? A little bat with weird fur. A little bat who wasn't special in any way, wasn't brave or daring or anything.

"Rotten humans," Falstaff was saying. "We should fly down and scare them."

"We should tangle up their hair," said Rowan.

"We should pee on them," said Skye.

When everyone finished laughing there was a short silence, and then:

"We should steal some fire."

No one was more surprised by this than Griffin, for it was he himself who'd spoken the words. He'd never said anything so outrageous in his life, and now everyone was staring at him, Luna with a smile pulling at the corners of her mouth – almost in a look of admiration.

"Steal fire," she said, as if mulling over an interesting possibility.

"What for?" Falstaff wanted to know.

Griffin's eyes darted back to the lapping flames, mind churning. Why had he gone and said that?

"Well," he began uncertainly, "the owls have it; why shouldn't we?"

A couple of years ago, the owls had used their fire to burn down Tree Haven. That was his father's fault. Shade had peeked at the sun, back when it was against the law, and been spotted by sentry owls.

"But what would we do with it?" Skye wanted to know.

"All I'm saying," Griffin repeated, "is we should have what they have. It's only fair."

"But we're at peace with the birds now."

"Doesn't mean we'll always be at peace," Griffin pointed out. "And what about the beasts? Or the Humans? What if they want to make war on us? Isn't it better we have fire just in case?"

They all had their eyes on him, and he thought: *I love this. They're listening to me.* And the words just kept coming. From where, he didn't know. Then again, this is what he did in his mind anyway. Imagine things. Sure, they were usually colossal doomsday scenarios, but wasn't it all really the same? Seeing something, and imagining what might, just *might* happen with it.

"There's something else, too," he said, and allowed himself a dramatic pause.

"What?" Rowan asked, almost in a whisper.

"We could use it to keep warm."

They all looked at one another, uncertain about this.

"Oh sure, the weather's warm *now*," Griffin hurried on, "but before long it'll get cold, so cold we have to leave here or *freeze to death*!"

The other newborns jerked in surprise.

"But that's why we migrate," Luna reminded him.

"Exactly. But that's the whole problem. I've been thinking about the migration, and I think it's really a bad idea."

"We've been doing it for millions of years!" exclaimed Skye.

"I know. It's ridiculous," said Griffin with a sad shake of his head. "We've got Tree Haven right here, this amazing roost, and every fall we have to leave and fly over a million wingbeats to Hibernaculum, sleep away the winter, and then next spring, fly all the way back here. Doesn't it seem like just a bit of a waste of time? But, we get some fire, keep it burning in the base of Tree Haven all winter, and we don't need to bother migrating any more!"

"But I want to migrate," said Luna, smiling. "It's going to be fun."

"Yeah," Rowan, Skye and Falstaff agreed simultaneously but without, Griffin noticed, wholehearted enthusiasm.

"Fun?" Griffin said, puffing out his breath thoughtfully. "I don't know if I'd call it *fun*. It's an awfully long journey. You've got storms, high winds, lightning, hail, freezing cold. Every year there's some who don't make it. I mean look at some of those older females in the colony. They're pretty weak, they can hardly hunt for themselves any more! And what about *us*? We've never done it before. Who says we're strong enough to make it?"

"We'll make it," said Skye, looking at the others for reassurance.

"Look what happened to my father," Griffin reminded them. "Caught in a storm, swept out to sea."

This stopped them for a moment.

"But he *made* it," Luna said.

"He was lucky. Just imagine yourself flying along the coast and a storm kicks up and you get blasted out over the ocean, the waves churning, the rain and hail smashing down so you can't see or hear – and then *wham* right into the water! It's up your nose and soaking your wings and making you so heavy and freezing that you can only sink down and down and down to the ocean's depths!"

Falstaff swallowed. Rowan's wings gave a creak as he shifted anxiously from claw to claw. They were all staring, riveted, at Griffin and he almost smiled.

"I'm not saying that's going to happen to any of us," he went on. "But don't you think we should at least get to *choose* whether we migrate or stay at Tree Haven? We steal some fire, we have a choice." He took a deep breath, revving himself up. "A *choice*! So the weak need not fear, or the elderly and infirm! So we need not be victims of the elements, but *control* them and so become *masters of our destiny*!"

He was out of words and breath. He looked at the newborns, who stared back at him, mouths ajar. Probably he'd overdone it a bit with that destiny stuff.

"I think it's a good idea," said Luna, and all heads swivelled to her.

"You do?" Griffin asked, startled.

"Absolutely. Me personally, I'm going to migrate, but I think you're right. Why shouldn't we be able to stay here all winter? Why not? Let's get ourselves some fire!"

Griffin nodded weakly, glancing back at the flames. Somehow he hadn't expected it to go this far. He'd just talked and talked and the words had spun out of him like some dazzling, chaotic spider's web.

"Maybe we should ask the elders first," Griffin said, feeling queasy.

Luna shook her head, eyes flashing with mischievous delight. "No, I think we should just go ahead and surprise them. So, how're we going to do this, Griff?"

Griffin liked it when she called him Griff. She was the only one who did it, and it made him feel special. Not only was he her friend, but he was a friend deserving of a nickname. He didn't want to let her down now.

"Well," he said, thinking fast, "a tall stalk of grass, maybe. We could shove it into the flames until it catches fire, and then . . . fly it back to the roost and put it in a little nest like theirs, with some dry twigs and leaves at the bottom. Somewhere near Tree Haven, close to the stream maybe. Someone'll have to go on ahead and get that ready."

"I *like* it!" Luna said, turning to the other newborns. "So who's going to steal the fire?"

Skye, Rowan and Falstaff shifted uncomfortably on the branch, then looked at one another expectantly, all talking at once.

"Probably best if you—"

"You're stronger—"

"Need someone really fast—"

Griffin noticed they didn't even glance his way.

"Me," Griffin blurted out. "I'll do it."

They all turned to him, incredulous.

"You?" Skye said.

Griffin nodded slowly, as if trying to balance a heavy stone on his head. "Sure. Why not?"

Maybe this was the way you did it, he thought. He wasn't brave. But maybe if he faked it, *pretended* to be brave enough times, it would get easier. And then it would come naturally. And he'd be truly brave.

"I don't know," Rowan said uncertainly. "Maybe Luna should do it."

"Not me," said Luna. "It was Griffin's idea. He's the one we need." She looked straight at Griffin as she said this, smiling, as if to say she knew all along he'd volunteer, and that he could do it. Then she turned to the others. "You three go on and make the nest."

"Come on," said Falstaff with a laugh. "He's not really going to do it."

"Just make sure that nest is ready," Griffin said, and before he could give himself time to start thinking, he dropped from the branch, unfurled his wings and dived.

In the deep shadows at the edge of the clearing he

sighted a clump of tall grass. He came in low, spraying out sound to check for predators, then touched down. It was not a graceful landing. He skidded on his rear claws, then pitched forward, his face in the mud. Scrambling up, he twitched dirt from his fur. He hated being on the ground. *Hated* it. Bats were made for flight, not for scuttling around. Laboriously he moved towards the grass, dragging himself forwards with his thumb claws and elbows. He pushed with his legs, but they were too weak to be of much use. Anything could be lurking in that grass. Rats, snakes, a crazed skunk.

The first stalks he examined were too wet to catch fire easily. Further in, beneath the shade of a large oak, he found some drier grass and peered up to pick out the tallest stalk. For a moment he felt like he was circling overhead from some safe distance, watching himself. He was crazy! What was he doing down there? His heart began to race, and his teeth started chattering, even though he didn't feel cold. He forced himself to pay attention to what he was doing.

He started chewing at the base of the stalk of grass, spitting out its sour tang. He bit through, and the stalk fell flat. Awkwardly he took it in his rear claws, lengthwise beneath his body. Then, flapping furiously, he managed to get airborne.

Hidden in shadow he made a full circle of the clearing, then came in low so he wouldn't be seen. He made sure to approach the fire on the far side from the two Humans, and when he was about twenty wingbeats away, he made another clumsy landing on his chin. He dragged himself forward, the stalk of grass still clutched in his rear claws. He looked up at the Humans, their torsos and heads towering above the flames. They were still sitting, and they hadn't noticed him. He wondered if he'd be able to take flight fast enough if they tried to catch him.

Griffin hesitated, glancing up at the pines, hoping Luna was seeing all this. He wanted her to be able to tell the colony all about this amazing thing he'd done. This amazing, *dangerous* thing. He grimaced. *My father'd better be impressed by this*, he thought.

He dragged himself closer, until the fire's heat lapped angrily against his face.

He watched the flames doing their hot jittery dance down amongst the glowing sticks and rocks, and he felt like they were urging him onward, closer, closer. Deep in the fire something popped and Griffin flinched, nearly taking flight. Luna should've done this. He'd tried to fake it, but he wasn't fearless. He was *all* fear, heart blasting, mouth dry, a terrible weakness seeping through his limbs. His wings felt mushy. But he thought of Luna watching – thought of his father – and knew he couldn't quit now.

Crouched right up against one of the big rocks, there was a bit of relief from the heat. Griffin took the end of the stalk in his teeth. He knew he'd have to be quick – the longer he took, the more chance there was of being seen. With his thumb claws, he pulled himself up on to the stone. Scalding heat poured over him, wilting his fur, bringing water streaming from his eyes. Squinting, he tried to swing the stalk into the flames, but it deflected off a big block of wood at the fire's edge. The stalk of grass was unwieldy, and he managed to pull it back a bit with his claw, so less was protruding from his jaws.

With a forward thrust of his shoulders, he drove the stalk deep into the embers, saw the tip flare, and pulled back. At first he thought he'd lost the fire, but then saw a glint from the tip, and a ghost of smoke curl up from it.

Got it!

Carefully he transferred the stalk to his rear claws. Wings churning, he took flight, climbing away from the ground, from the Humans and their fire, up towards the pine where he knew Luna was waiting. He took a quick backwards glance. If the Humans even noticed, they weren't doing anything about it. They were still sitting there like big mountainous blobs, staring at the fire, and grunting their slow, low words to one another.

"You did it!" Luna cried out, swirling around him in amazement.

"Is it still lit?" he asked. It was awkward holding the fire stick, and he had to fly carefully, afraid his down-strokes might accidentally blow out the flame, or even knock the stalk right out of his claws.

"Yeah, it's fine!" said Luna. "Griffin, I can't believe you did it!"

"I did it," he said, feeling her excitement fuel his own. "Yeah, I did it!"

"Fire!" she said. "You've got fire! Come on, let's get it to the nest!"

They talked giddily as they flew, Luna swirling around him and underneath him to check on the flame and make sure it was still burning. She was giggling. Griffin was giggling. It was contagious, and almost impossible to stop. This was amazing! He wanted his father to see him, right now, bearing stolen fire from witless Humans. Sitting right there at the campfire, and they didn't even know it was gone. And he'd done it. *Him.* He'd had this great idea, and he'd seen it through!

Through the forest they flew, back towards Tree Haven and the stone nest the others were building. Griffin ducked his head down to look, and was surprised at how quickly the flame was eating up the stalk, the intense bead of liquid light sliding towards his claws.

"Almost there," said Luna, seeing his worried frown. "You'll make it, Griff."

He flapped harder, but saw the flame gutter with too much wind against it. He slowed down. Still the flame continued its hungry advance. He could feel its heat now, along his left flank, in his foot. His mind began to dance with worry. He couldn't help it. He wished he hadn't done this. He wanted to get rid of it, but he couldn't just drop it. What if it started a fire, and the fire spread, and got out of control and burned down Tree Haven all over again? What a *stupid* idea this was.

"Luna," he said, "it's burning too fast!"

"No, we're almost there, don't worry, you'll make it."

No, she was wrong. There was still a long way to go. He looked and couldn't even see the tip of the stalk any more, it had burned down so close to his body. Heat lashed his fur and claws. He remembered the scalding force of the fire, imagined himself alight, spiralling to the ground in flames.

"Luna! I'm not gonna make it!"

"Wait, wait, I'll check, hang on."

Luna swooped below him again, and almost at the same moment, Griffin felt a searing pain in his left claw. He cried out, and before he could check himself, he let go of the fire stick.

"Look out!" he yelled but—

He heard her grunt of surprise, tilted sharply and looked down.

Luna was on fire, her back dancing with flame. The stick had bounced off, leaving its burning tip embedded in her fur.

"Griffin!" she cried, swirling round and round, flapping desperately but only fanning the flames.

"Land!" Griffin shouted to her, but she was panicking now, as the flames leapt nimbly towards her shoulders, licking out across her wings. Griffin whirled round her, slapping at the fire, but it was no good, Luna was moving too much, and the flames seemed to have burrowed deep into her fur. She was crying, a high, piercing wail.

"Land!" he shouted at her again in despair. "Land and I can put it out!"

Luna was tilting earthwards, though it didn't seem of her own doing. She slewed through the air at a reckless angle, gathering speed, too much, and slammed into a mound of hardened mud and leaves. She didn't move.

Griffin crashed down beside her, scrambled up and started sweeping mud and earth on to her with his claws and wings, trying to smother the flames. Suddenly he was shoved back out of the way and there was his mother, Marina – and Luna's mother, and a dozen other mothers, landing around the smoking newborn, throwing themselves on her to extinguish the fire. It took them only a few seconds, but still Luna didn't move. Her fur, Griffin saw, was terribly burned, patches of inflamed skin showing through. Her wings were seared and melted in places.

Griffin couldn't tear his eyes from her, and he realized he was moaning, a low, toneless cry that he couldn't stop.

"She's alive," he heard one of the mothers say. "Let's take her back to Tree Haven."

STONEHOLD

Shade stirred restlessly, frowning as he woke. He opened one eye, then the other, and looked around at the thousands of Silverwing males hanging from the cave's ridged walls and ceiling. Wrapped tightly in their wings, they were all still fast asleep. He held his breath, listening. He couldn't tell if it was a sound, or a vibration through the stone that had brought him out of sleep. Maybe it was just Chinook, snoring beside him. Or Cassiel, his father, muttering in his dreams.

Shade glanced at the long vertical gash which was the cave's opening, and judged from the light it was still an hour or so till sunset. At midnight, he knew that Orion, the chief male elder, would be choosing five messengers to make the journey to Tree Haven. Shade wanted to be one of them.

He wanted to see his son.

Griffin. The name was pretty much all Shade knew about him, and that he'd been born healthy in the spring. How could anyone be satisfied with just that? But this was the way it had been done for millions of years. Every spring the females roosted at Tree Haven and gave birth, and the males spent the summer at Stonehold, a hundred thousand wingbeats to the south-east. None of the other males seemed to want to visit their mates and newborns; they were perfectly happy to be apart until the fall, knowing nothing except the news the messengers brought back periodically after the birthing season. But that was months ago now! How could they stand it? It was too bizarre. He was desperate to see Marina again – and meet his son for the very first time.

Shade sighed. Well, he was awake now. For just a moment, he thought he felt the slightest of vibrations through his claws, as if something immensely powerful within the earth were stirring, testing its strength. Then it was gone. Probably it was just the wind off the ocean, or the great ceaseless stirring of the sea itself – or his own nervousness about tonight.

He wanted to be outside. Dropping from his roost, he stretched his wings, streaked through the opening, and was instantly over the sea. The sun was still high enough above the horizon to set the water alight. Shade banked sharply and soared over the rocky coastline, notched by countless coves and inlets. The tides here were fierce and sudden, and the sea had carved the land into high, blunt cliffs. Stonehold was deep within the tallest cliff of all, its craggy head crowned with moss-covered rocks, and a few hardy spruce trees, bowed by the wind.

Far away, Shade could hear a pod of whales singing their strange song, somehow mournful and ecstatic all at once, resonating through the water and air, gusted landward. Shade skimmed over the dense forest, intent on hunting now. From the topmost branch of a pine, a raven stared suspiciously as he passed, but said nothing. Shade watched the powerful bird carefully. He'd quickly realized that being *allowed* to fly in sunlight was not the same as being welcome.

Though the owls had agreed to a peace treaty with the bats, Shade and the other Silverwings still felt wary in the day. Most avoided it, choosing to hunt and fly under the moon and stars, as they had done for millennia. Sometimes Shade wondered what the point had been, fighting to get the sun back. But he knew it wasn't the daylight itself that was important: it was the freedom. The freedom to choose if you flew at night or day, and, most of all, the freedom from fear of owl attack.

Shade veered and caught a monarch butterfly. That was one good thing about flying in the sunlight – there were all sorts of new bugs to eat, ones that rarely came out at night.

"You're up early," said a voice behind him, and he glanced over his wing to see his father, Cassiel, pulling alongside.

"Did you feel the cave shake?" Shade asked.

Cassiel shook his head. "You did?"

"I don't know if it was real. I'm pretty sure I felt a little tremor."

"Could be," said his father. "Years ago there were a few earthquakes. Nothing very big though."

His father was trying to reassure him, but Shade remembered the low, controlled rhythm of the vibration, like a suggestion of greater things to come. He wondered if they'd felt it at Tree Haven.

"Do you think Orion will pick me?" he asked.

"All I know is he always chooses fast, reliable flyers."

"Well, I'm not the fastest, sure, but I'm reliable."

His father looked at him with a grin.

"You don't think I'm reliable?" Shade asked, hurt.

"Of course I do. You saved my life. But Orion's probably worried you might get *distracted* along the way. Discover some evil plan to destroy the world, or accidentally start a war. Something like that."

Shade snorted, but he knew his father was right. Even after all his adventures, maybe even *because* of them, he still noticed that the Silverwing elders didn't exactly *trust* him.

"They trust Chinook," Shade said irritably.

"Well, he is very trustworthy," his father agreed.

It rankled Shade that Chinook had been one of the first messengers. He'd been to Tree Haven and seen his mate, and his own child. And he'd brought news back about a hundred other newborns as well, among them, Griffin.

"What did he look like?" Shade had demanded, moments after an exhausted Chinook lurched into Stonehold.

"Looked fine. Healthy."

Shade's surge of relief and gratitude had quickly given way to intense curiosity.

"What else?" he'd asked Chinook. "Come on, a few more details!"

"They all look kind of the same at that age, Shade. I mean, they're all sort of red and floppy-skinned and they don't have any fur yet and, well, to be honest, they're pretty weird-looking."

Weird-looking. And that was all Chinook had been able to tell him. But Shade wanted to know everything, and not a single night passed when his mind wasn't filled with questions. Was Griffin growing well? Was he a good flier and hunter? What did he look like – more like Marina or him? Did he have lots of friends, or was he a loner? Was he curious, talkative, daring? Or quiet and watchful?

"It's ridiculous we have to wait so long," Shade muttered as he and his father sailed through the twilight forest, snapping up darkling beetles and mosquitoes. "Anyone should be able to go to Tree Haven if he wants. Splitting up the colony makes no sense."

"Only the mothers can feed the newborns," Cassiel reminded him. "We wouldn't be any use early on."

"But later we would. We could help teach them to fly and hunt."

"The females seem to be doing just fine on their own. It's the way it's always been, Shade."

"I think it's stupid," he said firmly. "And I can't believe no one else feels the same. Doesn't anyone else miss their mates and newborns?"

"Well, I don't think many males are in a hurry to leave Stonehold," his father said with a grin. "They know we've got it easy here. Apparently it's very noisy in the nursery roost. Newborns are pretty demanding. A lot of crying, a lot of shouting, a lot of commotion."

"A little commotion would be a nice change about now," Shade said.

The truth was, he was bored at Stonehold. He liked being with Chinook, and especially his father, but every night was virtually the same. They woke at sunset, took to the skies, and hunted. When they weren't hunting, they were hanging around, telling stories. The stories he always enjoyed, but then there were the councils, the endless councils about migration preparations: who would lead, who would take up the rear; the quality of the mealworms this year; the rainfall reports and prevailing wind reports and . . . it made his skull go numb just thinking about it.

He knew he shouldn't complain – but he wanted to anyway. Things were good right now. There was peace with the owls, food was plentiful and – there was just *nothing* to do. He was bored and he felt like he was getting boring himself.

He wanted to be back with Marina; he wanted to be with his new family.

"Do you think . . ." he began, and then stopped himself, embarrassed.

"What?" Cassiel asked.

He coughed. "Do you think I'll make a good father?"

The fact was, he still didn't feel like a father at all. The very idea seemed ridiculous. Even though he could barely wait to meet his son, he was still worried that Griffin might think he was a fake. Shade certainly felt like a fake. A father? How could he possibly take care of a newborn when he still practically felt like a newborn himself? He simply could not imagine himself saying, with conviction, things like, "You shouldn't do that," or "That's just the way things are," or "Do what your mother and I tell you." There was no way Griffin would take him seriously.

He was worried he wouldn't be vigilant enough or strong enough to rescue him if anything should happen, worried that he wouldn't be patient enough or firm enough – or *something* enough.

"You'll be a great father," Cassiel told him. "I think almost everyone worries about it, though."

"You?" Shade asked, surprised.

"Especially me," Cassiel replied. "I was hardly the most responsible father. I wasn't even around when you were born."

"Well, no fathers were."

"I was a little more absent than most."

"That wasn't your fault."

"Well, I took risks I shouldn't have, not when I had a

newborn coming." He flew in close to give Shade an affectionate nuzzle. "It'll be fine."

They hunted side by side for a while in contented silence, and then Shade sighted a tiger moth and went spinning off on his own in pursuit. The moth was wily, dipping and veering through the weave of the forest, spraying out a barrage of echo mirages. But Shade, after long experience, was focused with both sight and sound, and wasn't going to be thrown off. He came in fast with his tail flared, ready to scoop the moth up. Moths always tended to drop straight down, and his trajectory took this into account, but this moth didn't just drop – it plummeted heavy as a hailstone.

Shade did a backward somersault, and twisted round in time to see the moth hit the earth and disappear. This was not tiger moth behaviour. With his echo vision he probed the rocky ground and saw now there was actually a hole there. Moths, as far as he knew, did not make burrows. Carefully, he made a pass, shooting down sound. The hole was deep, and no echoes returned, nor any sign of the moth. Directly overhead, he noticed a powerful downward current.

Shade settled on the ground and warily advanced towards the hole, which seemed to have been split from the rock itself. He wondered if it had been opened by the tremor he'd felt earlier. The hole was noisily sucking in air. Dust and shards of stone drizzled over its rim. With his rear claws locked firmly in the earth, Shade stretched his head over the opening, feeling the current pull ominously at his fur. The tunnel slanted steeply into blackness. Maybe it led down towards the coastal caves, but he heard no slap of water, or shushing of wind. Far, far away he picked up the faint but frenzied flutter of the moth's wings, fighting the current, until it dissolved to nothingness. Wherever this hole went, it was very deep.

His ears pricked. A sound, like the faintest exhalation, rose from the depths, and a ripple of horror swept Shade's flesh. Perhaps it was just a whisper his own ears had superimposed over the silence. With all his concentration he listened, and heard once again the same sigh, like the slow measured breath of some living creature that wanted to speak. That wanted to come up.

"Who's there!" Shade shouted.

His voice echoed down the hole, rapidly dwindling. *Who's there! Who's there who's there there there . . .*

Then silence, as after a sharp intake of breath, the silence of something listening for you in the dark. Shade instantly regretted calling out. Cold sweat prickled his neck and shoulders. He couldn't move. He was waiting to hear the breathing resume.

He blinked, dizzy with the sudden overwhelming certainty that this tunnel plunged to the earth's very centre, to some terrible place that was not entirely unfamiliar to him. For in his mind's eye, though his ears detected no sound, he caught a pale flash of images he had seen before: a feathered serpent, a jaguar, a pair of unblinking eyes with no pupils. And he knew their origin: Cama Zotz, god of the Underworld.

"Yes," a voice whispered, and Shade jerked back in terror, but not quickly enough, for at that moment, the earth around the tunnel mouth collapsed, and Shade's upper body pitched down into the hole, his rear claws straining to keep their grip. The current plucked at him fiercely as he scrabbled with his thumbs to push back and out. One of his rear claws tore free of the earth and he was about to fall, to fall down into that terrible hole when suddenly he was hauled back and his father was with him, seizing him with his wings and teeth and claws.

They scuttled clear and took flight, panting and shaken. Roosting on a nearby cedar, heart still pumping painfully, Shade told his father what had happened.

Cassiel looked grimly at the hole. "We should go back to Stonehold and tell the elders. We'll need help to properly block off that tunnel. Don't want anyone getting sucked down."

"Or anything coming out," Shade said.

His father looked at him. "You're sure you heard someone?"

"I think so." He sighed. "There was something down there, and not just one thing, it felt like . . . a world." He did not want to imagine the kind of creatures which populated it, or what they might be capable of.

Shade stared up through the branches into a sky heavy with stars. By their position he could tell it was almost midnight. Orion would be making his decision soon. More than ever now, he wanted to travel to Tree Haven. He wanted to see Marina, and his son. He wanted to make sure that everything was all right. That the ominous tremor he'd felt earlier hadn't cracked the earth near them.

As he flew with his father back towards Stonehold, he'd already made up his mind: even if Orion didn't choose him as a messenger, he was leaving for Tree Haven before sunrise.

AWAKE

He woke to an enormous weight of stone, crushing down on him. The stench of seared rock and dust clogged his nostrils. Sluggishly at first, and then with increasing panic, he dredged his mind for memories. He could not remember what he was, or whether he had a name. He tried to lift a shoulder, dig in with a hind leg.

Push.

Exhausted by the effort, he wheezed, coughing dust from his mouth and nostrils.

What happened?

Who am I?

Fight, he told himself. *Fight this.*

Shoulders hunched, claws digging in, he pulled. His legs found purchase and he felt the leaden weight above him shift, allow him a few precious inches. His head was molten with pain, fire raging in all his joints. His left wing was still extended, pinned flat by stone. He tried to pull it in, feeling as though he were dragging it inch by inch through serrated jaws. He bellowed with all his might to dull the pain, and finally had his wing folded tight against him. Shuddering, he took a few moments to recover. He made the mistake of trying to open his eyes, only to have silt pour into them. Shutting them tight, he cracked open his mouth, and sang out sound. Almost instantly his echoes were slammed back to him, painting an unintelligible silver din in his mind's eye.

Buried alive.

He had a sudden image of himself, hundreds of feet below the earth, unable to reach the surface, the air slowly being forced from his lungs. Roaring with terror and rage, he flexed and thrashed, shoulders and back buckling against the stone. He felt it give, tumble down around him. Again and again he heaved himself upwards, rear claws pushing against anything they touched.

Slashing up through the rubble like a blade, his snout broke the surface first. Greedily sucking air, he pushed out the rest of his head. He opened his eyes slowly, ablur with tears and dust, and saw before him in the gloom a barren plain, stretching to all horizons. He heard no trees or vegetation or life of any kind. Just earth and sky – and a gritty wind that assumed its own ghostly silver shape in his echo vision.

Is this normal?

No, he was expecting something else – but what?

Think, he urged himself. *Remember.*

He hauled the rest of his body free, and shivered, wings drawn tight, chin pressed into his chest. His mind throbbed, trying to unlock itself. And then a few images flared in his mind's eye—

Trees that soared to the sky and formed a canopy.

Below, a world of lush vegetation. Creepers and vines and mosses and flowers.

A pyramid of stone, with other creatures like him, swirling around it.

Home.

He looked round at the rubble strewn in all directions. This was not home. Then how had he come to be here? Again he thought of that stone pyramid, stared at it in his memory.

A flash of light. The premonition of some cataclysmic noise – nothing more.

An explosion? Some kind of disaster? And this, was this all there was left, everything flattened to this rocky plain? Tilting his aching neck, he squinted up at the heavens and saw, through the swirling dust, stars glimmering. They reminded him of nothing.

Instinctively he spread his wings to fly, but the earth would not release him. He felt immeasurably heavy and tired. *Rest*, he told himself. *After a rest, you will be able to fly*. Instead, he began a slow crawl, moving with the wind, opening his wings a little and angling them so he was shoved along by it.

He didn't know where he was going, but sooner or later he would have to meet another living thing who could tell him.

Then he stopped. His nose twitched, as if trying to catch a scent. Hunching forward, head cocked, he listened. Something was wrong. Not outside, but inside. Deep inside him, something was all wrong.

He tried to breathe calmly, to listen, to think.

Then it came to him.

His heart wasn't beating.

In a panic, he coughed and thrashed about, hoping to force his heart into action. He pounded his chest against the rocky ground. Beat! *Beat!* Desperate for air, his vision flared and swam – then suddenly cleared.

And he realized he wasn't dying.

He was already dead.

At the same moment, his name came surging back to him. He opened his mouth to speak it and his voice sounded alien to him, saturated with grime and exhaustion.

"Goth."

A CRACK IN THE SKY

Inside Tree Haven, Griffin watched as they placed Luna on a soft bed of moss. With their noses they gently nudged out her wounded wings. His own mother was among the helpers, and his grandmother, Ariel. In small niches carved from the bark were mounds of different berries and dried leaves and strips of bark. Ariel took some of these things into her mouth, chewing not swallowing. Then she roosted above Luna and proceeded to drizzle the potion from her mouth on to the patches of raw burned skin.

Luna was shivering. Why was she shivering, Griffin wondered, when she'd just been on fire? She said nothing, made no sound, just stared straight ahead, eyes wide and unblinking. She didn't look like herself. It was like the things that made her Luna were gone away, or deep in hiding somewhere. She just gazed right through things. Maybe she was concentrating, using all her energy to get better.

Griffin had always found Tree Haven immensely comforting. He loved the reassuring thickness of its great trunk, and the geography of its craggy grey bark, knotted and gouged with valleys deep enough to hide in. Most of all he loved the inside, hollowed out by the Silverwings into a series of interconnected roosts, radiating from the trunk into the larger branches, all the way up to the elders' roost at the very summit. At sunset the entire colony would burst through the central knothole into the night with the sound of a torrential river. But his favourite time of all was sunrise, when everyone would return from the night's hunting, find their roosts, and talk while combing the dust and grit from their fur, and licking their wings clean. Then all the mothers and newborns, roosting snugly side by side, would sleep.

But now, he felt only shame and dread as he looked at Luna.

No one had spoken to him yet. There hadn't been time. In the forest, when all the grown-ups had arrived, his own mother had only looked at him anxiously for a moment, and asked, "You're all right?", and when he'd nodded numbly, she had returned to Luna, helping to carry her back to Tree Haven, and up to the healer's roost. Griffin had followed at a distance. As they'd flown up through the trunk, the silence was suffocating. Everyone already seemed to know what had happened. He tried not to look at the hundreds of horrified bats watching as they passed. He didn't want to look or be looked at. He didn't want them to see what he'd done.

Now the other mothers were taking turns blending the leaves and berries in their mouths, mulching them into a thick liquid and spreading it over Luna's wounds. Watching this made Griffin feel hopeful. He wished they would work even faster, cover all Luna's angry welts and burns with the dark unguent, cover up her pain, take it away.

When at last they were finished, his mother flew over and roosted beside him.

"Griffin, what happened?" she whispered.

He had childishly hoped this moment would never come. His voice shook as he spoke. "We saw some Humans in the forest and they had a fire, and . . . we thought we should take some. I got some fire on a stalk of grass and was flying with it, but it started burning me and I dropped it on to Luna by accident." He had to choke out the last words, he was sobbing so hard.

He wanted her to be furious with him. He deserved it. He hoped she would shout and punish him and when all that was over, somehow things would be better. Things would be fixed. But his mother looked so far from anger, was so still and mournful, that Griffin felt more frightened than he ever had in his life.

"You foolish, foolish children," she said, so softly Griffin could barely hear her.

"I didn't mean to," he said. "I didn't know she was underneath me, and I was scared I was going to get burned. I tried to help put the flames out but they wouldn't go away."

She wrapped her wings around him and held him tightly, and Griffin didn't know what to think. She shouldn't be holding him – this was his fault. He hardly dared breathe, wishing he could vanish.

"You're so lucky. It could've—" His mother cut herself short. "Why did you let them talk you into it?"

He said nothing, feeling as if all the air were being squeezed out of his lungs.

He had to tell her.

"It was my idea," he wheezed.

She looked at him, stunned. "Why?" she managed to ask.

He couldn't look at her as he spoke. "So we could have some like the owls. And I thought maybe we could use it to stay warm in the winter. So we could stay here, without having to migrate." *And so maybe my father would think I had some courage*, he thought, but didn't say this.

His mother shut her eyes tight, as though not trusting herself to speak. When she did, anger flickered through her voice. "Griffin, we don't want fire. We don't *need* it. Its only use is for war. We couldn't keep it inside. It would set the tree on fire. Even if it didn't, we'd still have nothing to eat through the winter. We'd starve."

He nodded so hard his neck hurt. "It was . . . a really bad idea," he said. "I'm sorry."

"You should have come and told us the moment you saw the Humans."

"I know."

"You're sensible, Griffin. Even if the others aren't. *You* should have known better. I don't know what you were thinking, stealing fire. If you'd only thought a bit . . ." She trailed off, as if unable to summon any more energy. Her eyes drifted back to Luna, and Roma, her mother, nuzzling her gently, talking to her quietly. Luna wasn't saying anything back.

"When will she be better?" Griffin asked his mother.

"I don't know." She paused, then added, "Maybe never."

"What d'you mean?" He felt panic moving through him like a crazed June bug, wings slashing the air, slamming itself everywhere. Did his mother mean she might be crippled her whole life? That she'd never fly again?

"She might die, Griffin."

He frowned, not understanding, shaking his head. "But you were all spreading potions on her, the elders know how to fix things like that, right?"

"She's very badly hurt."

The fur around her eyes was matted with tears. This was all his doing. Griffin knew she was ashamed of him now. He'd disappointed her so badly, how could she ever love him again? And what would his father say?

"What can I do?" he said, his voice sounding unfamiliar to him, thin and breathless. He wanted his mother to tell him to do something hard or painful – anything would be better than just being frozen with his feelings.

"There's nothing we can do," his mother said. "We just have to wait."

He looked around, this place he'd loved so much his whole life, and felt like he had no right to be here. All the other mothers were looking at him – hating him, he was sure. And Luna's mother – she would hate him most of all, and for ever. The tree seemed to echo with his own shame and grief. He couldn't stand it.

Griffin flew. Down away from the healer's roost, all the way down the trunk to Tree Haven's base where myriad passageways twisted into the ground amongst the maple's roots. He didn't know where he was going, and didn't care. He just wanted to go down, and down, far away from everything.

But his thoughts came with him. *Shut up*, he screamed inwardly. The tunnel was narrowing, and he was glad when it scraped against his face and back, when dirt got driven up his nostrils and against his teeth. He clawed his way along until the passage was blocked by a large slab of stone. It was totally dark, and he shut his eyes and his mouth, letting no sound light the world for him. If only he could make his mind this dark. Stop seeing Luna's burning wings spinning earthwards. Stop hearing that scream she made as she fell.

* * *

Unless the wind turned against them, Shade knew they'd make Tree Haven before sunrise.

He'd been chosen as one of the five messengers. Maybe the chief elder had sensed, just by looking at his eyes, that he was going whether chosen or not. Still, it had taken Shade so completely by surprise, that he couldn't help smiling. Orion had probably thought it was better to have him part of a group (where the others could keep an eye on him) than have him flapping off on his own.

They'd set off immediately. Around him flew the four other Silverwing males: Cirrus, Laertes, Urriel, and Vikram. They were faster than him; they knew it, and so did he. And he also knew he was slowing them down. But rather than streaking on ahead, and circling back impatiently for him every once in a while, they let *him* set the pace, and never showed any signs of restlessness. Shade was grateful. He hadn't known them particularly well at Stonehold, and none of them were big talkers, but he enjoyed their company. When they did talk, it was to remember Tree Haven, and wonder about their mates and their newborns, and trade stories about when they themselves were young.

Sometimes Cirrus or Laertes would awkwardly ask him questions about the jungle, or Goth and the Vampyrum Spectrum, or the rat kingdoms. Shade had told these stories enough times now that they hardly seemed things that had actually happened to him. Still, he liked telling them, and never tired of the stunned amazement in the faces of his listeners.

The weather had been so warm and the winds so fair that he was almost able to forget the fears which had urged him on this journey: the earthquake, the hissing crack in the earth, and the horrible presence he'd sensed down there. When Shade departed two nights ago, Chinook and his father were busily assembling a team of males to go and block the opening. As he'd said goodbye to his father, Shade felt a peculiar clutching at his heart. He knew he'd be back in a matter of nights, but he still didn't like leaving his father, especially when it was not so long ago they'd first met. Cassiel had told him to have a safe trip, and that he loved him.

Soaring over the dense forest, Shade's pulse quickened as he recognized the familiar landmarks which told him Tree Haven was near. A few hours ago they'd passed over the derelict barn where he and his colony had roosted on his very first migration. Now the Human roads faded into deep forest, winding rivers. The sky began to brighten to the east. The sparse birdsong they'd been hearing for the past half-hour was building into a dawn chorus. Shade's thoughts leapt ahead to his arrival. The fast ride down into the valley, skimming over pines and firs and hardwoods towards the silver maple they had chosen for the new Tree Haven. Once they crested the next ridge, maybe they'd even meet some of the Silverwings out hunting. Maybe he'd cross paths with his mother, or Marina. Maybe even his son! He wondered if he would recognize him.

"Listen," he said suddenly.

And there was nothing to listen to. No frogs, no crickets chirruping, not even the sound of insects wings. For a moment even the light breeze evaporated and then the air thickened ominously as though foreshadowing a lightning storm. Yet the sky overhead was almost entirely clear.

The air began to sing, a low, unbroken tone that he felt in every hair of his body. The tone gathered force, buffeting the underside of his wings, numbing his face. Without warning, the trees heaved up towards him, spiky branches almost impaling him as he veered wildly, flapping desperately against the leaden air. He cast around anxiously to make sure Cirrus and the others were all right. They all circled together, gazing down in horror. Below he saw the earth heave and grind, whole swaths of forest buckling up and crumpling against one another. He flattened his ears against the colossal noise, as if the earth's very bones were being smashed together, snapped and crushed. The air churned, hard as water, and Shade slewed about, as if he were no more than a seed pod.

The sky was aswirl with birds, woken by the earth's violent shaking. They'd taken wing in terror, their poor night vision making them career dangerously. On the lurching forest floor Shade could see moose and bears and lynx baying and roaring as they ran headlong, trying to escape the thrashing of the ground beneath them. The sight made him gasp in pity: unlike himself, they had no easy escape, no flinging themselves safe and high into the air. They were locked to the earth, their home that had in a second become their enemy. The river which meandered through the forest was frothing, water leaping over its banks. Dust erupted across the land.

Then, impossibly, it was over. With a great groaning of rock and wood, the earth slowly exhaled and lay still. Shrieks of pain and dismay rose up from the birds and beasts as they returned to their ruined roosts and dens. Shade stared down at the wreckage of the forest, his mouth dry, heart throbbing against his ribs.

Marina, he thought. *Griffin.*

Griffin must have fallen asleep.

Waking, there were a few merciful seconds when

everything was forgotten. He wondered where he was, and why his body felt so heavy, as if he'd just finished a long night's hunting. Then everything came back to him, and he wished he'd never woken up. Up in Tree Haven, Luna was suffering, maybe even dying. All because of his idea, his stupid, pointless idea. He wagged his head, trying to shake out the pictures flooding his head. He should go back up, help them, do something useful . . .

How could he face them all? Feel their eyes on him, hating him?

Especially his mother. She would try to be kind, and try to forgive him, but how could she, after what he'd done?

He tried not to cry. Then he stopped abruptly. What he'd thought was his body shaking was actually the ground beneath his belly. The shuddering intensified so his vision sang with sound, the very air throbbing with light. The tunnel was so tight it took him a moment to turn around. Scrambling forwards, spraying out sound, he heard the low grinding of rock against rock, and was suddenly shoved hard against the wall as a great fist of stone punched through the tunnel ahead of him. Griffin lurched back, cowering beneath his wings as a choking cascade of debris rained down upon him. The earth shivered violently for a moment, and then was still. Griffin waited, listening to the patter of settling grit.

"OK," he panted, trying to rein in his panic. "OK. No more shaking. That's good. That's excellent."

He lifted his wing to take a look and was immediately seized by a coughing fit, eyes and nose streaming. After a minute or so he managed to croak out a few tendrils of sound, and saw what he had most feared. The passage was blocked. Carefully he probed the wall of debris with his echo vision, but found no gaps. He stared for a few moments, numb, still half-expecting something to happen: the wall to crumble away and reveal a passage, or someone to call him from the other side.

"All right," he said, needing to talk. Talking aloud made things better somehow. If he could control his words, maybe he could control other things too. "What we have here is a cave-in kind of situation. Perfectly straightforward. The earthquake just shook loose a bunch of rock and dirt and dumped it here in my tunnel, so all I need to do is . . . um . . . *move* some of that rock and dirt so I can squeeze by. That really sums it all up. So. Let's just do that."

He scuttled towards the wall of debris. Clawing at it, butting it with his head and shoulders, he managed to dislodge some smaller bits of rubble, but mostly just churned up more dust. He prised out a larger rock, and an ominous tremor moved through the wall, and the roof of the tunnel wobbled and sent down a meteor shower of dirt.

"Not too good," he muttered, taking little sips of air to avoid coughing. "I keep digging and I might trigger another cave-in. If I don't dig, I don't get out. So we've got a bit of a dilemma here. But if I just sit around, another earthquake might bury me anyway, and I really have no idea how much air is left down here . . ."

Words were no longer helping, and he started gasping, panic squeezing at his lungs. He couldn't stave off the terrible truth any longer. He was trapped, and there was nothing he could do about it, and no one even knew he was here!

"Help!" he called hoarsely. "Help!" But now the fear in his voice just upset him more, and he stopped. He tried to calm his breathing. He would have to think of something.

He felt cold, very cold, especially at his tail and legs, and then realized there was a gentle breeze nudging past him.

With difficulty he turned himself around again, and fixed his sonic gaze towards the dead-end.

It wasn't a dead-end any more.

In what had once been a solid slab of stone was now a broad gash, big enough for him to fit through. He hurried towards it, sniffing. The breeze wasn't coming *from* the hole, it was going *into* the hole with a faint shushing sound.

"This is good," wheezed Griffin. "This is really good. A breeze. That means air. That means outside. That means we've got an escape kind of situation here . . ."

He hurried to the opening, but when he sang sound into it, his returning echoes showed him that the passageway angled down, deeper beneath the earth. He didn't like that. All that earth and stone above him, and what if there was another quake?

He took a look back over his shoulder at the cave-in. He could still try to claw through, but how long would that take? This other tunnel *must* lead back to the surface, or there wouldn't be a breeze.

"Nice fresh little breeze," he said. That decided it.

Cautiously, he squeezed into the crack. It was as if the earthquake had effortlessly opened a long fissure through solid rock. His claws clicked against the stone. The breeze was getting stronger, gently tugging the fur on his face and shoulders. After another minute, he paused, troubled that the passageway was still sloping downwards. He'd go on a little further, and then if it didn't angle up he'd . . .

What?

Turn back? Return to the cave-in, and wait around until all the air was sucked out of the tunnel and he suffocated?

"It's OK," he said to himself. "Air comes from the sky. This has got to take me back to the sky." It would just take a little longer than he thought. But he was far from reassured and for just a moment his mother hovered before his mind's eye and he felt like crying. It was fear that stopped his crying, a sudden attack of breathlessness in the cramped tunnel, deep beneath the earth. *Don't*, he told himself. *Don't think about it.*

He hurried on, trying to outrun his terror now. At least the breeze was getting stronger, a steady low moan, with the occasional sharp whistling edge, which reminded him of high winds in a summer storm. Little bits of stone were skittering across the tunnel, dragged by the wind, and Griffin could actually feel it speeding him along whenever his thumbs or feet left the ground – almost pulling him off balance.

For a sickening moment, he thought he'd hit a dead-end, but then he saw it was just a sharp upward bend in the tunnel.

"Here we go!" he said happily.

He hurried up and around the bend and then there was another sharp turn to the left and—

The wind wrenched Griffin around the corner, flaring his wings open from behind, and thrust him headlong down the tunnel. With a cry he tried to furl his wings, dig in with his rear claws, but the wind was too powerful. His wrists buckled and he fell against the ground hard on his chin, stunning himself, the wind blasting him along.

Desperately casting out sound, he saw that the slope of the tunnel was slowly but surely curving into a sheer vertical shaft, and he was careening helplessly towards it. The pull was overwhelming now and his thumbs and rear claws cut furrows into the rock. Heaving his body to one side, he managed to lever himself sideways across the tunnel. He lasted only a few seconds before the shrieking wind smacked him loose. Now he was falling, picking up speed, the stone searing his flesh whenever he tried to open his wings to slow down.

Freefall.

Down and down. Nose over tail, and suddenly—

Stars blazing overhead.

Falling from a hole in the sky.

He'd been plunging down into the earth, and now he was in the sky, plunging fast. Even when he managed to wrench his wings out, his speed seemed scarcely diminished.

Gulping air, he saw below him the entire world like an immense ball of dark stone, slowly revolving, so far away. He couldn't believe he was this high, level with the stars almost but plunging fast, dragged down towards the surface as if his wings were weighted. Wind screaming at his face, he spiralled in tight circles, blinking frantically to clear his streaming eyes.

Gradually the world below him started to reveal itself: furrowed ridges of hills, the dark scars of valleys or rivers, black smudges of forest. Trying to find his own forest, his stream, Tree Haven, but this vague landscape was completely unrecognizable.

A forest swelled beneath him. Still coming in too fast. He was used to the downward plunge of a landing, but this was too much. Desperately spraying out sound, he tried to pick out a suitable landing site. He pulled back, angling his wings to brake. He saw the trees hurtling up, and then he was amongst them, slashed by leaves and twigs and pine needles, and grabbing wildly for anything that might break his fall.

TREE HAVEN

Shade and his four companions cleared the last ridge and followed the tree line down into the valley. Whole swaths of forest looked like they'd been swatted over by a giant paw. He could hear the consternation of birds and beasts as he sailed overhead. *Please*, he thought fervently, *let Tree Haven be all right*. Not far now, not far.

There, up ahead, still standing!

But as he drew closer to Tree Haven, Shade saw that a large branch had snapped off, leaving a jagged hole midway up the trunk. Without hesitating he trimmed his wings and flew through the knothole.

Inside it was a chaos of wings and voices, newborns and mothers crying out for one another. Shade swiftly added his own voice to the clamour.

"Marina!"

He fluttered laboriously through the aerial tangle, crying out Marina's name. Around him he could hear his other Silverwing companions calling out for their own mates. Shade had helped hollow out this tree, but its passageways and roosts had been enlarged even more by the females, and he was no longer familiar with its twisting geography.

"Shade?"

He locked on to her voice instantly and wheeled. When he saw her, his throat tightened. She wasn't roosting, but lying flat on her belly on a ledge, her right wing extended awkwardly.

"Marina," he said, landing beside her, and for a few moments, neither of them said a word, their faces and bodies pressed into one another, revelling in the other's scent and touch.

"I'm so glad you came," she whispered into his neck.

Finally he pulled back. "Your wing."

"I'm not sure. It doesn't feel too good. The earthquake snapped the branch and I was on it. I got knocked around a bit before I got clear."

He cast a tender wash of sound over her wing, and could see the swelling in her forearm, though he didn't make out any obvious fractures. He was hopeful it was just a sprain, but knew she wouldn't be able to fly for a while.

"Is the pain bad?" he asked.

She shook her head impatiently. "I don't know where Griffin is, I asked Penumbra to find him, but she hasn't come back yet."

"He's probably still out hunting," Shade said, not wanting to worry her – but he felt drenched with worry. She hadn't seen what it was like out there – trees mangled, the earth wrenched up. If Griffin had been out there, Shade could only hope his son had been aloft when the quake hit.

"He was upset, Shade. He flew off somewhere to be alone, I think."

"Why?"

Her face was pinched. "There was a terrible accident."

"Not with Griffin," he blurted instinctively.

"Griffin's OK. It was his friend, Luna. One of the other newborns. They stole some fire from the Humans."

He listened in growing horror as she told him all that had happened.

"How's Luna now?"

"Not good. We tended to her burns but . . ." She shook her head. "And the whole time . . ." She lowered her voice as if ashamed. "Over and over again I kept thinking, I'm so glad it wasn't Griffin. So glad."

She started to cry, and Shade nuzzled her tenderly, trying to hold his own tears at bay.

"I think he did it to impress you," Marina said.

"Impress me?" he said, startled.

"I should've known it would happen. They all tell stories about you, the things you did and – he's not like you, Shade. He hangs back, he worries about things. He was probably afraid you wouldn't like him unless he did something clever and heroic."

Shade didn't know what to say. He hadn't even met his son, and it seemed he'd already made him unhappy, forced him into doing something foolish and dangerous that might cost a newborn her life.

Penumbra fluttered towards them, her face grave. "I'm sorry, Marina, we haven't seen him yet. But there are still plenty of newborns outside. We're still looking."

"I'll look, too," Shade reassured Marina. He put his head close to hers. "Tell me what he looks like."

He listened carefully as she sang an echo picture into his ears, and watched as his son appeared before his mind's eye, etched in silver. It was the first time he'd beheld his son, and Shade's heart swelled. He didn't know if Griffin strongly resembled either Marina or himself, but looking at him, he felt an overwhelming sense of familiarity. This small creature belonged to him.

"Where did you last see him?" he asked.

"The healer's roost. He flew off before I could stop him, and when I went after him he'd already disappeared. I thought maybe he needed to be alone." She shifted anxiously, wincing at the pain it caused her wing. "I should've gone after him."

"It's OK. I'm going to find him." When he saw her confusion, he added, "I'm going to listen for him."

Shade knew he could waste hours flapping around, looking. The best way would be to track him with sound. Long ago, Zephyr, the Keeper of the Spire, had told him that you could hear noises from the past, and even the future if your hearing was sharp enough. Shade had never had any success listening to the future, but he'd found if he concentrated enough, he could *hear* the echoes of things that had already happened – though how far back he didn't really know.

He stroked Marina one last time and flew for the healer's roost near the summit of Tree Haven. At the entrance he faltered when he saw the wounded newborn, so still, tended by her mother.

"How is she?" Shade asked.

"I don't know." Her mother barely lifted her head.

"Is there anything else you need?"

"Everything's been done," said the mother. "Thank you."

Shade fluttered to the back of the healer's roost and tried to clear his mind. He listened. He started by screening out the biggest sounds, those that were being made now within Tree Haven, and then tried to hear the smaller ones, the echoes of sounds made just a few seconds ago, then a few seconds more . . .

As he listened deeper and deeper into the past, he felt a strange weightless sensation, somewhere between flying and floating in water. He did not know how far back he was going, and had to guess, pausing sometimes and letting the echoes draw pictures in his mind's eye:

Luna, and her mother crouched over her, nuzzling her cheek.

Further back: Ariel and many other females, gathered round the newborn, doubtless discussing her injuries, though Shade didn't want to spend time deciphering their words . . .

Off to one side he saw Marina, roosting alone, watching . . .

A little further back in time and—

A newborn was suddenly beside her, talking, and Shade recognized Griffin at once.

I've found him, Shade thought to himself. Now he had to follow him, listening forwards through time.

Feeling as though he were hovering in an immense black void, Shade strained to catch the echoes that formed his son: the image was silvery, hazy, and threatened to dissolve altogether sometimes. Listening intently, he saw Griffin take flight and careen from the healer's roost.

Shade too had to take flight and follow his son's path, staying close to the echoes his wings made. It was like chasing a smear of liquid light, moving down through the great trunk of Tree Haven, and Shade flew with one eye open, so he could match his own course with his son's – and avoid colliding with other bats.

He followed Griffin's sonic trail lower, until it hesitated briefly at the base of Tree Haven. It took all Shade's concentration to focus, to stopper his ears against all the noise in the roost, and the competing echoes from the past.

When he saw his son's echo image disappear into the tunnels, he felt ill. He could only hope Griffin hadn't been underground. Shade paused, listening forward in time, hoping he'd hear another sonic mirage coming back out of the passageway. But there was nothing, except a long concussion of light, created by something very, very loud. The earthquake.

Shade launched himself into the tunnel, scrambling as fast as he could, following Griffin's trail. Past the junction to the echo chamber, and down even further. *Griffin, why did you go so deep? Why did you have to hide down here?*

So intent was he on the trail that he almost crashed headlong into the wall of rubble and rock created by the earthquake. Panting, he cast back into the past, before the earthquake, until he caught sight of his son's smudgy silver image in the tunnel. With horror, Shade watched as Griffin dissolved into the wall of rubble and disappeared.

That meant he'd gone *past* this point.

Or that he was trapped somewhere within the debris.

"Griffin!" he shouted, his voice clattering about in the cramped tunnel. Immediately he started clawing at the rubble, coughing and sneezing as dust swirled around him. The cave-in might be only a few wingbeats deep, or a few hundred. Didn't matter. But after a few minutes he realized he was getting nowhere this way. He backed up, closed his eyes. He knew it was dangerous, that it might cause an even more disastrous cave-in, but Griffin could be in there, trapped, and it was the only way to shift the rubble. Shade took a deep breath and with all his might barked out a bolt of sound.

The sound struck against the wall of rubble and the returning echo blinded him in both ears. The ground shuddered and rock and earth pelted his fur, but when he opened his eyes, he saw that his blast had triggered a small avalanche and opened a hole in the wall of debris. He sang out once more, carefully, to enlarge the opening, and then hurried towards it.

"Griffin!"

Nothing.

He clambered through, using careful washes of sound to search the debris. His heart fluttered, sick with the fear he might see the edge of a shattered wing, a bit of lifeless fur. Matted with grit, he dragged himself out the other side, trembling with exhaustion and relief. He'd seen nothing. Surely Griffin was on this side, safe.

"Griffin?"

But the tunnel was empty. Then he saw it. At the far end, the rock had been split into a narrow gash, big enough for a bat to squeeze through. It was hissing faintly. Shade instantly thought of the tiger moth, sucked down into the earth.

No.

It was still possible his son was trapped somewhere in the cave-in . . . only one way to be sure. Again Shade flared his ears and listened. It was simpler this time: fewer echoes to distract him as he sifted back through the sound of time, and then suddenly there was Griffin, hunched up in the tunnel, trapped.

Shade's throat thickened as he watched the worried movements of his son, scratching uselessly at the rubble which cut him off, then turning to move closer to the hissing opening which promised his only exit. Shade stared, his breath frozen, as Griffin ducked into the fissure and disappeared.

"I fear your son may already be lost to you," said Lucretia, the chief Silverwing elder.

Shade shook his head, trying to expel her terrible words. "There's no way we can know that yet."

It had taken all his resolve to return to Tree Haven. Underground, he had crawled into the hissing crevice, following Griffin's echo image down and down until suddenly it evaporated in the powerful current. Shade knew that unless he turned back immediately, he too would be dragged headlong to whatever waited beneath. He'd wanted to go anyway, to hurtle himself after his son. But he couldn't. Not yet. At the very least he had to tell Marina. Laboriously, he'd dragged himself back up the tunnel into Tree Haven. And now, at its summit, he shifted impatiently as he listened to the four elders roosting above him.

"Over the centuries," said Lucretia, "similar cracks in the earth have opened. We have accounts of bats who fell down them. None ever returned. Shade, where your son has gone, there can be no rescue."

"I'm going," he said hoarsely. "I only came back to tell you."

"Our legends tell us it is the Underworld. The land Cama Zotz created for the cannibal bats after their death. It's a place of utter darkness and torment. For our kind, Nocturna created a different afterlife, a wonderful one. But in Zotz's Underworld, there are only the Vampyrum Spectrum, all the billions of them who were ever born."

The thought of his son in this hellish place – the *wrong*

place – was almost too terrible for Shade to endure. "I won't leave him there."

"It is said that those who enter the world of the dead, become the dead."

"Legends," Shade muttered.

"They are all we have," Lucretia reminded him kindly, but firmly.

"I've never even heard these legends," Shade said, unable to contain his frustration – and indignation too. "Why don't the elders ever talk about Cama Zotz or this Underworld?" He'd spent a lot of time in the echo chamber, the perfectly spherical cave where the Silverwing colony stored its history. He'd even sung some stories of his own to the polished walls. So how was it possible that he – a *hero*, in case anyone needed reminding! – should be shut out like this? It was outrageous.

"There are some legends that are meant only for the elders," said Lucretia. "Unless we feel they serve a useful purpose in their telling."

Shade said nothing, not trusting himself to speak. He hated the idea of secrets being kept from him, as if he were some silly newborn. Why shouldn't he – why shouldn't *everyone* – know all there was to know?

"Well," he said, his mind already leaping ahead, "who started these legends?"

"We don't know that, Shade."

"All I'm getting at," he pressed on, "is that someone must've gone down to the Underworld, and learned all this stuff, about the billions of dead cannibal bats and the darkness and Zotz . . ."

"Perhaps . . ."

". . . and he must've come back alive – or how would *we* know?"

"This is all conjecture, Shade."

"If he came back, *I* can come back!"

The elders exhaled in unison, momentarily at a loss.

"There's something else to consider, Shade."

This time the speaker was his own mother, Ariel. He still wasn't used to seeing her like this: hanging above him, looking wise and impartial. To be perfectly honest, it unnerved him, made him feel like a newborn all over again. "If the earth opened this tunnel," she said to him, "it may close it. Without warning."

"That's why I need to go right away. Mom, Griffin's down there!"

"My grandson," Ariel reminded him. "And if you go, my heart tells me I will lose my son as well. And Marina her mate."

"Anything we say will only seem cruel to you," Lucretia said, addressing Shade again. "We know that. But the opening must be shut immediately, to prevent anyone else being lost – and to prevent anything from coming up."

"I know it's got to be closed, I know that. But not yet. Please." He looked up at his mother in confusion. "You would've done the same for me, wouldn't you?"

"Of course I would've." She fluttered down beside him, pushing her face against his. He breathed in her scent, wished momentarily he could go back in time – not that his past had ever been particularly easy. "But I'm not just your mother any more, Shade," said Ariel. "I'm also an elder. And my own wishes are not always those of the council."

"The council can't stop me," he said.

"Shade," Lucretia said sharply, "it is inviting death to go after your son. It is unlikely there is any food down there, or any water. There may not even be air to breathe.

No Silverwing was meant to go to the Underworld of Cama Zotz."

"But Griffin *has*! Two nights is all I want," Shade persisted. "If I haven't returned by then, block the opening."

The elders were silent for a moment. Then Lucretia sighed and looked down at Ariel. Sadly, she nodded up at the chief elder.

"Very well," Lucretia said, "two nights. But that is all."

"I'm coming too!" Marina raged at him.

"You can't," Shade told her. "You've got to let your wing heal. If you don't, you might never fly again."

"It's not fair!" she said through her tears. "It's not fair you get to go, and leave me behind where all I can do is worry!"

She looked so angry, he couldn't help smiling just a little.

"And you," she said. "What if I lose you too?"

He sighed, spreading his wings around her. "Tell me what you want me to do."

"Go get him," she said. "Go get him and bring him home."

"Yes," he told her. "Yes."

OASIS

For a long time, Griffin stared blearily, trying to understand what he was looking at. Slowly, things began to make sense. He was peering up at a complicated tangle of branches and leaves, and beyond them, stars blazing in the night sky.

Flat on his back, wings sprawled, jagged images of his crash-landing flickered in his memory. His body tensed. What if he'd broken something . . . A wing? He swallowed, afraid to move; he certainly didn't feel any pain. But maybe he was in shock. Maybe he'd broken his back and wouldn't feel anything ever again. Cautiously Griffin turned his head. Good, that worked. He inspected first his left wing, then his right. They didn't seem damaged. He twitched his fingers, one at a time, then slowly furled both wings tight against his body. Gently he rocked himself from side to side until he had enough momentum to flip on to his belly. He grunted as the bruised muscles all across his back and chest clenched. But at least nothing seemed to be broken. The thick bed of leaves and moss on the forest floor must have broken his fall, saved his life.

Stupid of him to linger so long on the ground. Just asking to be eaten. He wasted no more time. Wincing, he beat his wings hard, working up some lift before shoving off with his legs. Slowly he ascended in a series of jerky spirals. He wondered how long he'd been lying stunned down there. Lucky he hadn't been wolfed down by some passing beast. He reached the peak of a tall tree, and there he roosted.

He took a good long look around. Forest everywhere, looking enough like home that he felt a surge of hope. But when he turned his gaze to the sky, his hope seeped away. He couldn't find the north star.

All the stars were arranged in constellations he'd never seen before. He began shaking, a deep inner tremor that had nothing to do with cold.

Where am I?

He couldn't rip his eyes away. The stars were bigger than he remembered, and extraordinarily bright. Even with no moon in the sky, the light from the stars alone was enough to bathe the forest in a silver that was more like approaching dawn. Something else about them, too . . . what was it? Then it came to him. The stars weren't twinkling at all. Their light was pure and unwavering.

He clamped his jaws together, tried to stop his teeth chattering.

How did I get here?

He'd fallen down a hole.

Then fallen from the sky.

It sounded like something from a terrible dream, but he knew it wasn't. He'd had plenty of bad dreams – he was an expert – and right now this did not feel like a dream. But how had he gone from the *hole* to the *sky*?

"It's not possible," he said quietly to himself, trying to reason this out. "I mean, that just doesn't happen. Except . . . well, what about this? The tunnel goes right through the entire earth and spits me out the other side into the heavens, and somehow I just crash-landed on a totally different world?" His breath snagged. That felt worse. *Much* worse. Now he wasn't even on the same *world*?

Wrapping his wings tightly around himself, he covered his head. His stomach roiled. He tried to think of something positive. At least he wasn't dead. After a landing like that, he was lucky.

"So I'm here, and I'm not dead," he muttered aloud, not feeling lucky in the slightest. He wanted this to be over now. He wanted to be back at Tree Haven. He'd face his mother, the elders. Luna. Maybe if he just slept, everything would be fixed when he woke up.

As if he could sleep.

Timidly he unfurled his wings and took another look. Same forest. Same strange stars. A beetle, bigger and spikier than any beetle had a right to be, droned past his nose, and Griffin grunted, momentarily distracted.

"That is one ugly bug," he said. But he was too dispirited to pursue it. He felt no hunger at all, just a heavy crushing despair.

There must be other bats here. He should go and look. Maybe they could tell him where he was, help him get back home. But he stayed locked to his roost, gazing around fretfully. There was something weird about this place . . . something *wrong* with it.

Then it came to him.

No smell.

This forest had absolutely no smell. He blew hard through his nostrils, in case they were clogged, then tried again. No rich, loamy fragrance of soil, no leaf mould, no sharp tang of bark and pitch. He swung up on to the branch, and put his nose right against it. Nothing. He tried a leaf – same thing. There was something terribly disturbing about all this. He frowned as he took a closer look at the leaves. Couldn't quite place them. Some sort of oak maybe. But a little further down, sprouting from the very same branch, was a tuft of pine needles. Leaves and needles on the same tree? Completely freakish.

Instinctively he flattened his entire body against the bark.

He was being watched.

Not just by one creature, but many. His fur tingled unpleasantly as dozens of sonic gazes bombarded him from all sides. They were taking a good long look at him. With his own echo vision he cautiously scanned the branches and caught sight of a multitude of bats, roosting deep in the trees. His body relaxed a little. He'd been afraid they might be owls. But why were they just hanging there silently, staring at him?

"Hello?" he called out.

His greeting triggered a collective gasp, a brief silence, and then a chorus of hushed chittering.

". . . fell from the sky . . ."

". . . Corona saw him . . ."

". . . came down like a shooting star . . ."

". . . not a Vampyrum . . ."

". . . maybe a Pilgrim . . ."

A Pilgrim? Griffin's head was starting to ache from the effort of catching all these muted voices.

". . . look at him . . ."

". . . at his wings, see . . ."

". . . the way the light moves . . ."

". . . the glow of him . . ."

Glow? Griffin thought in alarm, glancing at his wings. He wasn't glowing. What were they talking about?

"Oh, do you mean my fur?" he called out, hoping to clear up the confusion. "My father's a Silverwing, but my mother's a Brightwing, so I sort of got fur from both of them. That's why I have all these bands of bright hair. Maybe that's why you thought I was glowing . . . you know, just the, um, contrast between the dark fur and the light? It's pretty weird, I know . . ."

He trailed off, discouraged. He didn't get the feeling he was convincing anyone. He took another look at his wings and chest hair, and still didn't see anything glowing. Was there something wrong with these bats? Maybe this was some kind of weird joke.

"I really don't see anything," he said, trying to stifle a nervous chuckle. "I'm sorry, if I glow, but I really . . . don't have anything to do with it." It sounded ridiculous, but he felt it was best to apologize for pretty much everything at this point. He wished these bats would just show themselves.

". . . ghost . . ." came an anxious whisper from the trees, and then that one word was transmitted across the clearing, round and round him, like a tornado, faster and faster.

". . . ghost . . . a ghost . . . ghost, ghost, ghostghost ghost . . ."

He felt like he himself was spinning, the air whipped away from his nostrils by this maelstrom of whispers. They thought he was a ghost. Starlight in his fur. He remembered his plunge from the sky, how fast the trees had come up, branches thrashing and slashing all around him. Then nothing. And then waking up—

Waking up alive?

Or dead?

Griffin's breath congealed in his throat. Panicked, he

folded his wings around himself, felt the warmth trapped against his fur; felt his furious heartbeat. Beating heart. That meant not dead. Alive.

"I'm not a ghost!" he shouted out, more to reassure himself than the others. "I'm a Silverwing! I'm just lost!"

A long silence stretched out, and for a moment, Griffin wondered if they'd all silently flown away. But then he heard the rustle of unfurling wings, the squeak of claws pulling free from bark, and a flurry of bats emerged from their hiding places, curiously circling around him but keeping their distance. They were all Silverwings, males and females both. Many were extremely old, and kind of mangy looking, even more so than Lucretia and the other ancient elders back at Tree Haven. A lot of these bats had fur that looked like it had been chewed up by a racoon and then stuck back on. Even some of the younger ones looked a little grizzled and squished out of shape. *And they think* I'm *weird*, Griffin thought.

His eyes skittered from one to the next, hoping he'd recognize someone. A knot of bats parted respectfully and a silver-streaked female – no older than Ariel, his grandmother – flew towards him, and roosted on a branch overhead. Of all the Silverwings he'd seen here, she looked the most normal, barely bashed or chewed up at all. Even though she was comparatively young she had the bearing of someone in authority. Her eyes did not meet his, but strayed across his body, as if following some kind of moving pattern. The glowing thing again, Griffin guessed. Her ears had a suspicious forward tilt, making her demeanour rather fierce, and he noticed she kept her knees flexed, as if ready to take flight at any moment. Still, just being in the presence of a grown-up made Griffin feel calmer and more hopeful. She would be able to help him.

"My name is Corona," she said. "I am chief elder here. Where are you from?" Her voice was gruff, not unkind, but not exactly welcoming either.

"The northern forests. From Tree Haven."

The tips of Corona's ears twitched together into a peak, and Griffin heard startled squeaks erupt from the other bats. He glanced around in alarm. What had he done now?

"*The* Tree?" Corona demanded – angry or frightened, Griffin couldn't tell.

"Well," he stammered, "it is *a* tree, an old silver maple actually, but Tree Haven is just what we call it. It's our colony's nursery roost."

Corona's ears relaxed. "I see," she said.

"You've heard of it, then?" Griffin said hopefully. "Maybe you know Lucretia, she's our chief elder, or Ariel, she's my grandmother actually, you might have heard of her too . . ."

He trailed off as Corona shook her head. "I haven't heard of this place, or these elders."

"Well, what about Stonehold, that's the males' summer roost. Near the ocean?"

"I know of no ocean here."

Griffin swallowed. "Where am I?"

"This is Oasis."

Oasis. He'd never heard of it. Then again, he didn't know very much about the world. He'd never been beyond the valley that sheltered Tree Haven. His mother hadn't even sung him the sound map to Hibernaculum yet.

"But we're *near* the northern forests, aren't we?" he asked. "Maybe you can tell me how to get back there?"

Again Corona shook her head. "How is it you fell from the sky?" she asked.

Griffin tensed. He didn't really want to try to explain this part right now. They thought he was enough of a freak already, with the glowing and all. But he figured there was no going back. He took a breath.

"I was in the tunnels under Tree Haven, and there was an earthquake and I got cut off by a cave-in kind of situation, and the only way out was down. Through this crack in the rock. There was a breeze and I thought it would take me back to the surface but it just went down and down some more, until I fell . . . well, really, I got sucked down by the wind. I couldn't stop, and I came out really fast from . . . this hole, I guess . . . and into your . . . um . . . sky."

He paused, watching Corona's face. She was motionless, only her nostrils flaring and contracting as she breathed.

"I'm as confused as you are, really," Griffin said. "I just want to get home."

"You're not a Pilgrim?" Corona asked intently.

"No. I mean, I don't even know what a Pilgrim is," he replied, feeling close to tears.

"I am sorry you are lost," she said, without sounding terribly sorry. "Perhaps someone else here has heard of Tree Haven, but I am doubtful. Beyond Oasis is only desert. But I wish you the best of luck on your journey."

And with that, she gave a curt nod and flew off, the other bats streaking after her through the forest.

"Journey?" muttered Griffin. "How am I supposed to go on a journey? I don't even know where I'm going!" And for a moment, his anxiety was doused by anger. Corona hadn't helped him at all, hadn't told him anything useful! She just wanted to get rid of him! This was no way to treat a fellow Silverwing! If she only knew who his parents were, she wouldn't have treated him like that! But that was the problem: she didn't seem to know anything about his colony, or where he came from. Stupid bat. He'd find someone who did. Must be plenty of bats in this forest. He'd get directions from them.

He dropped from his branch, and flapped into the trees. Right away he realized this wasn't going to be so easy. At the mere sight of him, the Silverwings scattered as if he were a demented owl. He couldn't get within fifty wingbeats without them pelting for cover. *Must be my glow*, he thought. Still, how scary was a glowing newborn?

He tried calling out to them.

"Hi, excuse me, I—"

"I was wondering if you knew where—"

"Please ignore the glow, I just wanted to ask you—"

It was no use. Without fail the Silverwings fled before he could get more than a few words out.

"These bats are *pathetic*," he said, throbbing with loneliness. What was he supposed to do now? He looked up at the sky again. Still no sign of the moon but the stars had shifted. He wondered how long it was until dawn.

His stomach hurt, and he felt strangely reassured by it. Hunger. Something familiar. This he could deal with. He remembered that big bug he'd seen earlier. Hadn't looked particularly appetizing, but a few of those would be the same as a thousand mosquitoes. Pricking up his ears, he listened for the whine of insect wings as he soared through the forest.

Strange that he hadn't seen any other kind of creature here. At night he was used to spotting deer, flying squirrels and kangaroo rats, sometimes even a bear shambling through the undergrowth, or a moose stepping softly through the trees. Here, the forest floor was deserted.

An insect swooped up before his nose, some kind of

winged spider by the looks of it, not something he'd ever seen. He switched over to his echo vision and locked on. It wasn't too fast, and he came in quickly and smacked it from his wing into his open mouth. With a bit of trepidation he clamped down on the bug and—

There was nothing there. His eyes snapped open and he looked around in confusion, sending out a barrage of sound. Maybe it had just gotten away. But there was no sign of it. He'd felt it in his wing, then in his mouth . . .

He tried again. This time, he locked on to a freaky-looking moth, overtook it and, with painstaking care, curled it from his left wingtip into his mouth. He felt the gauzy fabric of its wings against his skin, then brought his jaws together. There was a quick pulse of light, a faint pop and the bug melted away. Gone.

Panting, Griffin tried to land, missing the branch on his first approach and nearly plummeting to the ground. The second time he shakily gripped the bark.

The bugs were not *real*.

They were just little bits of sound and light. What else wasn't real here? What about those odourless trees? His eyes darted anxiously across the branch, noticing the leaves. There were buds just unfurling, others fully grown, and some hard curled dead ones, still clinging on. It was spring, summer and fall all at once here. It wasn't normal. This place was *not normal*.

Then he saw her.

Maybe it was her distinctive upstroke, or her sleek profile as she streaked past – but he knew.

"Luna!" he cried out.

She shot him a quick backwards glance, then came around for a better look. As she flew closer, his heart leapt. It was definitely her, no question! She roosted at the end of his branch, staring at him in amazement.

"How did *you* get here?" Griffin exclaimed, words pouring out of him in sheer, giddy joy. "This is the weirdest place, Luna! Have you seen the trees and the leaves – and the bugs? Bizarre! These huge spiny bugs that you can't even eat! And the other bats here, have you talked to any of them yet? They're kind of unusual, to say the least. They keep telling me I'm glowing!"

"You are," she said.

"Oh." He felt taken aback. "You can see it too? Because I can't, you know. I can't see anything glowing at all."

"It's like you have starlight trapped in your fur."

He paused to catch his breath, and noticed the shiny patches of scar tissue on her wings. But her fur didn't look too bad. He couldn't believe how quickly it had all healed. All those potions the elders had must be amazing.

"You're all better," he said, overwhelmed with gratitude and relief. "Everyone was really worried about you. Mom said they were afraid you were going to die."

"What're you talking about?" Luna asked, frowning.

He blinked. Maybe no one had told her how badly injured she'd been. Made sense, he supposed. No point scaring her when she needed to be calm and rest.

"Well," he said. "I'm really sorry about everything. You know, it just happened before I could even think. I just—"

Her look of total confusion stopped him. She had no idea what he was talking about. Had the accident wiped out her memory or something? For a second he was almost glad. At least this way she wouldn't remember the horrible accident, the fear and pain – and how it was all his fault.

Didn't matter. Now that Luna was here, everything

would be all right again. She would know what to do. Even if she didn't know the way back, she would have a plan. She always had a plan.

"Luna, it is so *good* you're here. I was beginning to panic. I know, I know, I always panic. But this time, I was *really* freaking out. I didn't even have to imagine a worst case scenario, because this one was taking care of itself just fine."

"Who *are* you?" Luna demanded. "And how d'you know my name?"

Griffin laughed. It was just a joke, but there was a hardness in her face, a wary crease in her forehead. Maybe she *did* remember what had happened, and was angry with him. Punishing him a bit. Well, he deserved it.

He forced another nervous little chuckle from his throat. "How did you get down here anyway?" he asked. "Did you get sucked down that tunnel too? After the earthquake?"

"I don't know what you're talking about."

She seemed so serious that for a moment he wondered if this bat only *looked* like Luna. But no. Her voice, her name, the scars on her wings . . . It was definitely her.

"Come on, Luna . . ."

"How do you know my name?" she demanded.

Could she have lost so much of her memory that she didn't remember him at all?

"Look, Luna, we've got to figure out how to get home."

"This *is* my home."

"No. We're from the northern forest. From Tree Haven," he told her, hearing the quaver in his voice. "There was an earthquake, and we got sucked down some tunnel and ended up here."

Slowly Luna was backing away from him. She looked

scared. "I don't know you," she said, "and I don't know what you're talking about."

"Yes, you do!" Griffin shouted, so overcome with dismay and frustration that he began to cry. It wasn't fair. He was in this weird, freaky place where the trees didn't even know how to be trees and the bugs were nothing but air. And his best friend didn't even *know* him. He turned away from her, trying to hide his tears.

"Why are you glowing?" she asked. She must have edged towards him, because her voice was very close.

He cleared his throat. "I don't know."

"It's kind of interesting. It has a sound," she said. "Can you hear it?"

He shook his head, turning. Head cocked, she was listening intently. "It sounds like . . ." For a moment her face had a faraway look. "I don't know. Something familiar."

He was glad she hadn't left, glad she'd moved close to him; he longed to jostle wings and shoulders with her, feel the comforting warmth of a body near his.

"You OK now?" she asked.

"Yeah. Thanks."

"I'm sorry you're lost. If I could help you, I would, but I've never heard of any of those places you mentioned."

Griffin felt a lightning charge of fear spike his fur on end. His claws clenched deep into the bark.

"What's wrong?" he heard her ask, as though from a great distance.

She had no smell.

Before he could stop himself, he unfurled his right wing and, with its tip, touched Luna on the chest. He jerked back as if he'd been seared. But she wasn't hot. The opposite.

She was colder than any living creature could be.

"You're . . ."

But Griffin couldn't say it, because he was suddenly mute with fear, and in that moment he finally understood. The bugs, the trees, all those bats . . .

Dead.

And Luna, too.

"What's wrong with you?" he heard her ask.

Griffin blinked, trying to focus.

Can't breathe, no air, everything's dead.

Up.

That was all he could think. Up.

Away from here. He'd come from the sky, he would go back to the sky. It made no sense, but instinct had taken over, and his body told him to fly high. It was harder than he thought. As he rose above the forest, the air did not want to keep him aloft. Pounding his wings, it was as if there was nothing beneath them, nothing to push against. And how heavy he felt! Sweat beaded his eyebrows, prickling his fur. He remembered the fierce pull that had dragged him to earth. This world, whatever it was, was greedy. It didn't want you to fly, didn't want you to escape.

High above the trees, he could see how big the forest really was, and realized it was set into some kind of vast crater. Beyond, on all sides, stretched desert.

His thoughts fluttered anxiously through his mind: Luna, how cold she was, no scent, dead, dead. His fault. And now she was in this terrible, terrible place, and she didn't even know she was dead. None of them did. They thought *he* was the ghost.

Keep flapping!

But what was he hoping for? You fly into the sky, and then what? You had the sky, then the stars. Just air and more air and then nothing! You couldn't fly all the way to the stars! It was crazy, but maybe if he flew high enough, something would happen and magically he'd be back in the tunnel, or even back in Tree Haven, and this would all be over.

He didn't know how much longer he could fly, fighting against the immense pull of gravity, and his own exhaustion. But the stars, he realized, had definitely become larger and brighter and—

He nearly hit them.

He hadn't been paying attention with his echo vision, and with a choked cry he braked, flaring his wings and almost pitching over backwards. The sky had suddenly ended and above him was a dome of solid black rock. What he'd thought were stars were deposits of blazing stone embedded in the shell of the sky.

He dug in with his claws and hung, panting with fatigue. Even now the hungry backwards pull of the world tore at his knee joints, making him wince. He knew it was only a matter of time before he'd have to let go. Frantically, he sprayed sound across the stone. So this was what he had fallen through, thinking he'd been spat out into the heavens. Hope pulsed at his temples.

If he could find the hole, he could heave himself in, crawl inch by inch back up into the real world.

The opening must be here somewhere. Upside down, he scuttled across the stone sky, every step making his knees and wrists bark with pain. If only he'd noticed when he'd first come hurtling through, taken his bearings – but he'd been so scared and disoriented. Wasn't this roughly the right place? But his barrage of echoes painted only a wall of solid light in his head. Not so much as a crack.

When he peered back down through the cloudless sky he saw the great stone planet slowly turning. With a sick heart he realized that as the world shifted so too did the sky overhead.

His crack could be anywhere in the vastness of all this stone sky.

He kept looking anyway, dragging himself inch by inch, trying not to cry so he wouldn't blur his vision and hearing.

No one knows where you are.

Keep looking!

You told no one.

Maybe it's just over here a little more.

No one will come for you.

"Help!" he cried out, hoping that maybe some little bit of his voice would echo back home. The words were instinctive, wrenched up from his belly. "Mom! Help, please!" He pushed his face into the stone of the sky and noticed that it had a smell. The cold, gritty scent of rock, normally unappealing, was now everything he had lost: the smell of the living world. And he breathed it in as if it were the perfume of honeysuckle, the fragrance of his mother's fur.

Don't go, he thought. *Don't.*

He had to keep looking. But with a grunt, his knees buckled and he fell, sucked viciously earthwards. He unfurled his wings, fighting the pull, trying to guide himself back towards the forest crater. Where else was there to go? On all sides was only desert, rolling out to the ends of this terrible dead world.

THE MINES

Without night or day, moon or sun, it was impossible to keep track of time, and Goth had no idea how long he'd been dragging himself across the cracked plain. Eventually, after many failed attempts, he managed to take flight, only for a few seconds, before the ground dragged him back down. Was he just weak, or was the earthward pull stronger here than . . . than where? Where he used to be?

And so he carried on, hoping he was going in a straight line, and that he would eventually reach something – or someone who could explain this new world to him. If he was indeed dead, then this must be the land of the dead, the Underworld of Cama Zotz. He remembered that much at least: the name of his god. But he had always assumed the Underworld would be teeming with the dead. Where were they?

And where was Zotz?

A flurry of wings caught his attention, and he called out, "Stop!", but the bats, perhaps a dozen of them, continued on over the plain, heedless of his cries. Anger seethed through him. He would've flown after them, broken their necks for their insolence, but his limbs were still too weak. Would he always feel this way?

On and on he scrambled and flew, for hours or perhaps

nights, until at last he saw that the land appeared to drop away in the near distance. Hopeful of a vantage point, he hurried on and reached the very edge of the desert, where the earth simply plunged straight down into a cliff. Goth stared for a long time, his eyes blazing with the reflected brilliance of what he beheld.

There was a lake, and in the lake was an island and from the island rose a city more glorious than he had ever seen.

Impulsively he launched himself off the cliff, wings extended to their full three-foot span. For several seconds he plunged before his strokes became powerful enough to pull him out of his dive. Dazzling starlight shattered the placid water as he beat a course for the island. Dense rainforest grew up the steep coastline, and Goth laughed delightedly at the growing cacophony of toucans and macaws, the shriek of spider monkeys.

The entire island rose to a central plateau, and from a distance the city built upon it looked like one great gleaming pyramid. Closer Goth flew, and could see it was actually composed of innumerable buildings of pale stone, beautifully smooth and luminous in the stars' glow. Stretching through the city's middle was a monumental plaza paved with jewelled flagstones, and flanked by pyramids, each taller and more magnificent than the one before. All were crowned with an enormous tablet bearing a glyph of a majestic bat with jagged open jaws, tongue extended hungrily, nose flaring upwards into a spike. Cama Zotz, Goth knew instinctively.

Ornamental pools ran the length of the plaza, pulsing with tall geysers of steaming water. What a grand place this was, Goth thought. Was this like the place he came from? There was something familiar about it: the pyramids, the rainforest, the shriek of animals. But surely no place could be as magnificent as this.

Goth heard the bats before he saw them. An explosion of wings, like a crack of thunder, preceded them as they burst from the pyramids. Billions there must have been, like a single many-headed serpent coiling darkly through the air, and into the jungle to feed.

Goth was still high in the air, too high to be noticed by them, but he could tell they were all his kind. Vampyrum Spectrum – there, the name came back to him now. Nation upon nation of the dead, gathered over the millennia to live here in the splendour Zotz had created for them. He felt a profound rush of kinship with them, but something more too. A sense of power over them – but why?

In the distance, at the head of the plaza, rose a mountain, and Goth inexplicably felt drawn to it. But as he flew closer, he could make out terraces of luminous stone and realized with shock this was no mountain but yet another pyramid, the highest of them all.

To reach its summit was his one desire now, but he had exhausted himself with so long a flight, and it was all he could do to make a clumsy landing no more than halfway up. He could understand why he had mistaken the pyramid for a mountain. Miraculously, a rainforest grew from the stone of the terraces, trees whose trunks opened into a canopy of vast leaves. Giant ferns sprouted everywhere. Creepers and vines twisted over the stone, bearing fleshy flowers, some of which snapped open and closed, as if hungrily seeking air, or prey.

For just a moment, the rock beneath Goth's claws seemed to quiver, and he staggered off balance. He wondered uneasily if the pyramid itself was a living thing. He shook his head, feeling dizzy: it was merely fatigue.

The terraces were broad and steep, and Goth found he could flap up only one at a time, resting frequently.

Up and up he leapt and finally he could see the summit. A huge protrusion, like a flared wing, curved high over the pyramid, trailing thick vines which cascaded down to the luminous stone. Thousands of bats roosted here, and Goth felt an overwhelming sense of homecoming. Leaping into the air, he was determined to make a graceful entrance, and he soared towards the roosting bats.

"My fathers, my brothers and sisters, it is I, Goth! I am here to join you!"

He got no reply except for a few snorts and muttered words he couldn't make out. Four large Vampyrum dropped from their roosts and swirled around him. A female with a mighty crest of fur atop her skull swept in close. With immediate dislike, Goth noted that she was even larger than him, with muscular shoulders, and savage eyes that glinted in the starlight.

"Goth, you say?"

"Yes." He stared at her teeth in shock. They were not bone white, but black, as dark and lustrous as obsidian. He glanced at the other three Vampyrum and saw, embedded in their jaws, the same black, chiselled fangs.

"Excellent," the female said to him. "We've been awaiting your arrival with great anticipation."

"You have?" asked Goth, allowing himself a smile. Clearly his instincts were correct. He *was* someone of status here.

"You're to join the work crew," the female snapped.

"Work crew?"

"Shackle him," the female told her companions. Before Goth knew what was happening, the three Vampyrum had knocked him to the pyramid's summit and were looping a vine around both his ankles. This was no ordinary vine. Rivulets of pale light streamed over its braided surface, and it seemed to move of its own will, knotting itself with an eerie speed and strength. On his back, enraged at this indignity, Goth struggled, but the other bats easily overpowered him. And the vine held tight. Then, hauling at a second gleaming vine with their teeth and claws, the Vampyrum hoisted him, ankles first, up into the air towards the multitude of other roosting bats.

"Release me!" Goth roared.

"You speak as if you had authority," the female said mockingly.

"Who are you?" Goth demanded, volcanic anger pounding at his temples.

The female thrust her face close. "Phoenix. Chief Builder, under direct orders from Cama Zotz. This is all his bidding."

"I have committed no crime!"

"Is that so?" Phoenix laughed.

Goth lunged for her throat. But the female recoiled easily, and smacked him across the face with her right wing, sending him spinning from his vine. He glared at Phoenix, enraged that this creature had struck him, and even more disgusted by his own helplessness. He thrashed against his restraints, but seemed only to pull the vine tighter around his ankles.

"Let me give you some advice," Phoenix said. "Rest while you can. Your shift will be starting soon."

She withdrew with her three Vampyrum guards. Goth looked about through the jungle of vines and realized that all these bats were imprisoned like him, tethered by the ankles to what seemed to be the same colossal length of luminous vine. With surprise he noted that most were not Vampyrum, but other species of bat, most of them significantly smaller than himself, with fur of varying brightness and thickness. His resentment grew: why was he being herded together with these slaves and weaklings, creatures whom he had feasted on when alive? He should be among the millions of free Vampyrum he had seen earlier, bursting from the glorious pyramids, streaking over city and jungle. Clearly the Vampyrum tethered here had also displeased Zotz in some way. He looked around at this huge assortment of bats, united only in their misery. Their flanks rose and fell as though recovering from some great exertion. They looked more than exhausted; they looked defeated.

"What work is this?" he demanded of the large-eared bat closest to him.

The bat stared at him dully. "You'll see soon enough."

Goth bristled at this disrespect, but said nothing more. He was too fatigued, and perplexed. With difficulty he bent his neck towards his feet, and managed to get his jaws around the vine which bound him. He bit and his teeth sang with pain. It was harder than stone.

"Only the guards can cut the vine," the large-eared bat informed him.

Goth grunted, remembering their obsidian teeth.

So why then was he here? Surely some terrible mistake had been made. But how could he be certain? He scoured his memory again, and saw only flashes of things. A giant stone tablet with a hole in its centre, the sun blotted out, a sacrifice about to begin and then—

The rest would not come.

He hung in a kind of stupefied limbo, staring at the enormous stars. They seemed close enough to touch. As they drifted slowly overhead, he noticed in the heavens a vast dark circle within which no stars shone. He blinked. It seemed that some kind of dust or rubble was raining from this circle, glittering in the starlight as it fell. Like the stars, this colossal circle of darkness was moving across the heavens, and its path would bring it directly over the pyramid.

"Take wing! Take wing!" shouted an army of Vampyrum guards, and at once, the thousands of bats around him began to stir. Goth looked up and saw the first of the workers lurch into the sky, followed closely by the second, the third and on and on, all tethered together by this endless vine, flying heavenwards in a giant chain. They seemed to be beating straight for the huge dark circle in the sky's fabric. And as Goth stared in amazement, he saw a second chain of shackled bats, descending from on high, as if they'd issued from this very same void.

There was a sharp tug at his ankles and now he too was being dragged skyward. He spread his wings, though his own strokes seemed almost unnecessary, for the chain was moving with surprising swiftness, and he was carried along by sheer momentum. He was the last in the chain, and overhead burly Vampyrum guards swirled, making sure no one broke ranks.

"Faster!" he could hear them shouting.

"You're off course!"

"You, Deadweight!" Phoenix's face was suddenly against his, and Goth flinched in surprise. "Flap harder! You're dragging the line!"

Goth increased his power strokes, hating Phoenix, but refusing to be the weak link. Apparently satisfied, Phoenix flew upwards to supervise another section. Goth turned his attention back to the descending column of bats he'd seen earlier. Their flight path was now almost parallel to his, not more than a hundred wingbeats distant. Their wing strokes were laboured as they lurched down, fur coated in grit, and their eyes and nostrils heavily rimmed with dust. What was it they were doing? What work could possibly be done in the sky?

Was it an illusion, or were the stars getting bigger and brighter? The bodies of the other bats ahead of him were gleaming more brightly than before. Upwards they flew.

A fine silt of dust blew into his face and Goth blinked it away in irritation. His eyes could see only the stars and beyond them the eternal emptiness of the heavens. But when he cast out sound, his echoes bounced back at him. In alarm, he swept his sonic eye heavenwards again and again and somehow, inexplicably, the sky was coming to an end.

The sky was stone, the stars nothing more than deposits of glowing ore. Was the Underworld some enormous cavern, then, and this was its ceiling? Above he saw the leading bat in the chain disappear into the great circular void. Then the second bat disappeared, then the third – swallowed up one by one into darkness. Goth shot sound into it, and this time no echoes bounced back.

A tunnel, Goth now realized. But where did it lead?

He could see the opening now, hundreds of wingbeats across, its rim roughly hewn as if it had been laboriously gouged by millions of claws. Bat claws. He understood now. The bats had made this, had hewn it from the sky itself.

Finally he was pulled up inside. Without the fake starlight it was instantly much darker. He switched over to his sonic vision. The walls of the shaft led straight up, ridged with ledges from which roosted Vampyrum guards, watching over the workers as they continued their ascent.

The speed of the line slowed dramatically. A long stone bridge jutted halfway into the shaft. As each bat in the chain neared it, he roosted for a brief moment, and a Vampyrum guard stationed at the edge would shove something into the worker's mouth. A rock, Goth realized, as he drew closer. The worker bats would take the rock between their jaws, so only the tip was protruding.

Goth flew past the ledge, refusing to roost.

"Take it!" the guard roared at him, but Goth would not have a rock shoved into his mouth. The guard did not pursue him, as Goth had expected, but simply shook his head with a grim laugh.

Finally the tunnel dead-ended and as Goth approached he could see the thousands of worker bats, scattered across the ceiling, still tethered together. Goth flipped over and made an awkward landing, hanging upside down. All the others had swung their bodies up flat with the rock, using their thumbs and rear claws to hold tight. With the rocks in their mouths, they were already busily chipping away at the stone. A constant drizzle of shards and grit rained down from the ceiling, down the shaft, down to the earth below.

They were miners, digging this shaft deeper and deeper. Or was it higher and higher? How could they endure this forced labour, the indignity of using their heads as tools?

"Where's your rock?" Phoenix demanded, roosting beside him.

"I don't have one," Goth told her haughtily. "What is the purpose of this labour?"

"No rock? Then you must use your teeth!"

She slammed her body against Goth's, forcing his head towards the ceiling, and pushing his muzzle against the stone.

"Now! Dig!"

Goth had no choice. Baring his upper canines he reared back and brought his teeth forward to chip at the stone. It was very dense and each blow sent a lightning bolt of pain through the roots of his teeth into his skull. His mouth filled with grit and rubble and he spat it out.

"Next time, you'll take a rock," Phoenix said. Over her shoulder she said, "I'm watching you."

All around him, the bats worked in grim silence, the staccato click of rock on rock echoing through the shaft. The repetitive labour sent his mind into a reverie. How long had they been working to create this shaft? Where was it meant to go? All the way to the Upper World? Surely it would take millions of years to get any distance, even with thousands of bats ceaselessly working. He lost all track of time, and then felt a tug on his ankle. His mining team was beginning its descent. It was exquisitely painful to release his grip on the ceiling, his claws had been clenched for so long. He coughed grit from his mouth.

As the chain passed the long stone bridge, each bat spat out his mining rock. When Goth limped past, the guard gave him a mocking smile.

The descent was, if anything, more laborious than the ascent. He was even more tired now, and the fierce gravity of the Underworld made it necessary to flap hard simply to slow his fall, wings billowing. Halfway down, they passed another crew, returning for its shift. A spasm of panic, almost like a clattering heartbeat, racked Goth's chest. Was this the afterlife that awaited him, this mindless scrabbling, repeated eternally?

INTO THE UNDERWORLD

It wasn't like falling.

It was like being inhaled by some colossal beast. Shade hurtled through the narrow tunnel, scalded by the rock, the smell of his singed fur sharp in his nostrils. Far, far below, he caught a small ragged patch of light. He was accelerating towards it, could barely snatch air through his nostrils. Ears pinned flat, he shut his eyes for fear the wind would pluck them from his head. He furled his wings, folded his body small, and steeled himself for what awaited him.

Land of the Dead.

Would he die the moment he passed the threshold?

Would there be air?

Frantic images flashed before his mind's eye. A cave teeming with millions of cannibal bats. Cama Zotz coiling his shadowy presence towards him. And somewhere down there, his son—

Out.

Shade knew it instantly, the gut sensation of space and sound opening around him. He was still alive, still breathing: there *was* air. One legend wrong. Slowly he stretched his wings, fighting the monstrous downward pull. He felt like he was carrying a large stone in each claw.

Levelling off and circling, he peered down, and his stomach lurched. This was no cave. Far below him was an entire world, revolving like a small planet deep within the earth.

How will I ever find him?

He glanced back up at the stone ceiling, vast as the sky. It was scattered with large deposits of glowing rock, casting a light more powerful than real stars. Shade flew closer, knowing he had to find the hole he'd come through.

His way in. His only way out.

He bombarded the stone with sound. All that rock above him, all that weight just massed there, hanging, waiting to crush him like a midge. In his echo vision, a small crack of darkness appeared in the blazing silver of the sky. With effort, he flew for it, flipped upside down, and sank his claws deep, flanks heaving.

The unearthly light from a clump of phosphorescent minerals washed over him, turning his fur ghostly white. He peered back up the crack. The wind shrieked down at him, nearly blasting his head off. Far, far up and away was Marina, Tree Haven, his world. It seemed impossible there was a passageway between here and his home.

He needed to mark the crack somehow, so he could find it again when he had Griffin. He coughed to cleanse his throat, closed his eyes, and shouted at the rim of the tunnel entrance. The sound hit the stone at the proper angle, and bounced between the two sides, but the fierce wind sucked the echoes away instantly.

Discouraged, he let himself fall away from the rock, taking a good look. The clumps of minerals really did look like stars once you moved further back. *So use them like stars.* He found his crack and memorized the little constellation around it – seven stars arranged in a rough circle. Remember that. How they would claw their way back up that shaft was another question, one he didn't want to think about right now.

Griffin.

He flared his ears, and listened for his son. Moving backwards in time through the bright haze of silence until—

He caught just a ghostly trace of movement, a shape that could be wings, a head, a pair of panicked outstretched claws hurtling through the crack. But then the image dissolved like mist dispersed by a breeze.

"No . . ." Shade muttered as he swerved and dipped after the scattered little shards of sound. The last sparkling sonic motes dissolved. Shade circled, despairing, looking down at the world far below.

Where do I begin?

Just begin.

He tried to imagine his newborn son, spat out into this strange world, weak with terror – and felt his own muscles weaken sympathetically as he spiralled down, fighting the earth's pull. Would Griffin have been able to make a proper landing? He might have crash-landed somewhere, and was now injured, unconscious . . . dead. Shade peered down, trying to find a likely spot: forest, caves, trees, anything that would beckon a frightened bat. Shade was still too high to use sound, and with his eyes could only make out shades of darkness below.

You've only got two nights.

Lower still, and now he saw an arid, pockmarked plain spreading before him. No trees, little vegetation, and no kind of creature on the ground. Quickly he scanned the skies for Vampyrum, but saw nothing, not even the sonic flare of a mosquito. This place was so inhospitable, perhaps it had never known inhabitants. But where were they, he wondered uneasily, all the inhabitants of the Underworld? Where were the billions of Zotz's dead?

And where was his son? Griffin wouldn't stay *here*. He'd fly on, try to find somewhere with food, shelter, trees where he could roost. Or hide. Would he hide somewhere and just wait . . . for what though? He would try to get out. Perhaps he'd already tried to make it back to the ceiling, but wasn't strong enough.

"Griffin!" he called out, flinching at the noise, half expecting to see a thundercloud of cannibal bats boiling towards him. He didn't like the idea of drawing attention to himself, but what else could he do?

"Griffin Silverwing!"

His voice echoed back at him from the flat earth, and evaporated. Over his wing he peered upwards and found his circle of stars, marking the escape route. It seemed to have slid further across the sky, and he realized that either the earth was revolving, or the sky was. His heart sank. That meant Griffin hadn't necessarily come down around here. He might very well be on the opposite side of the world.

Doesn't matter. Keep going.

This wasn't a good plan. This was barely a plan at all. But he was afraid to stop and think, afraid of wasting more precious time. He wished Marina were with him now, to help him – to advise him.

"Griffin! Griffin!"

He called out his son's name so many times the sound became a part of him, like a heartbeat, or a breath. He would not stop until he heard his son's return cry.

PART TWO

PILGRIMS

Near the edge of Oasis, where the forest met the great cracked plains of mud, Griffin picked a tree shrouded with hanging moss, and roosted hidden against the trunk. He hadn't wanted to return at all, but where else could he go?

Alive, he kept telling himself. *You're alive*. But he didn't feel very good. Trembling, his joints felt like they might snap apart, his muscle and sinew pulpy. His stomach gulped. He tried to concentrate. He needed a plan.

"OK, how's this," he muttered to himself. "You take a little rest, then fly back up to the stone sky and keep looking for the crack. That's a plan. Pretty big sky, though, and I can only stay up there ten, fifteen minutes at a time before I get sucked back. I could keep going up for years and not find it, and anyway, I wouldn't have the energy to keep going back because there's nothing for me to eat down here. I'd just get more and more worn out and—"

He stopped himself. Sometimes the words didn't do what they were supposed to. They were *supposed* to make him think more clearly. Right now they were just scaring his fur out by the roots. He decided to try once more.

"Forget the crack in the sky. Maybe there's another way out. I leave Oasis and . . . fly out over that terrifying desert . . . oh yeah, that's great, *very* promising. But it can't go on for ever, can it? And maybe I'd meet someone who could help me. Someone friendlier than the bats here – wouldn't be hard. But what kind of crazies would live out there in that desert anyway?"

He rustled his wings anxiously, gripping and regripping the branch. He wasn't good at this. Every time he thought of a plan, he just kept coming up with all the drawbacks. And look what happened with his last plan anyway. Steal some fire, what a great idea! And now Luna was down here and it was all his fault. Guiltily he thought of her confused, startled look as he'd leapt away from her in terror, wings churning to escape. Leaving her behind.

What would your father do?

His father? Oh, well, if his father were here, he'd do something amazing like blast a hole in the sky, or bring all the bats back to life and deliver them into the sunlight. Give him a couple of hours and Shade could probably solve everyone's problems. Then there would be a big celebration, and they'd have to sing his praises to the echo chamber again, and the echo chamber would be so full it would blow up and blast little bits of Shade's heroics all over the northern forests so every living thing could hear them!

Griffin's heart raced with anger. Then, as his pulse slowed, he felt his energy and hope leave him like an exhalation. How he wished his father were here. He squeezed shut his eyes.

Do something, he told himself.

Go find Luna.

The thought surged into his head, and he wasn't quite sure why. He was terrified of seeing her again. Nothing he could do would help her. And what was he supposed to say? "Oh, by the way, you're dead. Just thought I'd let you know." But she was his best friend, whether she knew it or not, and he needed her right now. Maybe she would help him. Maybe she could make a plan.

He set off at once, hoping he could remember the place he'd met her. This was good; this was doing something. He was aware of the Oasis bats flapping clear as he approached. *Just me, the fabulous glowing bat!* Despite himself, he smiled.

When he saw the stream, he felt even more cheered up. He swallowed in anticipation, mouth parched. The surface sparkled in the starlight – if you could still call it starlight. He was too thirsty to be cautious now, so he strafed the stream, mouth open to catch the water—

And veered up, coughing violently at the gritty swirl that poured down his throat. Not water at all, just a kind of dusty nothing disguised as water. Like the bugs, the water wasn't even there.

"Gah!" he exclaimed angrily. "I *hate* this place!"

A new worry pounced into his head now. He remembered his mother telling him once that you could survive longer without food than water. So how long would he last?

"Join us! Join us! Come with us to the Tree!"

Griffin peered up through the branches and saw a tight group of bats streak past, maybe three dozen, all different species, flying low over the forest.

"Join us!" the lead bat called out again.

Griffin flew after them, keeping just below the tree line for cover.

"Pilgrims . . ." he could hear some of the Oasis bats muttering around him, ". . . the Pilgrims are back . . ."

Griffin saw that the leader was a Silverwing female, and an old one at that. Her fur was mostly grey, and sparse in places, showing patches of wrinkled skin. Her whole body conveyed age and weariness. As she flew her shoulders were hunched, her long fingers disfigured by swollen joints, her wing saggy and blistered. Her gnarled thumb claws looked ancient, like turned-up roots. Nonetheless she was an arresting figure, and her still-strong voice commanded attention. Griffin couldn't help but feel hopeful at the sight of her, but then again, he'd been disappointed by the last Silverwing female he'd thought was an elder.

"You must not remain here!" the lead Pilgrim called out. "This is not your final destination. Come with us."

As the Pilgrims circled overhead, a huge number of the Oasis Silverwings gathered in the higher branches, peering up curiously, muttering amongst themselves. None dared go closer. Griffin hurriedly looked for Luna, but could find her nowhere amongst the crowd.

"Go away!" someone called out to the Pilgrims, and Griffin recognized the voice as Corona's. "You're not wanted here!"

From the trees, other bats started shouting now.

"You're crazy!"

"Clear off!"

"We're happy where we are!"

"Stop bothering us!"

"Go! Go! Go!"

It became a chant, a horrible din that sounded like the hoarse bark of ravens, trying to drown out the old Pilgrim. But Griffin thought there was more than just derision in their voices; there was an edge of desperation, too. Their hardened faces held a frightened intensity. Even as their shouts and cries echoed through the forest, somehow the aged Pilgrim's voice could still be heard.

"We are no longer of the living!" she cried out as she flew. "You must accept that. You. Are. All. Dead!"

Griffin gasped, feeling a huge rush of surprise and relief. This Silverwing *knew*! How come she knew, and all the others didn't?

"This is the Underworld," the Pilgrim cried out. "Every one of you is dead."

"I'm feeling fine, thanks very much!" a mocking voice cried from the trees. Harsh laughter echoed all round.

"We were not meant to stay here eternally," the Pilgrim persisted, the power of her voice undiminished. "In our lifetimes we undertook many journeys. There is one last journey you must make."

"You go on ahead!" someone else shouted.

"You all believe yourselves to be alive, but it is a delusion. Death has clouded your memories of your past life, but you must try hard to remember. Do not deny the truth. This is a dead place, but there is life to come. You need not stay here for ever. We can help set you on your way, but the journey must be yours. You must travel to the Tree."

The Tree? Griffin remembered the shock on Corona's face when she'd mistakenly thought the Tree was his home. Where was this Tree, and what was so special – and terrifying – about it?

"We've heard all about the Tree!" said Corona, breaking through the forest canopy and swirling around the Pilgrim. "It is a place of torment. Anyone who goes into the Tree never comes out! It burns you up, eats you up! It kills you!"

"No," said the Pilgrim forcefully. "It does the opposite. This pathetic imitation of a forest is death. These are not true trees. Look at them. These are not the leaves we have known! And where is the sun, the moon? All these things we once had? Think back! Think what came before this place."

"You are the one who is deluded," said Corona. "Listen to yourself! How can we be dead? We fly, we hunt, we think, we speak. I pity you, but you are not welcome here, spreading fear and lies!"

"Nocturna gave us the Tree as a way to a new life. We were meant only to pass through this place, and reach the Tree."

Griffin nodded eagerly to himself, reassured by the mention of Nocturna. His mother had told him a little about her, and her promise that bats would regain the light of day. That had come true.

"Those who want to come, join us!"

Griffin looked as two Oasis Silverwings flew out to join the Pilgrims. They looked bewildered, and more than a little afraid.

"Come back!" Corona called after them. "You fools, they're leading you to your death!"

The two bats faltered, but did not turn back. A third Silverwing flew out into the open, followed by another, until perhaps a dozen had joined the circling Pilgrims.

"Welcome, welcome," the lead Pilgrim greeted them warmly. Turning her gaze back to Corona and the others skulking in the treetops, she said, "Think on what I have told you. I will come again to speak more to you."

"No! Don't come back!" Corona told her.

"Goodbye," said the Pilgrim, and she led her group away over the treetops of Oasis.

Griffin followed at a distance, still hidden. Where were they going now? Where was this Tree? Part of him wanted to join them. Maybe it was simply that the lead Pilgrim was a Silverwing, and he instinctively trusted her. If she knew about being dead, maybe she knew other things too. But maybe his glow would turn them against him. And what was this Tree? And why was everyone else so afraid of it?

At the very edge of Oasis all the Pilgrims landed in the trees. As Griffin watched, the Silverwing female roosted beside each one in turn, pressed her face close and sang quietly. Griffin couldn't hear the song, of course, but after each bat had heard it, he spread his wings and launched himself over the desert.

Soon only the Silverwing female was left. Griffin didn't know if he could endure seeing her fly away as well. He saw her sigh as she gazed after the departing bats, and then her knees flexed and her wings opened, ready for flight.

"Wait!" Griffin called out, and at the same moment – or a split second before, he wasn't sure – the old Silverwing turned. It was as if she'd been anticipating his voice, or maybe she'd just glimpsed his glowing body through the mangy branches. Griffin saw her gaze sweep across and lock on him. She stared. Then she dropped from her branch and came hurtling towards him with such speed and intent that Griffin scuttled back against the trunk, suddenly wishing himself invisible. With a snap of her aged wings, she roosted, overlooking him. For a moment she said nothing.

"You're alive," she breathed in wonder.

"I think so," Griffin said, a little frightened by her piercing eyes. Then he frowned. "How did you know?"

"The glow," she said. "It's the same as the Tree's. How did you get here?"

"There was an earthquake," he said, so thankful to be

telling someone who would understand. "I got caught in a cave-in, and the only way out was down, and the wind sucked me right down here."

"Fissures sometimes open," said the old Silverwing. "Usually the earth closes them almost instantly, but sometimes the living get dragged down. Burrowing animals mostly, who spend their lives deep in the soil. You are lucky you have wings, my young friend, or you would have plunged to your death."

"Lucky," he said, "yeah."

"What is your name?"

"Griffin. I'm from Tree Haven. In the northern forests?"

"Tree Haven," said the old bat with a smile.

"You know it?"

"Very well. I was its colony's chief elder. My name is Frieda."

Griffin stared. *Frieda Silverwing?* Everyone had heard of her; she was still considered one of the greatest elders the colony had ever known.

"You knew my parents, then!" he exclaimed happily.

She studied his face and fur and ears so keenly he had to glance away in embarrassment.

"Yes," she said, a smile of genuine pleasure sweeping her aged face, "I believe I do. I thought you looked familiar. Shade Silverwing and Marina Brightwing are your parents."

Griffin nodded so hard his neck hurt.

"Do they know what has happened to you?"

"I don't think so. My mother—" He didn't want to tell her about Luna's accident, how he'd flown away in shame to hide. "She didn't even know I was down in the tunnels when the earthquake happened."

"How long have you been here?"

"It's hard to tell without the sun. Maybe a night and day?"

The sadness in her eyes frightened him.

"I *can* get home, can't I?"

"The crack you fell through has probably already closed. Even if it hasn't, you could waste precious time searching, and still never find it. And by then it might be too late."

"Too late?"

Frieda dropped from her branch and fluttered to roost beside him. Her body was cold and odourless, but he still found it comforting to have her near him, this bat who had known his parents.

"Griffin," she said gently, "there is no sun here, no food, nothing to nourish the living. Linger too long, and you will sicken and die."

"Well, it's not like I *want* to linger," Griffin blurted, needing to talk, to drown out her terrible words echoing in his head. *Sicken. Die.* "Believe me, I have absolutely no interest in lingering. None whatsoever. I want to get out of here. This place is the worst – no offence or anything, I know it's your home now, but really, it's terrible. All I want is out. But no one's been able to help me so far and—"

"It's all right," Frieda said, touching a wing to his face, stopping him.

"Is it?" he said, almost believing her.

"There is a way out."

"The Tree, right?" he said numbly. "So why's everyone so afraid of it?"

The Silverwing elder smiled sadly. "When we die, we are born into this world. We open our eyes to trees and forest and other bats and these things instantly become our new reality. This, we think, is the way it's always been. These bats think themselves alive, and trick themselves into believing Oasis is their home, and always has been. Yet all have vague memories of their past lives. Most ignore them as troublesome dreams. But some dwell on them and gradually realize what has befallen them. Some find it very hard to understand they are dead – especially those who died suddenly or violently, or those who died so young they scarcely had time to understand life, much less the notion of death."

Griffin looked at his claws, thinking of Luna.

"And Cama Zotz, the god of the Underworld, does all he can to keep everyone in this state of delusion. The forest is his creation, and is convincing enough to satisfy most bats."

Zotz. The name itself seemed loaded with danger, like lightning. Griffin had heard all sorts of stories, traded from newborn to newborn, how much of it true he could only guess. The little he knew for sure was from his mother – stories about his own father's adventures in the southern jungles. He did know that Cama Zotz was the god of the Vampyrum Spectrum, the cannibal bats his father had defeated.

"So . . . where is Cama Zotz?" Griffin asked nervously.

"All around us," said Frieda, and Griffin felt his fur twitch across the nape of his neck. "This is his kingdom, and he would rather see it swell in size than diminish. He can't stop bats from seeking out the Tree and leaving this place, for the Tree was rooted here by Nocturna herself. But Zotz does all he can to convince us this is our true and final home. Most bats have willingly agreed to play along. And for those who come to accept their deaths, he makes their journey long and difficult, and puts many temptations and trials in their path. That is why there have always been Pilgrims to help the dead understand who and what they are. And set them on their final journey."

"They all go to this Tree and live inside it?" Griffin asked. "It must be huge."

Frieda chuckled. "It is huge. But no, the Tree is not the destination. The Tree is a conduit, a passageway to the next world."

"But I don't want to go to the *next* world," Griffin said in alarm. "I want to go back to my own world."

Frieda nodded. "From what I understand of the Tree, it is a kind of current, a slipstream that guides us where we most need to go. For the living, there would be a different path than for the dead."

"Have other living bats gone into it?"

"Not in the time that I have been a Pilgrim, no."

"See, that's what's got me worried. It just seems like the Tree would be all used to dead bats down here, and I go in there, alive, and maybe it makes a mistake and sends me to the wrong place, like this next world for instance. I'm sure it's nice and everything," he added hurriedly, not wanting to offend her, "but it's just . . . not where I want to go."

"I understand completely," said Frieda. "I believe that Nocturna will take care of you once you're in the Tree."

Nocturna. She wasn't exactly taking care of him now. Maybe he didn't deserve taking care of, after what he'd done.

"As long as it takes me home," he said. "I just want to be really clear about this."

Frieda smiled. "I have every confidence it will."

Griffin nodded. Frieda was wise, his mother had always said that. If Frieda said it, he would try to trust her.

"So what is the next world, anyway?"

"I'll only find out when I enter the Tree myself." Frieda sounded tired, and more than a little wistful.

"You've seen the Tree though, right?" He still wanted to be reassured it was a real place.

"Yes, Griffin. Many times."

"Why haven't you gone inside?"

"Believe me, every time I see it, it's all I can do to stop myself from hurtling through the knothole." She laughed ruefully. "I thought with death my responsibilities as elder would end, but no, it seems that even now I'm expected to look after all of you." She shook out her wrinkled wings. "I would have preferred to rest this old body of mine, but in time someone will replace me." She smiled. "Soon enough," she said. "Until then I'm needed here. Dying is a confusing business."

"The young ones," Griffin said, "the ones who die suddenly, what happens to them?"

"In time, most come to realize what has happened on their own, and travel for the Tree. But some, even with help, never make the journey."

"So they just—"

"Remain here eternally, yes."

Griffin shuddered inwardly at the thought.

"And time is a luxury you do not have, Griffin." Frieda reminded him firmly. "You must set out now."

He looked at her. "Alone?"

"You may meet other travellers on the way."

He inhaled, feeling a slow squeeze of panic around his heart. He wanted to stay with Frieda, be with someone who remembered the Upper World, who knew his parents.

"Come with me," he whispered, knowing it came out

sounding like a whine, weak and cowardly – but he couldn't help it.

She leaned her old, grey head against his. "I can't, child," she said. "Even if I could, I'd be of no help to you. The best I can do is set you on your path."

It wasn't fair, he thought, anger momentarily overtaking his fear. Why couldn't she make an exception? His parents were important. His father . . . his father was more famous than her, even! He'd won back the sun, made peace with the owls! She should be taking care of him down here, not deserting him.

Maybe she caught the flash of indignation in his eyes, because she said, "I know this must seem harsh, even cruel to you, but it has always been this way. There are many colonies like Oasis, all across the Underworld, and I must visit them all. That is my role."

"It's not like they even listen to you, anyway," Griffin muttered.

Frieda surprised him with her laugh. "No, it's not. The dead are notoriously stubborn. But nonetheless . . ."

"I know . . . you have to do it."

"Are you ready to hear the map?"

He blinked. "Hear it?"

"Ah, you haven't even had your first migration yet, have you? The mothers sing the maps to their newborns, a song made of echoes that they see in their mind's eye."

The simple image of his mother made his eyes fill with tears. Tree Haven, the other newborns. Feeding in the night, preparing for the upcoming migration. Would he be a part of it?

"Close your eyes," Frieda said to him.

He did so, and she sang sound into his ears. His breath snagged as the darkness inside his head suddenly exploded with light. A perfect silver forest flared before him, so real he jerked back, eyes snapping open.

Frieda was smiling. "Shade did the same when I first took him to the echo chamber."

Griffin looked at her eagerly, hungry for more about his father. But Frieda was already singing again, so he shut his eyes, flared his ears and—

The forest, Oasis, and the plain of cracked mud and rock encircling it and stretching to all horizons. He soared up, and his stomach plunged as if actually in flight, until he was high in the air.

"How am I supposed to find my way?" he asked, remembering at least to keep his eyes shut. The desert all looked the same. No trees or hills or landmarks of any kind.

"Listen," he heard Frieda tell him, as if from a great distance.

Suddenly he heard a new tone being sung, and he was streaming down over the plains now, frighteningly fast he thought, right towards the earth. He could see that the mud was cracked in a definite pattern, as if some ancient river had once flowed there. The riverbed filled with light as he neared it, coursing along its path to the horizon.

"Oh!" he said, "so I follow that old trail kind of thing. But then what?"

He was plunged back into darkness and then—

A single tree on a plain, a pudgy-looking thing with fat branches, bristling with thorns.

"It's called a cactus," came Frieda's faraway voice.

In his mind's eye Griffin was circling the cactus and then roosting on a high branch that split in half and then rejoined, forming a circular gap. Suddenly he was pelting towards the opening – would he fit through? – and shot straight through the other side.

"Why—" he began to say, but already the images were shimmering and shifting and he was flying again, over desert, and then a valley, and at the valley's end was the opening of a vast cavern. Around it, many bats fluttered. It looked inviting, but he was obviously not meant to linger there because he was jerked past, hurtling on into darkness for another moment before—

An immense canyon, whose walls plunged down into total darkness. It ran to both horizons, uninterrupted, like some huge terrible scar, and he was about to cross over it to the other side. As he did so he felt a terrible yawning pit in his stomach, and simultaneously the urge to look straight down – but, luckily perhaps, he couldn't because he was not in control of this flight. All he knew was that there was something terrible in that great canyon, and the thought of even flying over it made him feel sick.

Turning now. He soared between two tall spires of stone which flanked the canyon like the horns of a buried beast, and then, his new course set, the landscape blurred past him at impossible speed until—

A deep valley ringed by mountain ranges. The valley was empty, dead, but suddenly from the soil sprang a frail shoot, buds unfurling as it grew higher, thickening into a trunk, sheathing itself with bark. Up it grew with dizzying speed, a sapling now, reaching skywards, now a mature tree, its main trunk forking into yet more branches which sprouted leaves and branched again. The tree was higher than the mountains now, and Griffin had to flap out of the way as the trunk soared up past him, its hundreds of branches reaching skywards until they seemed to be scraping the very heavens.

"The Tree!" he said in delight. It was so tall, so beautiful. Then it ignited, its entire surface wreathed in flame.

Griffin cried out in surprise. After a moment it was so engorged that it seemed the Tree and all its branches were made entirely of fire. How could this be a way out? Midway up the trunk was a small knothole, the single gap in the Tree's seething skin of flame. Griffin could see nothing beyond the darkness, but it was like peering into the eye of some hypnotic animal. It beckoned, even as he felt his instincts holding him back. Fly into that? How could he? How could anyone? No wonder the Oasis bats thought the Tree was a place of death and torment. Fly too close and—

Luna. Spiralling to the ground, her wings ablaze.

His eyes snapped open. Frieda was looking at him patiently.

"You understand?" she said. "Those were all the landmarks. Do you remember them?"

He stole some air. "The path in the cracked mud. That fat tree, I mean cactus, and I squeeze through the hole in the branch and that sets me on course to the big cavern. Go past the cavern and over the canyon, not looking down, turn between those two weird skinny towers of stone. And that pretty much takes me to the Tree. Um, does it always, you know, burn so . . . brightly?"

"It does, but you musn't fear it."

"Don't fear raging inferno. I'll remember that." He started to giggle nervously, but managed to stifle himself when he saw that Frieda had more to tell him.

"The path can change," she said. "Zotz alters the landscape when he pleases. It's best if you leave immediately. Let no one distract you on your way. There may be those who try to slow you down or stop you."

"Who?" he wanted to know.

"Those jealous of your life. And there are also the Vampyrum."

Griffin's mouth fell open. "What about them?"

"Not so long ago they were content to remain in their own oasis, but now they have been raiding others, and enslaving the bats. Be watchful always."

Griffin swallowed, mouth parched. "Is there anything else I should know about? I'm not sure I'm quite terrified enough."

Frieda smiled. "You know everything you need to. But you must hurry."

He was glad she didn't mention the dying part again.

"I *will* make it, right?"

"It will be the stuff of legends, do you realize that?" Freida told him, her eyes dancing with starlight. "No living creature has come here and returned. You will be the first!"

"It'll make a good story," he said with an unexpected surge of enthusiasm.

"An excellent one."

"Maybe even something to tell to the echo chamber," he said, imagining it, the words he would speak to the smooth walls, his own echo voice joining Frieda's and the elders', and his father's too! The stuff of legends! He smiled, trying to feel brave, but he felt his face tightening like it might crack. What made *him* think he could be the first to do this thing?

"What if—" he began.

"Give my kindest wishes to your parents when you see them," Frieda said.

His parents. Her words filled his heart with hope: Frieda thought he'd make it back.

"Thanks," he said, and then, before he could check himself, "But Luna."

Frieda looked at him curiously. "Who?"

"My friend. I saw her down here. She doesn't know she's dead."

"She will have to find that out in her own time."

"But she needs to get to the Tree, right? Could she get out if I took her with me? To the Upper World?"

Frieda shook her head.

"She's barely dead, though," Griffin hurried on anxiously. "Maybe a night or two at most. And she shouldn't be here—"

"She is dead, Griffin, and nothing can change that."

"Nothing?"

Frieda looked troubled.

"So there is a way?" Griffin persisted.

"Listen to me, Griffin, I did not intend to tell you this, but it affects you very much. Your life glows around you like a haze. The dead can see it; most may not know what it means, but some will. They will want it. They may do anything to get it."

"What can they do? I mean, they're dead."

"Dead or not, they can still kill you. They still have bodies, and weight, and strength, and if they have the will, they can steal your life away."

Griffin felt his insides start to coldly churn.

"How?" he heard himself ask.

"If they kill you, your life springs from your body, like a kind of current, like an echo, and they can suck it into themselves. I have never seen it happen, but I have heard of such things, and it is terrible. And so this is an answer to your earlier question about your friend. The only way the dead can live again is to steal the life of a living thing.

So you must be especially wary on your journey. Stay away from all others. Your trip is one that must truly be made alone. Even those who seem friendly may attack you out of fear or desperation."

Griffin nodded, looked to the horizon. "It's just that, it shouldn't have happened," he blurted out, needing to tell someone. "It was really stupid the way she died, an accident and . . . it was because of me."

Frieda exhaled sadly. "Death never seems just, Griffin. I'm sorry. And I'm sure it wasn't your fault."

"It was, though," he said. "And" – he heaved in a big breath – "I can't just leave her. Even if I can't bring her back to life, I could at least get her away from here and all the freaky trees and bad bugs." The idea of her here, thinking this was real, so confused – he just couldn't bear it.

"She may slow you down," Frieda warned him.

"Well, she used to wait around for me back at Tree Haven."

Frieda looked at him and nodded. "You are a good friend. Do what you must. And good luck."

She opened her wings.

"Wait. Um, I just wanted to know . . ."

"Yes?"

"Do I look like them?" he asked, not knowing why. "My parents."

"Yes. You look like both of them."

"I'm not like them, though, really."

"No," said Frieda. "But that doesn't matter."

He'd wanted her to disagree, he supposed. Say he was as valiant as his father and as smart as his mother. But that would be lying. He wondered why she said it didn't matter. It must matter if you were a coward.

"Goodbye, Griffin," Frieda said, looking straight into his eyes. "Whether you travel with your friend or not, you must depart now."

"Where are you going?"

"To another colony, across the Underworld."

"Well, bye then," he said. How did you say goodbye to someone in the land of the dead? The thought he might never see her again made him gloomy. "Thank you!" he called after her, as she sailed out over the desert along a different route from his. He stared, feeling a terrible squeeze in his stomach when finally she disappeared.

He should be leaving too now. Precious time.

Along the mud-cracked plains, he found the pattern which would lead him on his journey.

Then he turned back to Oasis, and went to find Luna.

CAMA ZOTZ

Goth clung to a vine, exhausted after his descent from the mines. All his limbs trembled, and he detested this weakness in himself. He detested too that he was tethered to these other inferior bats. To his surprise, the sight of them filled him with no hunger for meat. His only hunger now was for freedom – and life.

Through the weave of vines, Goth caught sight of another Vampyrum staring at him.

"I know you," Goth whispered to himself.

The other cannibal bat flinched and hurriedly turned, scuttling as far away as his tether would allow. Goth crawled after him. Since he was the last in the chain, he had more flexibility, but he still had to drag a few pulpy little bats off their roosts to get closer.

"I *know* you," he said again.

"No," said the other bat, not turning to face him.

"Throbb!" said Goth, surprising himself. How was it he had effortlessly summoned up this bat's name, when he'd had such difficulty remembering his own?

"Names are discouraged here," mumbled the other bat. "We don't really have names." He tried to scramble further away, but there was no slack left in his line.

Goth was now close enough to poke at him with the tip

of his wing. With a defeated sigh, Throbb turned. Goth's mouth split into a smile. The mere sight of Throbb's face triggered a flood of images from the past: an artificial jungle, Human captors, an escape, flying south with Throbb, trying to get back to the real jungle. And—

"You were hit by lightning!" said Goth, delighted by these new memories. "You were turned to ash."

"I really don't see any point talking about it," Throbb said petulantly.

Goth grunted with satisfaction. He never thought he would be glad to see Throbb again – a whining, cowardly creature, he now recalled – but in current circumstances, he was glad of anything that linked him to the world of the living. And Throbb might prove useful, as he had long ago.

"Surely you don't blame me for the lightning," Goth said pleasantly.

"No, that was bad luck," said Throbb. "But there were other things. The spinning blade you made me go through first, the cold, the freezing rain, the snow, the blizzards, the frostbite, the hunger, the humiliations. I'll say one thing about being dead – it got me away from you."

"There was a bat we were chasing," Goth said with a frown.

"Shade, a Silverwing from the northern forests. You wanted to—"

"Follow him to Hibernaculum, where his entire colony was sleeping through the winter," Goth cut in, for already another cataract of memory was spilling into his mind. Shade. That little northern runt had defied him, had led him into a lightning storm and nearly killed him. But that was not the end of the story with Shade. There was more, and it had to do with his homeland, the stone pyramid, that flash of light and noise which was cut off for ever.

"Why can't I remember everything?" Goth asked.

"Everyone's like that at first. It takes a while."

Goth grunted; he didn't like the fact Throbb was in a position to tell him anything, but he needed more information.

"Why are we set to work with these underlings?"

"Well," said Throbb uncomfortably, "we've both displeased Zotz. Not that I'm complaining. No, no, I toil willingly. Happily. I love my work."

"You're a slave," Goth said with contempt.

"It's really not so bad. It's very peaceful here. Frankly, being dead was a relief after travelling with you. And there's no hunger, no pain – as long as we serve Zotz."

Goth could understand Throbb being punished. But himself? What had he done to deserve this?

"Who was I?" Goth demanded.

"Best to forget all that. Not important. Work, work, work, that's all we need to think about now." Throbb tried to make a cheerful laugh, but it came out like a demented squawk.

"Tell me," hissed Goth.

"It won't make you any happier, I'm just warning you," said Throbb.

Goth snorted impatiently.

"Well, when I knew you, you were a prince."

Goth looked away, blinking as images from his past flickered before his mind's eye. A prince of the royal family Vampyrum Spectrum, favoured by Zotz himself . . .

"But then you got to be King," Throbb prattled on. "I wasn't around for that of course, on account of being sizzled by lightning. But congratulations, I guess. Of course, you weren't King for very long, but it's more than most of us get . . ."

Rage reduced Goth's voice to a slow, pungent whisper. "I should not be here. A terrible injustice has been committed against me."

"You hear a lot of that down here," Throbb said.

"I must speak to Cama Zotz."

"Probably not a good idea."

"Where is he?" Goth demanded.

"He's anywhere. Everywhere. But he only appears when he wants."

"You've seen him, then?"

Throbb's eyes flicked away. "Just once."

"I want to see him," said Goth. "There's been a mistake."

"Well, there's plenty of stories about you, actually," said Throbb, unable to hide his pleasure.

"Stories?" Goth growled. If he hadn't been restrained he would have closed his teeth around Throbb's neck.

"About the things you did in the Upper World. You're famous really – in a bad sort of way."

"Speak, then!"

"If you must know," said Throbb with a vindictive smile, "you're the reason we're all here. This mine didn't exist until after what happened at the pyramid, you know, the sacred temple. Not that I was alive to see it, but things get around down here. You don't know? You *really* don't know?"

"Tell me, Throbb, or I will—"

"No talking!" roared Phoenix, crashing down upon them.

Without hesitation, Goth lunged, and with his teeth tore fur from her shoulder. Phoenix punched Goth back with a furled wing, bared her obsidian fangs, and plunged at his throat. Instantly Goth kicked out with both rear claws, pushing the vine tethering them between Phoenix's jaws.

Instinctively she bit, severing the vine with a crack of light. Goth rolled free.

He opened his wings and flew, Phoenix at his tail. He cleared the jungle of vines and dived down the pyramid's far side, away from the plaza, away from the great Vampyrum city. Out over the rainforest, Phoenix and her guards pursued him, but could not overtake him, so powerful were his wing strokes, fuelled by rage and determination. He had once been King and he would not be defeated! He soared clear of the island's coast, and was over the lake now. When he glanced back, Phoenix and her guards were circling, as if afraid to cross the water's threshold. Cowards.

Beyond the lake stretched more of the same terrible desert he had seen on his awakening. He balked at the notion of flying deeper into it, but what else could he do? That glorious city could only be a prison to him now; he was an enemy to his own kind. But how? What were these terrible things he had done?

"Zotz!" he shouted to the wind. "Zotz, it is your servant, Goth. Please hear me!"

At first Goth thought it was only the fatigued trembling of his limbs, but then he realized the air itself was shaking. Even the stars overhead seemed to flicker. Below, the mud-cracked plain shimmered like a windswept pond. A mist of dancing stone rose from the earth as the tremors deepened. Goth felt the shuddering in the bones of his feet and legs, coursing along his spine and into his jaws and teeth. He was terrified, but felt a dark rush of anticipation too. Circling, he fixed his eyes on the epicentre of the earthquake.

Show me, he thought. *Show yourself.*

With a thunderous crack that reverberated against the

stone heavens, two massive spikes erupted from the earth, soaring up past him. As Goth shook his head, cleared the silt from his eyes, he saw that these spikes were not stone, but folded wings, now unfurling. Electricity crackled along their dark membranes as they shook dust and rock from the creases. The simple act of those wings extending to their full length – hundreds of feet, Goth guessed – created a shockwave of searing wind which blasted him backwards.

In a titanic convulsion, the ground between the wings heaved up, and Goth saw a darkly-furred back rising from the rubble, two powerful legs pushing clear, massive shoulders hunching to lift a long, leathery neck. Goth swallowed, nearly gagging, for his throat was so dry. Finally the head came into view. It was white, hairless, gaunt as a skull. From the back a long knobbly crest jutted high into the air. The jaws themselves were thrice the length of Goth's entire body, and when they split apart, he saw endless rows of jagged teeth. Eyes, set far back in the skull, blinked the dust clear, then turned to gaze straight at him.

Goth stared back, unable to look away. Despite his terror, his heart exalted. Finally he beheld Zotz. He had never seen any creature so massive, as big as a mountain. In his imagination, he had always pictured Zotz as a giant, but one who would look essentially like the other Vampyrum. But there was something altogether more bestial about him, and slightly reptilian. His thumbs had developed into a kind of paw, so that he stood on four feet, like a beast, his wings spiking up high. His skin had a scaly look, especially around the furless face. He looked like something unspeakably ancient.

Zotz's head plunged down towards Goth, the wind

shrieking through the serrated crest like some bird of prey. His words came out like a scalding gale.

"I have heard you, Goth. Now behold me, and know that I am very displeased."

"My Lord," Goth said, struggling to keep his voice strong, "I do not know what I have done."

Zotz's head stopped, wingbeats from Goth, and hovered. From the god's parted jaws, welling from the depths of his throat, Goth heard a faraway chorus of screams.

"When you were injured," said Zotz, "I healed your wings."

Goth remembered instantly. "Yes, Lord Zotz."

"And did I not make you King as I promised?"

"You did, Lord Zotz."

"Did I not favour you with visions? Did I not make you my mouthpiece? All I asked was for you to do my bidding. You had only to sacrifice one hundred hearts while the sun was eclipsed – and so liberate me from the Underworld."

Goth winced, desperately dragging memories from his mind's vault. He could see it now: the temple filled with sacrificial offerings, the sun at its very zenith, being swallowed by the moon.

"I tried—"

"Did you?" Zotz's angry voice reverberated over the plains. "You gathered the sacrificial offerings, yes. But you let yourself become distracted by your hatred of Shade Silverwing. You had only seven minutes during the eclipse, but you put your own bloodlust ahead of your duty to your god. And you missed your chance."

Images cascaded before his mind's eye, making him grunt with surprise. Yes. Shade, the young runt, had been in the temple, and he had brought rats and owls as allies and attacked during the sacrifices. And he, Goth . . . he winced in shame now as he recalled it. He had left his place at the sacrificial altar and tried to kill Shade Silverwing.

"I beg your forgiveness, my Lord." He dared not meet the eyes of his god.

"There is worse. I have waited thousands of years. But now there is no purpose in waiting. There can be no other opportunity for sacrifice."

Goth looked up in shock. "I don't understand."

"The prophetic stone was destroyed, Goth, the royal pyramid was destroyed, and with it, the last of my priesthood. They alone knew how to liberate me. There are other Vampyrum Spectrum, but they do not know me – and without blood sacrifice, my powers to project myself to the Upper World are vanquished. You have imprisoned me in my own kingdom!"

A terrible weakness swept through Goth's limbs as he tried to understand. He remembered Shade escaping the temple, and then—

A flash of light, the beginnings of some cataclysmic noise, then nothing more.

"How did this happen?" Goth asked.

Zotz's head swayed from side to side, like some enormous cobra before it struck. "The high-priest, Voxzaco, do you remember him? He dropped one of the Human's explosive discs on the temple, thinking he might this way fulfil the sacrifices. A daring plan, and I might have rewarded him, had he not been too late. The eclipse had already ended, and Voxzaco succeeded only in turning the royal pyramid into a tomb for the Vampyrum Spectrum. Perhaps you are thinking, Goth, that Voxzaco is to blame. Rest assured, he will spend his eternity in a place of suffering. But so shall you."

It happened so quickly Goth scarcely had time to flinch. Zotz's jaws snapped wider and plunged around him. He was in total darkness, casting about with his sonic eye, glimpsing the vast array of jagged incisors, each as big as himself. Beneath him pitched a great black river of tongue. It leapt high, knocking him deeper into the mouth, back towards the cavernous entrance to Zotz's throat.

And from that opening – it was unmistakable now – emanated the most terrible cacophony of screams and cries and strangled pleas Goth had ever heard.

"No!" Goth shrieked. "Please, no!"

The tongue pitched once more and, with a terrible wet constriction, he was squeezed down into the throat. Pummelled and punched by the spasms of Zotz's gullet, he tumbled head over wing in darkness.

With a splash he landed in a churning pool.

And started screaming in pain.

It was not water, but acid, and he was in Zotz's stomach, roaring in agony as he felt his fur and flesh being scorched from every inch of his body. He thrashed in vain, trying to claw his way out, but he was being swirled round and around too quickly. With his frenzied echo vision he caught jagged silver glimpses of other bats, hundreds of them, spinning in this whirlpool of acid, faceless, screaming in torment. And he was screaming too, there was no stopping it, adding to the hellish din.

Swirling and swirling at great speed, yet time had stopped.

He was here for ever and no time at all, for the pain was so intense it was all he could comprehend. This was for ever. For ever had already happened and was yet to come.

This maelstrom of acid and spray and noise and pain. He wished for oblivion.

"Zotz!" he roared. "Forgive me! Let me serve you again!"

He was tugged violently under the surface, acid searing his nostrils, gushing down his throat. Eaten away, from within and without. Caught in a powerful undertow he was sucked through the liquid, away from the whirlpool's eternal grasp, and agonizingly squeezed down the undulating tunnels of Zotz's bowels. The smell of bile and putrefaction made him retch again and again.

One final suffocating squeeze, and he was spat out into open air. He hit the ground wheezing. Gratefully he pressed his claws and face into the earth. He was still alive – no, not truly alive, of course, but the pain was over. His flesh and fur were miraculously unscathed.

"Thank you," he exhaled raggedly. "Thank you."

"Do not think this is an end to your suffering."

Goth jerked up, expecting to see Zotz towering over him. But instead he saw that he was on the narrow ledge of a mountain face. Wind plastered his fur, made him squint. Far below stretched desolate mud-cracked plains. Zotz was nowhere to be seen. Then the rock face shimmered, and Zotz's enormous eye opened from the mountain itself, gazing down at Goth.

"I have always favoured you, Goth." Zotz's voice vibrated in the rock beneath Goth's claws, pulsed in the tips of his fur. "But you have made me doubt your loyalty. You have much to atone for."

"I will serve you without fail, Lord Zotz. What is your bidding?"

"You will return to the mines, and labour there." Zotz's eye never once blinked.

"I will serve you eternally, Lord Zotz."

Low laughter crumpled the air. "Not an eternity, Goth. Merely thousands of years, until you bore a tunnel to the Upper World."

Goth was so stunned he could say nothing for a moment. He'd stupidly assumed the mining was nothing but punishment.

"After the destruction of my temple, I realized a tunnel was the only chance of liberating myself. During an eclipse we will breech the Upper World, and our tunnel will be so vast it will suck the living down by the thousands. And when one hundred have been sacrificed to me, I will rise and kill the sun. The two worlds of the living and dead will be collapsed into one, and I will reign."

Goth marvelled at the grandeur of the plan: finally Zotz would rule over all creation – and the Vampyrum with him. Perhaps, after all his labour, his god would reward him with a position of great power.

"But you will have no part in my reign," said Zotz, as if hearing his thoughts. "You squandered your chance in the Upper World. When the tunnel is finished, you will join Voxzaco and the others who have gravely displeased me."

Goth said nothing, trying to fathom the endless horror of his fate. To labour in those mines for millennia, only to swill around in Zotz's stomach for an eternity. The idea swelled in his mind, threatening to explode his skull. He clenched his teeth.

"No," he said.

Zotz's eye seemed to darken in the mountain face. The silence stretched out, congealing malignantly.

"You dare defy me?" Zotz hissed, his voice right up against Goth's ear. "You would prefer to begin your eternity of pain now?"

"Yes!" Goth said savagely. "If that's all that awaits me in the end. It would be a greater torment to bore your tunnel to the Upper World, to see life again, and then be struck down for ever. I will not do it!"

Cracks splintered the mountain, radiating from Zotz's enormous eye. Shards rained down on Goth. Thunder split the air.

"You speak as if you had a choice, Goth!"

"Devour me, then!" Goth cried wildly, flaring his wings, not caring what happened to him any more. A strange calm seeped over him, filled him as black as night, and in that instant an idea came to him.

"Devour me now, Lord Zotz," he said, "but if you do you will lose a servant whose talents could glorify your kingdom and liberate you from the Underworld!"

He winced, waiting for something terrible to happen, for jaws to soar from the mountain and devour him. The thunder evaporated, the mountain stilled. The air shimmered with laughter.

"Your arrogance is astounding, Goth. But I no longer find it so appealing. I fear your pride and vanity have outpaced your ability."

"Send me back to the Upper World," said Goth. "I will be your mouthpiece. I will win you new followers, more zealous than the last. I will wait for the next eclipse and I will perform the sacrifices and raise you from the Underworld. Do not languish down here for millennia, waiting for the tunnel to be completed. Your triumph is closer at hand than that! Send me back to the Upper World now, and with the next eclipse you will be liberated!"

"An impressive speech," came Zotz's voice. "But your plan is flawed. What makes you think I can send you back to the Upper World?"

Goth faltered, surprised but also intrigued. He had always thought Zotz omnipotent.

"Surely, my Lord, there are no limits to your might."

"My kingdom is the dead," Zotz said, his voice shifting with the wind. "Over them I have absolute power. But I have no authority over the living. I can give life no more than I can take it away. There is only one way for you to regain the Upper World, and that is to steal the life of a living creature."

"How is that possible?" Goth asked, feeling the power and promise of his plan drain away. "Down here?"

Zotz's eye stared at him from the mountain, unblinking, stern. "It is rare, very rare, but from time to time, a fissure opens in the earth and some living creature gets sucked down to my world: a rat, even a bat occasionally." Zotz paused. "There is one here now."

"Where?" Goth asked, the word exploding from his mouth. "Let me take it!"

"You are eager, Goth."

"Eager only to do your bidding, my Lord."

"Why should I choose you as my missionary?"

"It was my idea. No one else before had envisaged it."

"True," said Zotz's voice, riding the wind, "but perhaps there are others more suitable to the task. Your father for instance. Other kings before you who might serve me better."

"They would all be excellent servants, I am sure," Goth said carefully, "but they have been down here a very long time, and perhaps they have forgotten the Upper World, its ways. Perhaps their earthly appetites have been dulled, but I can still taste life. I know the jungle, and I can find new Vampyrum colonies and make them converts. No one will strive harder than me, for I have the most to lose, and the most to atone for."

"Most convincing, yes," said Zotz. "But why should I allow you to take this life for yourself? Should it not rather be offered up for me?"

Goth considered his words. "Truly it would be a most suitable sacrifice for you, my Lord, but far less than you deserve. One life, after all, will not liberate you from the Underworld."

"True, and yet even a single living sacrifice would give me some solace after so long an absence."

"I would gladly give it to you, my Lord. But is it not better to wait and allow me to bring you all the sacrifices you need from the Upper World?"

"Are you bargaining with me, Goth?"

Goth looked away from Zotz's huge, hypnotic eye. "Yes, my Lord, I am."

Laughter trembled through the rock and air.

"How am I to know you would not take this life for yourself? So you might live again, and thus defy me?"

"I would not do such a thing!"

"Your plan is a bold one, Goth, and I admire it. But first you must prove your discipline and loyalty. Hunt down the living newborn and kill him – but do not take the life which rises from his body. That will be mine to inhale. Do this for me, and when the next living creature enters my kingdom, its life will be yours."

Goth clenched his teeth. How long would that take? Decades, perhaps even centuries?

"Are you ready to make such a sacrifice for your god, Goth?"

"Yes, my Lord, I am ready."

"Across the desert," Zotz told him, "there is a forest

called Oasis, one of the many places where the newly dead come. A newborn has fallen through a fissure and is there now. I have sensed him. Behold."

Goth shut his eyes as Zotz sang an image into his mind: a small male, some strange Silverwing and Brightwing hybrid perhaps. But what was most interesting was the lightning travelling the membrane of his wings, sparking from the tips of his fur. Goth's mouth flooded with saliva. When alive, it was meat he wanted; now it was the life which coursed through it. He hungered for that strange glimmering light, could imagine it seeping down his throat, better than any food. He swallowed. It was not to be his. Not yet.

Goth opened his eyes.

"I can guide you to him," said Zotz, "but expect little help from me. I can confuse and frighten the living, but can not inflict harm in any way. It must be you who makes the sacrifice."

Goth nodded, puzzling over this weakness in his god. Zotz could not kill. He needed it done for him. Zotz needed him. Goth felt a pulse of pride: he was more useful than he'd imagined.

"I will not fail, my Lord."

"The living wither quickly in my kingdom. You must reach the newborn before he weakens and dies. I will be watching. Here is your path."

The earth rumbled, and a ridge poked up through the surface, like the spine of some skeletal beast waking after a long dormancy.

"Now go," said Cama Zotz. "Catch the newborn and summon me, so you may make an offering to your god."

CAPTURE

Never had Shade seen such a desolate landscape. He flew higher, trying to guess when it might give way to something different. With a sudden chill he wondered if this was all the Underworld was, a place where you would be alone eternally, flying over nothingness, calling out for your loved ones.

Again he checked the sky and saw that his circle of stars was about to disappear below the horizon. He hoped it would come back again. In the Upper World, the stars always came back. But this place was clearly different. There wasn't even a moon or a sun as far as he could tell.

Feverish with exhaustion, he knew he had to rest for a bit. He spied some boulders strewn across the earth, some heaped up into great mounds. Maybe he could roost down there, and still have a good vantage point to keep watch. He couldn't believe he hadn't seen a single Vampyrum yet – or any other creature for that matter.

He dived down, made a pass, then picked out a massive boulder with a number of outcroppings. He roosted. He hated being still, not doing something.

"Griffin!" he called out. "Griffin!"

Turn, he told himself, but before he could, something cold and supple and very strong wrapped itself around him, squeezing him into darkness, and dragging him off his roost.

The icy grip was so tight he could barely struggle. Or breathe. It was a huge wing that held him, he could tell by its leathery feel, and the hard ridges of finger bones gouging into him. Only a Vampyrum had wings this big. Desperately Shade tried to pull his claws free so he might slash his way out.

"I'm going to let you go," whispered a voice near his head, "but you must be quiet."

The voice didn't sound at all like the hoarse bark of a Vampyrum, though Shade couldn't be sure, it was so muffled through the thick membrane. Slowly the huge wing loosened and unfurled, and he leapt free, flapping hard and nearly smashing his head against the stone ceiling. It seemed he'd been dragged from his roost into some tiny cave within the boulder. Dropping, he clung to the far wall and whirled to look at his captor.

Not a Vampyrum.

Something much, much bigger.

Hanging upside down from the ceiling, this enormous winged creature looked more beast than bat. Her body seemed to take up most of the cave. She was densely furred with long dark hair, and her age was obvious by the abundant streaks of grey. Her face tapered into a long muzzle and a neat pointy nose. Bigger eyes Shade had never seen: dark, round and penetrating, but surprisingly gentle. Her triangular ears were extremely small – how could you *see* with ears so small? She looked like a fox with wings. And what wings they were. They would easily span five feet when fully extended.

Shade stared warily. He noticed she kept one of her wings half-flared against the cave wall, blocking the only exit. But she didn't seem to have any carnivorous designs on him. Was she some kind of bizarre native creature of the Underworld? Before he even had time to speak, a second winged creature scuttled into view from behind the first, smaller but no less unusual looking.

Twice Shade's size, this new beast had a most peculiar, squashed-looking face. His fleshy upper lip arched in the middle, giving him what seemed to be a permanent snarl. A pair of curved incisors jutted from both upper and lower jaws. He had a tiny two-pronged nose, and his cheeks were very whiskery and bumpy with moles. His eyes, though, seemed less fierce, flashing quick-wittedness and something like mischief. Then Shade's gaze gravitated towards the huge, wickedly sharp rear claws: they looked like they were designed for more than simply gripping bark. Nothing fun about those. If this thing were a bat, he thought, it was a species he'd never seen or heard of. Shade's surprise and confusion only grew when a third creature fluttered out from behind the others. He gasped.

A Silverwing.

It was a male, no more than a year or two older than Shade, but his right shoulder and wing looked strangely crumpled, as if injured in some terrible crash. He had a painful, lopsided flight. But what was a *Silverwing* doing down here in the Underworld?

"How did you get here?" Shade asked him, overwhelmed. Had this bat, like Griffin, been sucked down some terrible fissure?

"Why is he glowing?" the misshapen Silverwing hissed to the fox-faced creature, sounding both alarmed and disdainful. "Look at him, Java, he's some kind of glowing *thing*, and you brought him in here with us?"

"I needed to shush him up," Java whispered.

"That boy's got glow enough to cut through fog," the whiskery-faced creature remarked, looking Shade over curiously.

"Glow?" Shade asked, peering down at himself.

"Shhhh," hissed the fox-faced Java, drawing back her huge wing a touch to reveal the opening in the cave wall. "They're coming."

They? Shade's heart thudded. Quietly he scuttled towards the gap, wanting to see, but the misshapen Silverwing stopped him with a harsh shake of his head.

"You glow!" he whispered. "They'll see you!"

Shade had no idea what this Silverwing was talking about. Java, he noticed, had sealed the opening once more with her wing, but left a tiny gap at the top. With a twitch of her large head she gestured Shade over. He gave her a grateful nod and, hanging overhead, pressed his face to the sliver of an opening. Just enough to see through.

Three Vampyrum streaked past, and his breath snagged. Not more than fifty wingbeats distant, their heads swivelled methodically, screeching out sound. Searching. No wonder the Fox-face had dragged him off his roost. He'd been stupidly shouting his head off, leading the cannibal bats right to them. Shade was about to draw back when he caught sight of another bat, not a Vampyrum this time, but—

A Brightwing, by the size and silhouette of her. And she wasn't alone either. A stream of bats fluttered across the sky, one close after the other in single file. Shade squinted. They were actually tethered together, leg to leg, by some kind of luminous vine. Now he saw more Vampyrum on the flanks, shouting at the smaller bats to keep flying, occasionally veering in and snapping at one of them. Anger seeped into Shade's astonishment as he stared at the hundreds of prisoners, most of them species he'd known from the northern forests. His eyes and echo vision lingered on each one, making sure it was not his son. Only when the last bat in this terrible chain had disappeared did Shade turn away, sickened.

"Lucky they didn't find us, with him squawking out there," said the misshapen Silverwing, with a sour glance at Shade.

Java said peaceably, "They've passed, and we're fine." She looked apologetically at Shade. "Sorry about the wing grab, but you can see why now. I had to get you inside fast."

Shade nodded. He liked Java's voice. It had a gentle, mellifluous sound which reminded him of a lazy wind. "Where are they taking them?" he asked, his voice hoarse.

"Back to their city, I figure," said Whiskery-face with a grimace.

"What for?" Shade asked, fearing the reply.

"That we don't know," Java told him.

"And we don't plan to find out," snapped the grouchy Silverwing. "It was very diverting meeting you. You're very sparkly. But we've got a long way to go, and you're a liability. You're loud. You glow. You're fortunate we saved your twinkly skin. Now if you'd be so kind as to flutter off, we'd all appreciate it."

"I'm not glowing," said Shade, getting irritated. His mind was already seething with questions, and he didn't want any more distractions.

"Sorry, my boy, but you are," said Whiskery-face. "You'd scare fish out of water."

Shade looked at Java, somehow trusting her most of all of them. She nodded.

"All right, so I glow," said Shade impatiently. "I don't

know *why* I glow, but it's not important." He took a breath, tried to focus. "All those bats, those prisoners out there, where did they come from?"

Java looked at him strangely. "Surely you know about the raids. The cannibals have been attacking the Oases, and capturing all the Pilgrims they can."

Shade shook his head, uncomprehending. Oases? Pilgrims?

"He doesn't know," the misshapen Silverwing muttered to the others in annoyance. "He hasn't figured it out yet. He's not a Pilgrim."

"What's a Pilgrim?" Shade asked.

"If our little shooting star here ain't a Pilgrim," Whiskery-face commented, "what's he doing so far from an Oasis?"

"Look, what're you talking about?" Shade demanded.

Java sighed. "Oh, I do hate doing this. There's no easy way to tell you, Silverwing. You're dead. We're dead. All of us."

Stunned, Shade looked slowly at each of them in turn. So this was what the dead looked like. He'd expected different, something ghostly, wispy white as vapour on an autumn pond. These creatures had bodies, a solid shape in his echo vision. The Silverwing didn't even look that old! Java's fur was greyed with age, but she still seemed strong and healthy. Then he remembered the preternatural cold of her wings around him, and felt a sympathetic chill seep from his own marrow. He shivered.

"I know, it's a shock, isn't it, to hear that?" Java said kindly. "We all had to go through it, believe me. With a little time you won't find it so dreadful. Trust me."

"Um, well, I'm not dead, actually," said Shade.

"Denial," said the misshapen Silverwing in a bored voice. "Classic reaction."

"This is perfectly normal," Java told Shade in soothing tones. "You just need some time with it."

"No, really, I can see why there'd be a misunderstanding," Shade said. "But I'm not dead. There was an earthquake and—"

"This is all very poignant," said the misshapen Silverwing, "but do you think we could hurry it along?"

"Yorick," said Java, for the first time sounding testy, "surely a little patience wouldn't kill you."

"It did kill me actually," snapped Yorick. "And now that I'm dead, I find myself exceedingly *im*patient to get out of here!"

Shade looked from one to the other, dazed. "So those other bats I saw outside, they all came down here when they died?"

"Quick learner," muttered Yorick.

"Every bat from every part of the world comes here when they die," Java told him.

Shade couldn't speak, he was so shaken. This hideous netherworld was where Nocturna sent her own favoured creatures? Nocturna was supposed to look after them when they died! Send them to some wonderful place!

"All bats come here," he muttered, dazed. "But my elders . . . the legends say the Underworld is only for the Vampyrum."

"Wrong!" said Whiskery-face cheerfully.

"Can't be right . . ."

"It's true," Java told him gently. "You saw for yourself just now."

Shade snorted angrily. "This really spikes my fur up," he said. "They tell you things and you're supposed to believe it because they're elders, and it's some dusty old legend that's been staggering around the echo chamber for thousands of years . . ." The others were all staring at him in astonishment, and he trailed off. "Sorry, I just hate not knowing things. You, for instance," he said to Java and Whiskery-face, "no one ever told me about creatures like you. Never."

"I'm a Foxwing," she said. "A bat, but a fruit eater, from the other side of the ocean from you, I think. My name's Java."

"Shade," he said. "From the northern forests. Are you all so . . . big? Your species?"

"Bigger. I'm a runt."

"Really?" said Shade, ears pricking in surprise. "So am I."

"And I'm Nemo," said Whiskery-face, "from the coastal waters way down south. We're fish-eaters." Now Shade understood the wickedly elongated claws. He could imagine Nemo strafing streams and oceans, snatching food from the water. His eyesight and powers of echo location must be extraordinary.

"And the grouchy Silverwing here," said Java, "is Yorick."

"Do you know my colony?" Shade asked, trying to place him. "Tree Haven?"

"Never heard of your colony, never heard of you."

"Not surprising," said Nemo, his eyes flashing mischief, "since Yorick's probably been down here five hundred years or so."

Shade stared. Yorick looked the youngest of them all, yet he was five hundred years old? Five hundred years *down here*?

"Not such a quick learner yourself, are you, Yorick?" Java said with gentle mockery. "Took you some time to figure things out."

"I had some adjustment difficulties, if that's what you're referring to," Yorick said primly. "But I think I've made up for those now. You two wouldn't have gotten far without me as leader."

"Leader, is it?" Nemo said, amused. "My boy, we tolerate you because you've got the map, and you won't share it with us. It's not your charisma that keeps us bobbing alongside, believe me!"

"I'd appreciate it if you didn't call me *my boy*," Yorick replied tartly. "I'm approximately four hundred and fifty-two years your elder, by my calculation. And now, we really should be moving on."

"Where?" Shade asked.

"The Tree," Java told him. "The dead need to travel there. All of us."

"Really, I'm *not* dead." He sighed. "I have a heartbeat and everything. Come and listen."

Java looked sadly at the others.

"Humour him," Yorick said. "If it helps speed the grieving process . . ."

Java walked across the ceiling towards him. Her face was almost the same size as his entire torso and she had a hard time bending one of her triangular ears to his chest. Her cool ear had barely touched him when she jerked back in shock.

"It's beating," she yelped. "His heart *beats*."

"You're sure?" Yorick snapped.

"Listen for yourself." Java stared at Shade with such intense curiosity and awe that he looked away, self-conscious. "You're warm too. But how?"

"I came through a crack in the stone sky," Shade told them. "From the Upper World."

"Why?" Yorick demanded, incredulous.

"To find my son."

"Is he dead?" Java asked.

"Alive. There was an earthquake and a crack opened up and sucked him down." Shade felt all his frantic impatience seep back. "Do you know where he might go? He's a newborn. I tried to track him, but lost the trail, and I don't know where he would've landed."

Java, Yorick and Nemo all looked at him, mute, then turned to one another helplessly. Shade's anxiety felt amplified in their silence.

"What about these Oases you mentioned. How many are there?"

Java inhaled deeply. "Hundreds at least, all across the Underworld, and between them, stretches of badlands like this one."

Shade felt the breath leak out of him. Hundreds. He could search for months.

"We can't help you look," Yorick said sharply. "We've got to get to the Tree."

"What is that?" asked Shade, hopeful. Maybe it was just the way it sounded like Tree Haven, or maybe it was merely the image of a tree, a living thing that could only be good, give shelter. Was this a place Griffin might try to reach?

"We're Pilgrims," Java explained. "The three of us came from different Oases, on different sides of this world, but we all share the same journey, and that's how we met. We're not supposed to stay here. Once we accept our deaths, we're meant to travel to the Tree. It's the only way out for us."

"Where does it go?" Shade asked urgently.

Java shook her head. "A new world, better than this. All

we're told is that we must enter the Tree to begin our new lives."

"Who told you this?"

"The messenger Pilgrims. They fly over all the Oases with their message, and mostly they get ignored by everyone – me included for the longest time. But it was this latest Pilgrim that finally broke through to me. A Silverwing actually. Frieda."

Shade choked. "Frieda? Frieda Silverwing?"

"You know her?"

"She was my elder back home, before she died. Where do I find her?"

"She travels the Underworld," Java explained, "urging bats to begin their journey, and giving them maps to the Tree. I don't know where she is right now."

"And it doesn't matter," said Yorick. "We must go."

"The journey's not what you'd call clear sailing," Nemo explained to Shade. "There's the voyage itself, which is long, and the land can change on you, and then you've got to wait around for more Pilgrims to get a new map. There's the pain too. Once you've figured out you're dead, you start feeling pain again, whatever you had in the Upper World, only worse. So there's that to carry with you. And we've got these cannibal bats stirred into things too. So far we've managed to slip past them. But if we get caught, our voyage is over just like that."

Shade was silent, trying to fathom this huge depth of new information. All the dead, here. Silverwings and Brightwings and Vampyrum all swirled together. A journey to some Tree that would take the dead to a new world. But would his son know about the Tree? Would Griffin naturally fly for it – and was that even the right thing for the living? Maybe it was only for the dead. He longed to talk to Frieda. Wishing was useless. He needed a plan, something to keep his mind focused. Seconds streaming past.

"I don't know where to start looking," Shade admitted.

"Maybe you'd feel like travelling with us for a bit," Java offered kindly.

Yorick's ears nearly shot off his head. "Honestly, Java, all those years eating fruit have made your brain mushy! Hasn't anyone been listening to me? He's going to attract all sorts of attention to us, the worst kind! He'll make bats curious, he'll make bats angry; they'll talk, and talk travels! And let's not forget you can see him coming a hundred wingbeats away! The cannibals will have us in a second!"

"I might be useful to have along," said Shade.

Yorick snorted.

"I say let him come if he chooses," Java said firmly.

"This is my voyage," Yorick said coldly. "I've got the map, I lead the way. I've been down here five hundred years, and I'm not going to risk getting caught because of a stranger with a tragic tale to tell!"

"Nemo, what do you think?" said Java.

"He has my welcome," Nemo said, giving Shade a wink.

"That's it, I'll go solo," blustered Yorick.

"All right," said Java solemnly. "If you must, you must."

"I don't need you all slowing me down."

"Good sailing, my boy," said Nemo fondly. "May you have favourable winds."

Yorick looked defiantly from Nemo to Java, then glanced out of the cave opening. His battered wings twitched nervously.

"If he comes," Yorick said sternly, "he does what I say, he keeps his mouth firmly closed and he flies close to you,

Java. If we see anything coming, you wrap him up tight so he's not like a beacon."

Shade smiled. "Seems fair," he said.

"Our route takes us over an Oasis soon," Yorick told Shade, more kindly. "Maybe someone there will have seen your son."

"Thank you." Shade's wings twitched impatiently. One Oasis out of hundreds. What were the chances? It was the best he had right now though.

"Good, good," muttered Yorick, "then let's depart."

Java gave a yelp and pulled back her wing as if she'd been nipped. A dark muscular shape thrust itself through the exposed cave opening and then enlarged into a Vampyrum Spectrum, jagged wings spread wide, blocking their only exit.

LUNA

Finding Luna was harder than he thought.

He went back to where he'd first seen her, and flew out in an ever-widening spiral. Streaking through the trees, he called her name. The other bats flashed out of his way in alarm. Oasis was huge. It could take him nights and nights to sweep its entire area. And he was running out of time – that was the thing that nagged at him like a burr on his cheek. With every wingbeat he was getting weaker, using up the energy he was supposed to be saving for his journey to the Tree.

But how could he leave without her?

"Luna!" he called. "Come on, Luna, I need to talk to you! Luna!"

She had either gone to a completely different part of Oasis, or was avoiding him. His mouth felt stale; he wanted water. He wanted food. He wanted to see the horizon brightening. His wings hurt. He roosted on a freaky-looking tree, trying to quell his growing panic.

"Why're you looking for me?"

He jumped and looked along the branch to see Luna, wrapped up tightly, her eyes watching him over her wings.

"You've been here all along?" he exclaimed.

"I've been following you."

"Following me?"

"Trying to decide if you're crazy or not. Why'd you fly away from me like that? Like you were scared of me."

He tried to say it. Couldn't. She did it for him.

"You think I'm dead."

"Well," he said, letting out a big breath of relief. "So you know."

"Yeah. That I'm *not* dead. I mean, come on, look at me!" She sprang from the branch, did a somersault, then nimbly flipped upside down in mid-air and roosted beside him. "Not bad for a dead bat, huh?"

"Look," he said, "all I know is—"

"Plenty of bats here think *you're* dead, though," Luna told him good-naturedly.

"Yes, I know."

"The whole glowing thing, the way you fell out of the sky. It's pretty suspicious."

"OK, but—"

"Do *you* feel dead?"

Griffin couldn't help chuckling in frustration. "I am not dead. All right?" He stopped laughing. "But you are."

She sniffed.

"It's not just you," Shade told her. "You're . . . well, you're all dead. I'm sorry, it's not a very polite thing to say, but you are. And I'm not the only one who thinks so."

"I saw you talking to one of the Pilgrims."

Griffin nodded. "Her name's Frieda. My parents knew her. She was the elder of our colony."

"Hmmm," said Luna dubiously. "And I suppose she's dead too, right?"

"Uh-huh."

"She seemed nice," Luna said, with a trace of sadness. "She didn't seem crazy or anything."

"I don't think she is."

Luna looked at him hard. "So prove it."

Griffin sucked in a big breath. "This place is not the real world. It's . . . totally different, and it's all wrong. The trees, take a good look."

Luna stared at the trees around her, unimpressed. "So?"

"They're all mixed up. Pine needles, oak leaves, maple leaves, all on the same branch. That doesn't seem weird to you?"

She flicked her wingtips carelessly. "No. That's what I'm used to. Maybe the trees where you come from are just different."

Griffin sighed. This might be harder than he thought.

"Eating," he said. "Those bugs don't taste like anything. Because they *aren't* anything. They're just sound or something, they just disappear when you chew them. And where's the sun, Luna? Where's the moon?"

"What are those?"

"The sun?" he said in disbelief. "That big bright ball in the sky. Feels warm on your fur. And the moon . . ."

For a crazy moment he wondered if he was the crazy one, spouting gibberish. Obviously he needed a better strategy.

"So how long have you lived here at Oasis?" he asked casually.

She shrugged. "Always."

"Since you were born?"

Her face clouded for a moment, and almost defiantly she said, "Yeah."

"Where's your nursery roost?"

She waved her wing vaguely. "Over there."

"Who's your mother?"

"What's the point of all these questions?"

"Do you know?"

"Of course I know who my mother is!"

"So what's her name?"

"This is stupid." But for the first time, Luna looked uneasy. "Um . . . it's . . . Serena."

"No."

"I think I know the name of my own mother," she insisted, indignant.

"Frieda said the dead don't remember anything. The memories are there, but you just have trouble seeing them – or don't want to."

"This is all just talk."

"You have no heartbeat," he said sadly. "And you're cold. Living things are warm. That's why I . . . I got scared and flew away. I'm sorry."

"A heartbeat?" she said, as if the idea was unfamiliar to her.

"Come closer. Put your head here, you can hear it."

Hesitantly she shifted along the branch and pressed her ear to the centre of his chest.

"Loud," she said, pulling back.

"Yeah, well, it gets louder and faster when you're scared."

She folded some of her wing against her own chest, attentive, listening.

"Maybe some bats just don't have one," she said.

"Look at your wings." He hated doing this. "Tell me how it happened."

She frowned at the scars, seemed about to speak, then gave a little shake of her head. "I think I just was born that way." But she said it without much conviction.

He watched her, waiting.

"*You* know, is that what you're saying?" she demanded.

"I know."

She shrugged, then a moment later, "So let's hear your story. I'm not saying I believe it or anything."

He didn't want to be doing this, but maybe if he could start her remembering, there'd be a landslide. But did he really want her remembering this particular thing? Carefully he chose his words, voice hoarse.

"There was a fire in our forest. And you got burned. The elders tried to heal you. Everyone was taking care of you, but you were too badly hurt. You died."

"But I don't *feel* dead."

"This is the Underworld, Luna."

"You seem to know everything," she said angrily. "All about me, too."

"We grew up together."

"News to me."

"When you first saw me down here, you flew right over, even though I was glowing! All the other bats are terrified of me. They just scatter. Not you. You came *right over*. Because you remembered me!"

She stared at him, then looked away. "I don't remember you. I don't remember anything."

"Well, I remember you," Griffin said. "And I'll tell you everything you want to know. If you come with me."

"Where?"

"The Tree."

Suddenly, he was aware of the other bats, dozens of them hanging in the branches, staring balefully.

"Out!" Corona shouted, darting from her branch and swirling angrily around Griffin. "You're poisoning this colony!"

"Spreading lies!" another bat cried, and then they were

all shouting at him, the air suddenly jagged with their wings.

"Bad as the Pilgrims!"

"Won't stand for these lies!"

"Out! Out!"

"Get him out!"

"Hey!" shouted Luna. "We were just talking!"

Griffin clung to his branch, paralysed. They seemed so angry, and there were so many of them he doubted he could have broken past. Then they attacked, battering him with their wings.

"Out! Out!"

"Lies!"

"Trying to destroy us!"

At first Griffin tried to fend them off, but there were too many, and they were relentless. He wrapped himself up in his wings, making himself small against the blows pelting down on him.

"What're you doing?" he heard Luna cry above the din of their shouting.

They were clambering all over him now, crowding in from the sides and above, trying to wrench his feet from the roost. He felt their terrible, cold bodies, oddly light, but still strong, gripping him with their claws. They were dead, so how could they hurt him? But they were! Could they kill him?

"Stop!" he cried out. "Stop it!"

His feet were dragged from the bark, and he fell, dozens of bats still riding on his back and chest. He landed hard on another branch, and more bats piled on.

"Leave him alone!" he could hear Luna's voice cry out, as if from far away. "Get off him! You'll crush him!"

They were clutching at his throat, stamping on his chest,

and he was having trouble breathing. Tried to swallow, couldn't, and now he was choking. *No air, no air. Please, get off!* His vision blurred, pulsed, began to darken around the edges.

And then he saw it.

He *was* glowing. Light was lifting off his body like tendrils of mist, from his nostrils, from his mouth. He could see it rising up into the air and ... singing. Yes, singing. The light had a sound unlike any he'd ever heard. It was like a song. It was like a scream. A single note, pure and mesmerizing, but insistent and painfully shrill. It was beautiful and terrifying both.

The other bats must have seen and heard it too because they pulled away with shrieks of fear, their ears pinned flat. At once, he felt the terrible, icy weight of the dead bats leave him, and he coughed and gagged air into his battered chest.

And with the air, he saw the light being sucked back into him too, reuniting itself with him. The wail faded and stopped. The light vanished. He could no longer see his glow. He blinked, wondering if it had all been a hallucination. But then why had the dead bats all left? He'd seen the looks of terror on their faces. Whatever the light and sound was, he needed it inside him, as much as blood and breath. He clenched his chest muscles, worried the light might fly out of him again.

When another bat landed suddenly beside him he flinched. It was Luna.

"You OK?"

"You were right," he grunted. "I glow."

"I can't believe they did that," she said, furious. "It's disgusting! I'm really sorry. I had no idea they'd get so angry, really I didn't, Griffin."

"Not your fault," he said, then stared at her in amazement. "Hey! You called me Griffin."

She looked confused. "That *is* your name, right?"

"Yeah, but I never told you!" Griffin exclaimed excitedly. "You must've . . ."

"No, I didn't! But you knew it anyway."

"So this proves what?"

"That you remember me from when you were alive!" he said, beaming. "That I'm telling the truth. That I'm *right*!"

"That I'm dead, you mean."

He stopped smiling, crestfallen. "Yeah."

"Griffin," she said, and looked at him intently. In her eyes, he thought he saw a translucence, a clear view into the past, as if she'd somehow caught a glimpse of it. Then her face clouded. "I still don't remember you. Or being dead, or anything."

He nuzzled his cheek against her cold fur. "You will. But you've got to come with me."

She sniffed, looking around the forest. "I can't believe what they did to you. They're crazy. You think the Pilgrims are right, that we're supposed to go to this Tree?"

He nodded fervently.

"And you'll tell me things, everything I want to know. You'll tell me about myself?"

"I promise."

"Then I'm coming with you," she said.

MURK

"Pilgrims, aren't you?"

The Vampyrum's face was taut with fatigue, and his flanks heaved as if from a long flight. He glanced out of the cave opening, anxiously scanned the skies, then swung his gaze back inside, eyes sparking with fear.

Shade wondered what he was so afraid of. Surely not them. True, the cannibal was outnumbered, and half the size of Java, but Shade could tell that the old Foxwing would be no match for the Vampyrum. Her fruit-eating jaws and teeth, all her instincts, made her ill-equipped to battle a savage carnivore. Shade wondered what power the dead still had in them, then remembered the strength of Java's cold wing around him. Strong enough to fight. And kill? Surely the dead couldn't be killed a second time. But what about him? He looked at Nemo and Yorick, frozen in mute shock. In the cramped cave everyone was now within a wingspan, eyes locked. Not even the Vampyrum seemed certain of what to do, and Shade didn't want to give him the time. For all he knew, the cannibal was waiting for reinforcements to ensnare them all. Shade inhaled silently, and prepared to sing out an echo illusion – a vulture, an owl – that would terrify the cannibal into retreat. He opened his mouth, closed his eyes, ready to paint with sound.

"Take me to the Tree," said the Vampyrum.

His words were such a surprise, and his tone so beseeching, that Shade faltered. He looked at the others.

"It's a trap," growled Nemo. "We lead him to the Tree and he'll send for an army to wait there and capture every single Pilgrim that reaches it."

"No. I want the Tree for the same reasons as you. Escape."

"Why should we trust you?" Shade demanded.

"I'm an advance scout for the convoy that just passed." He nodded at Shade. "I heard you calling out someone's name. I could have captured you."

"This is your fault," Yorick muttered bitterly to Shade. "Cawing out there like a raven, it's no wonder he found us!"

"I could've had you all taken prisoner," the cannibal continued. "But I didn't. Because I hoped you would lead me to the Tree."

"And if we don't," said Shade, "you'll have us chained up like the others?"

The cannibal took another anxious glance out at the sky. "No. I'm a deserter. If I get caught by the Vampyrum, I'll face the same fate as you."

"And what is that?" Yorick asked, trying to sound bold.

The cannibal's mouth clenched tightly shut.

"Tell us," Nemo said. "You want what we know, better tell us what *you* know."

"Above the Vampyrum City," the cannibal said with some reluctance, "they've started digging through the sky."

A tremor rippled Shade's flesh. Already he had a terrible premonition of what he was going to hear next.

150   Kenneth Oppel

"What for?" asked Java.

"To tunnel out," Shade answered dully. "To the Upper World."

The cannibal looked at him, surprised, and nodded. "That's why the raiding parties have begun. We need more labour to speed the work. They say it will take millennia."

"It's disgusting," said Java, sounding angry for the first time Shade had known her. "You can't keep making slaves of us all! That's not the way it's meant to be! How are we supposed to reach the Tree?"

The cannibal nodded. "The Vampyrum know nothing of the Tree. Cama Zotz keeps it secret from us. The little I have learned is from listening to the Pilgrims, and from rumours. Zotz does not want us to leave his kingdom either."

"But it's not you slaving in the mines," Shade said.

"Many of my kind do. Those who have displeased our god." He had lowered his voice to almost a hiss, and Shade's skin crawled at the idea of Zotz everywhere, listening.

"I want to come with you, to the Tree," the cannibal bat said again.

"What if they're searching for him!" said Yorick to the others. "He can't come with us. It's worse than having Sparklywing over here!"

"I won't travel with this meat-eater," Nemo spat.

"Finally, we agree about something," said Yorick gratefully.

Java sighed. "He has as much right to the Tree as us."

"What?" Shade said, aghast.

"Frieda Silverwing herself said so. The Tree is something Nocturna created for all bats, Vampyrum included. We can't stop anyone from making the journey."

"Does he have to make it with *us*, though?" Yorick moaned.

"There's no point talking about it," Shade said impatiently. The idea of this cannibal being entitled to Nocturna's Tree appalled him, too. But right now his whole body had become a clock, every thump of his heart a reminder of time lost in his search for Griffin. "I don't trust him either," he said, "but we have no choice. If he wants to follow us, he will. We should just go."

"Thank you," said the cannibal. "My name is Murk. You'll see that you need not fear me. I can make sure we have clear passage through the skies."

Shade just grunted. Murk. What kind of name was that anyway? Goth. Throbb. Murk. Who named these bats?

Murk peered cautiously through the cave opening, and then flew. Shade and the others followed. Outside, Yorick cleared his throat importantly.

"If everyone could just be silent a moment while I take my bearings." He circled above them, muttering to himself. "Now where were we . . . Ah, yes, I remember this part now . . . yes . . . or was it this way . . . very tricky, very tricky . . ."

Shade looked worriedly over at Java. "Does anyone else have the sound map?"

"Not me," Java said. "I'm blind in both ears. My whole species is. No echo vision for us. Good eyes though," she said with a blink. "Can see just fine by day or night. When the Pilgrims came to my Oasis, they described the map in words. But it's not as clear that way, I guess. Easier to forget than when it's sung right into your head. I was actually lost when Yorick found me, flying way off course. He said I could travel with him."

Shade looked over at Yorick, surprised by this act of kindness.

"And Nemo," Java went on, "he never even had the map. He'd been travelling in a big group of Pilgrims, and all but him were taken by the Vampyrum. So Yorick's the leader. He's taken us on the right course so far. At least I think he has."

In dismay Shade watched Yorick flitting about, wondering if he had any sense of direction at all. Maybe he should offer to help . . .

"Got it!" announced Yorick proudly, taking the lead. "This way!" His crimped wing gave him an odd, lopsided flight, but he was nimble enough. Relieved, Shade flew after him. Off to his left flapped Java, giving herself ample room so she didn't swat anyone with her massive, leisurely wing strokes. Even from a distance, Shade felt himself buffeted by their turbulence.

"You might want to pull ahead," she told Shade with a smile. "I stir up a bit of wind."

Shade nodded gratefully, climbing to smoother air. Up front, Nemo flew alongside Yorick. Shade looked back to see Murk in the rear, keeping pace several wingbeats behind. He didn't like it at all. When he'd last travelled with Vampyrum, it had not ended well.

For a long time they flew in silence over the badlands, Shade burying his anxiety and impatience in the simple labour of flight, plunging his wings down, lifting them high, over and over, all the while looking for Griffin. The landscape was so flat, there seemed few places where a bat could be concealed, though occasionally Shade would swing away from the others to investigate a mound of boulders, an outcropping, probing with sound, but reluctantly keeping to his promise not to call out Griffin's name. What he wanted was to shout it with all his might.

"If your son is alive, I think perhaps he will glow like you," Java said quietly.

Shade nodded in surprise; he hadn't thought of that. Then he frowned. "But *I* won't see that, will I?"

"I will though. And I am watching for him, too."

"Thank you, Java."

Looking up at the stone sky he could find his circle of stars nowhere. They must still be below the horizon, perhaps shining down on the other side of the Underworld. How long had he been down here anyway? In his mind he shuttled through all that had happened, trying to add up the minutes. Twelve hours maybe. A single night. His body told him he should be sleeping, so above, it must be day. If he didn't find Griffin soon their only escape route would be blocked. Unless . . .

"How far is it to the Tree?" he asked.

"Well, of course, the map doesn't really give distances," Yorick said over his shoulder. "Half a million wingbeats maybe."

Half a million wingbeats. That was two nights' journey; less if they didn't take time to rest or sleep. "Can the living enter the Tree?" he asked Java.

"That I don't know," she replied apologetically. "It's not something Frieda Silverwing talked about amongst the dead. She said Nocturna made the Tree for all bats, and that it would take us where we most needed to go."

If only Frieda were here now, Shade thought. She would be able to tell him whether the Tree was an escape route for Griffin and himself, or simply a dead-end. But: *It will take you where you most need to go*. Well, where they needed to go was home, and if his crack in the sky got blocked off, the Tree might be their only hope. Part of him wasn't even convinced there *was* a Tree. What if it was just another legend, a rumour started by the dead, desperate for another life?

"You're sure about the Vampyrum?" he whispered to Java. "About them being allowed into the Tree too?"

"You find the idea repellent, don't you," said Murk, and Shade turned in surprise to see the cannibal flying alongside him. Shade made no reply.

"You think we evil flesh-eaters should stay here for ever and that only you small, good bats deserve to travel to a new world."

"Exactly," muttered Nemo from up ahead.

"We are Nocturna's creatures too," Murk said matter-of-factly. "She made us what we are. That's why the Tree is for us as well."

"How convenient for you," Shade said, bristling. It seemed completely wrong. Unfair. Why should these flesh-eating fiends have a share of anything perfect? Especially when their god, Zotz, was only intent on feeding off the living, and creating eternal night so he could reign.

"Aren't you betraying Zotz by leaving?" Shade asked coldly. "Why would you want to leave the kingdom of your own god?"

For a while Murk said nothing, and Shade felt disappointed the conversation was over. In an odd way, he was enjoying it, interested in what Murk had to say. It was rare to have the chance to talk to a Vampyrum.

"Down here is like life, only less," Murk said. "We only pretend at life here. We have no more need of food or even sleep really. We do not dream. We are biding our time here, mimicking the world above. And I feel there must be more to eternity than this."

"Yes," said Java eagerly. "That is exactly the feeling I

have. It's not *more* of my old life I want. It's something *new* in the next world."

"Fine for you," snapped Yorick. "You got to live your full life. I was just flying along, nice and cheerful, taking my time, and got blasted against a tree during a storm. I had another twenty years coming to me."

"At least nobody *ate* you," muttered Nemo, looking darkly at Murk.

"I make no apologies for my species," said Murk. "I doubt you grieve for the fish you eat." He glanced over at Shade. "Or you for the insects you devour."

"I eat fruit," said Java. "No one's feelings get hurt that way."

"We do not choose our appetites," Murk said. "We are born with them."

"You eat your own kind," Shade said bluntly.

"Why is that evil? Many other creatures in the Upper World eat their own kind. It is simply the nature of things."

"You sacrifice living creatures," Shade said.

"Because it is pleasing to Zotz. What more precious gift can you offer your god than the gift of life. Would you not give your god whatever was asked of you?"

Shade faltered. Nocturna had never asked for anything as far as he knew. She was infuriatingly quiet. But what would he do if she asked him for another life? It wouldn't happen, he told himself, because she was not barbaric, like Zotz.

"Then he is an evil god," Shade said.

"Who should say what is good or evil but a god?"

"We have our own god."

"Yes, and was it not she who gave us our appetites? Who made us what we are? We are not monsters," said Murk. "We obey our natures, and our god. Like you."

Shade sighed, disconcerted by Murk's logic. "It means we will always be enemies."

"In the world of the living, yes. But not here perhaps."

Shade laughed bitterly. "You ate us in the Upper World, and now you use us as slaves in your mines! I don't think there's a very good chance of peace."

Murk grunted. "No. You are right. But it wasn't always like this here. The mines are recent. Before then, Zotz was content to let us inhabit his jungle paradise." For a moment Murk looked off wistfully. "A glorious city of pyramids, and rainforest the likes of which we never knew in the Upper World."

Shade sniffed. A paradise! It seemed outrageous that the cannibals got a paradise and the other bats were made to wallow in this gloom.

"Sounds great," said Shade irritably. "Why do you want to leave, then?"

"I'm not the only one," Murk said. "There are many like me who have already made their escape. More would leave, I'm sure, if Zotz told them of the Tree, and wasn't so greedy to swell his kingdom. A paradise without choice is tyranny."

Shade said nothing, thoroughly unsettled by Murk. He sounded far too reasonable.

"You mistrust me," said Murk, "and I understand that. But rest assured, the only appetite I have now is to escape this world for the next."

"I'd hoped for better neighbours," Nemo muttered.

Shade turned his full attention back to the sky and land. What a fearful place this was, all scarred earth and rock, a landscape never formed, never named. Murk continued to fly alongside him, and Shade wished he'd go back to the rear. Did he think they were all on friendly terms after their discussion? In the Upper World, this creature would have seen him with only one thought in his mind: food. Shade didn't like him being so close.

"Why do you glow?" Murk asked, and Shade tightened. He'd been worried this moment might come. He caught the worried flick of Java's eyes.

"Just lucky, I guess," said Shade.

Murk said nothing more, but Shade noticed that every so often he'd look over at him, and his nostrils would flare as if taking a sniff. Perhaps this cannibal didn't need food any more, but Shade wondered if a lifetime of instinct could be dulled so easily.

THE CACTUS

Luna kept looking back over her wing, and even Griffin felt a tug of regret when he saw the treetops of Oasis finally dissolve into the distant gloom. He returned his gaze to the terrible mud-cracked plain stretching endlessly before him. No wonder so few bats wanted to leave for the Tree. You'd have to be pretty determined to launch yourself out over this. Oasis was starting to look pretty appealing, even if it was filled with freaky trees and bats who tried to strangle the life out of him.

"It's OK," he said to Luna, hoping he sounded reassuring. Maybe she didn't need reassurance. She never had back home. Personally, he wanted plenty of reassurance. He looked at her off his left wingtip and felt better. They were together, so how bad could it be?

Bad, he thought. *It could always be bad.*

He felt tired and weak and they'd only been flying a couple of hours, following the deep straight gouge that Frieda had illuminated in her sound map. What amazed him was that, somehow, he was faster than Luna. His wing strokes kept pulling him into the lead. Back home, she used to be an amazing flier, stronger and faster than him. Now, Griffin was purposely slowing down so she could keep up. He didn't want her to notice and feel bad.

But it also started him worrying. *She may slow you down*, Frieda had warned him.

"So, we were friends, right?" Luna asked.

"Yeah. You had lots of other friends, too. You were very popular."

"Really?" She seemed pleased. "Why?"

"You were cheerful and brave and . . . just a lot of fun to be around."

"I like what I'm hearing," she said with a grin. "You can keep talking."

"Everyone wanted to be your friend. You always had good ideas. Well, *exciting* ideas anyway; I wasn't always sure they were *good* ideas, because they were obviously reckless and highly dangerous."

"You're not making this up?"

"Nope."

She laughed. "So what sort of things did I do?"

"Well, the owl game for starters . . ." and he told her all about it, and plenty of the other things she'd done back at Tree Haven.

"That sounds like fun," she said, and suddenly fell silent.

"You OK?" he asked, worried he'd done or said something wrong.

"Just the way you tell it. Like it's over and done with. And I can't even remember myself in it."

"You will."

"Yeah?" She looked at him with such yearning he felt his heart clench.

"Absolutely," he said, hoping he wasn't lying. "The more we talk about it, the more you'll think about it. It'll all come back."

"That'd be good," she said with a nod. "If I could remember, it wouldn't be so bad."

"I'll be your memory for now. Anything you want to know, just ask me."

"The fire," she said. "How did it happen?"

The sight of her scarred wings still made Griffin wince, and though he tried to avoid looking, he often found his eyes dragged back to them. He'd just promised her . . . but what was the use of telling the truth? Wouldn't do a bit of good. It would just make her hate him. And he needed her to be his friend down here. He wanted to help her get out of here – to make things right after the terrible thing he'd done. But that was only part of it. The truth was, he was too afraid to fly for the Tree alone. He wanted companionship, and right now he could think of no better companion than Luna.

"Well," he began, unable to look at her. "There was a storm, and lightning hit the tree you were roosting on, and a branch fell and knocked you out, and you caught fire."

"No one else died, did they? Like my mother?"

"Just you."

"Tell me her name."

"Roma."

"Yeah," she said. "That sounds right." She closed her eyes as she flew, and Griffin could only guess that she was trying hard to summon up an image of her mother. He watched, wondering what it was like to be her, what she must be feeling – and simply could not imagine. It made his mind lurch. Dead. Not alive ever again. Everything taken away.

Eyes opening, Luna sighed with disappointment.

"I just hope you're telling me the truth," she muttered, then smiled. "You could be telling me anything, and how would I know?"

Uneasily he smiled back.

"I can't believe how well you're taking all this," he said with admiration. "Being dead, I mean. If it were me, I'd be completely stressed out."

"Well, doesn't seem there's much I can do about it, does there?"

He laughed. "No. I guess not."

Suddenly she winced.

"What's wrong?" Griffin asked worriedly.

"My wings."

"They hurt?"

Luna hunched her shoulders, fluttered her wingtips, as if trying to shake the pain loose. "They never hurt before," she muttered.

"Is it bad?" Griffin asked.

"Not so bad." She forced a smile, but it didn't erase the furrow in her forehead. "So where are we headed exactly?"

"Well, we're supposed to follow this gully until we reach a kind of short fat tree with prickles all over it. It's called a cactus. That's the first landmark, and it should tell us the way to the next one."

They flew on in silence. Griffin reminded himself to keep sweeping the horizons, watching for Vampyrum. At least there wasn't much chance of being crept up on out here. Mostly he kept an eye on Luna, searching her face for signs of pain. Why had it started all of a sudden like that? Maybe that's what happened when the bats left Oasis. Or maybe it was something to do with him, reminding her of the accident. Now her body was starting to remember too.

"Home doesn't look like this, does it?" Luna asked suddenly.

"No."

"That's good. Because I may not remember much, but this is one sorry-looking place. Not even bugs live out here!"

"Wasn't like they were real anyway," Griffin said.

"I guess dead bats don't need food." Luna frowned. "But what about you? *You* must be hungry."

"I could sure use a few caterpillars right now," he said, and regretted it. He didn't really wanting to start thinking about food. It would only make him hungry.

"How long to the Tree?" Luna asked.

"Frieda said a couple of nights at most. Not long. You tired?"

"No. You?"

"Getting there." He wondered how long he could keep up the pace, with no food or water. All this dark was making him tired, too. He craved moonlight, the horizon's glow at sunset or sunrise. He craved sleep.

A change in the air made him sniff, but it wasn't a smell that set off his inner alarm; it was the *texture* of the air, a thickening that billowed from the fractured earth like the sun's heat. He looked down and saw the ground flinch, as if it were taut skin. Then, as Griffin watched in horror, it liquefied.

Gone was the earth below them, gone was the gully they had been following, all melted into a black sea. At first it sloshed thickly back and forth, but then it started to crest, as though whipped by a strong wind. And indeed, a wind did kick up, buffeting them as they flew.

"The map!" Griffin cried. Dissolved. Gone. He looked around in horror, not quite able to believe this. "You're seeing this, right? It's not just me."

"I'm seeing it," muttered Luna.

"Does this happen a lot here?"

"Not that I've seen."

"Because just in case you're wondering," Griffin shouted, "this is *not normal*!"

Big fat bubbles formed on the surface and popped, boiling up everywhere. Instinctively Griffin flew higher with Luna. How were they supposed to find their way now? Frieda had said the landscape could change, but he hadn't expected it so soon, or so drastically. Fighting the wind he tried to steer a straight course. A headache pounded at his temple in sync with his heartbeat. The whole desert was molten, a million black mouths, puckering open, slapping shut, eager to swallow him down.

"Luna," he said anxiously, "there's nowhere to roost now."

"We'll just have to keep flying, Griff."

She even remembered his nickname. It cheered him up somehow, and despite the burn in his chest, he gritted his teeth and concentrated on his wing strokes. Ten minutes ago he hadn't needed to roost – now it was all he could think of.

"This has got to clear up soon, right?" he panted.

"Absolutely," said Luna.

"Absolutely," he echoed, trying to believe it. "But, say if it doesn't clear up, we'll still have to land eventually, and I don't know about you, but I'm not crazy about the idea of crash-landing in that goo down there. It looks like a bog kind of situation. That really oozy mud that will just suck you right down and clog up your nose and mouth and—"

"Is that a tree?" Luna interrupted. "Over there?"

On the horizon, an odd, fat tree jutted crookedly from the earth.

"That's it!" Griffin cried in relief. "The cactus!"

As they flapped closer, he saw that it grew from a small hillock and somehow hadn't toppled into the boiling morass which slapped against its base. It had a number of smooth chubby arms, and amidst the wickedly sharp thorns bloomed strange flowers. Luna was already making for its spiny branches, but Griffin held back.

"You think it's safe?" he said. "I mean, *structurally*. There's quite a tilt on that thing."

Luna looked back over her wing in amazement. "Griff, do you see any other trees around here?"

"It's a cactus, actually. And no, I don't. But—"

"Come on, what's the worst that can happen?"

Griffin smiled.

"What's funny?" she asked.

"You used to say that to me back home; it was sort of a joke we had because . . . well, I always thought the worst would happen."

"So what *is* the worst?"

"The worst? We land and the cactus falls over and takes us down with it into the boiling muck."

"We'd fly off if it started to fall."

"Good. Good plan."

"Anything else?"

"It's a weird-looking thing. Not exactly inviting, you know what I mean? All those pointy bits and . . . oh, forget it," he said, exhausted. "You're right. Let's land." Wary of the thorns, he came in and grabbed the slippery bark, flipping upside down. Seemed solid enough. Didn't make sense that it was still standing, a little island in a churning sea. At least the waves didn't seem to be getting any worse.

"I guess this happens here all the time," he said, looking at the pitching horizon. Frieda had told him not to linger anywhere, to keep moving. But no way was he setting off again if there was no place to land. It would be like launching yourself out over the ocean – hoping for an island or a passing ship for refuge. He thought of his father, how he'd once nearly drowned in the sea during a storm. He'd survived. He'd survive anything.

"First landmark," said Luna.

"Yeah," said Griffin in surprise. In all the panic, he'd forgotten. He felt a small flicker of pride. He'd made it this far. Their trail was melted, but that didn't matter now. The cactus would give them their new route. He looked up and found the round hole in the centre of the branch.

"See that?" he told Luna. "We look through there and that's our new course."

He would do it later. Right now, he was too tired to move.

"Aren't you wiped out?" he asked Luna.

"I don't know," she replied thoughtfully. "I don't really feel any different from before."

"Well, I'm completely shattered. I'm finding this all very unsettling. I don't know how bats live down here, long term. I couldn't do it. I've only been down here a night or so and I'm already a nervous wreck."

"You're always a nervous wreck," said Luna.

"True," Griffin said with a laugh. "Very true." He felt better now, and gave a yawn that stretched every inch of his body.

"Why don't you get some sleep," Luna said. "We're not going anywhere until this calms down."

"You don't mind?" Griffin could think of nothing he wanted more right now. "But shouldn't someone—"

"I'll keep watch," Luna told him. "Just in case the goo rises, or the tree tips."

"Or if you see anything coming," he added, remembering the Vampyrum.

"I'll wake you instantly."

"Thank you," he said gratefully.

"Just one thing . . ."

"What?"

"Would you mind telling me more," Luna said, "about home and everything."

"Of course." He was glad she asked. He wanted to think about it, describe it and paint it into life with words – as if that would make it easier to reach again. Roosting from the highest branch, away from the hissing and bubbling earth, they drew close to one another. Her body was cold, and still unsettling to him, but nonetheless comforting. He was so glad to have her with him.

He began with Tree Haven itself, the first place in the world he remembered, describing it as clearly as he could. Then the forest outside, the different trees, the stream, the sugar maple he loved. He told her about the other newborns, Rowan, Skye, Falstaff, and how good it was at the end of the night to go back to Tree Haven where they would all roost together.

"I see her," Luna said suddenly.

Her voice made him jerk, she hadn't spoken in so long.

"My mother," Luna said. "I remember her." Quietly she began to cry. "I saw her, I really saw her. Oh, Griffin. I don't know what's worse. Seeing, or not seeing."

He met her gaze, transfixed by the grief in her eyes, not knowing what to say. She was sobbing, but she had no tears.

"Keep going," she said hoarsely. "Keep telling it."

"You sure?"

"I don't think I really believed it before now," she said,

"being dead. It just didn't seem like it could be true. But when I saw her, when I remembered, I knew it was. I really know now. But don't stop, please."

Haltingly, he continued. Her crying settled into a kind of shuddering, and he could feel her sorrow transmitted through his own fur and flesh, and sometimes he cried too. He lost track of how long he'd been talking. It made him feel safe, all the talking. As if, through all these words, he was controlling things, making things right. He glanced over at Luna, but she had her face turned away from him, so it was hard to tell if she was even awake. Sometimes he would pause, and after a second she would say, "I'm listening." And so he would continue as the earth hissed and boiled around them.

Finally, exhausted, he could think of no more to say, and slept.

ATTACK

"We're nearing the Oasis," said Yorick with obvious relief. "Right on course."

Shade saw how, in the distance, the badlands gently dipped away into a vast, shallow crater. After a few hundred more wingbeats, he made out the tops of trees. It was the first time he had seen any kind of living thing here – if you could use the word "living" at all – and the trees even looked familiar. His heart quickened. If he were a newborn – if he were any kind of bat – this place would instantly draw him in from the desert.

Yorick turned to him. "You can have a look around, but we won't be stopping long, remember. If you want to travel with us, you leave when we say." He grimaced sourly at Murk. "In any event, I shouldn't imagine we'll be very welcome with a Vampyrum in tow."

Shade nodded.

"Don't worry," Java told him. "I'll help you look."

"My eyes and ears are sharper than most," Nemo boasted. "I can hear a fish below the river's surface and snatch him out before he feels the water ripple."

"Thank you," Shade said.

"Look, the tallest tree, do you all see it?" Yorick pointed out. "That's our rendezvous. We continue our merry little journey from there." He studied the sky. "When that large star touches the horizon, we leave." Shade found the star. Already it was not far from the earth's rim. Now that they were near the boundary of Oasis, he could see how large it was. A vast forest to search, and only a breath of time to do it in.

"If we split up we can cover more territory," Java said to Shade. "Something you should know: the bats who live here, they will think they're still alive."

"Got it," said Shade.

"So be careful if you speak to them. Usually, they're not very happy to see Pilgrims. They think we're loony."

As Java and Nemo veered off, Yorick shook his head disapprovingly. "Just make sure you make it back to the rendezvous," he called after them. "I'm not waiting for anyone! I'd help you look, of course," he told Shade, "but my bad wing and all. I've got to rest it or I won't last ten more strokes." With that he fluttered off to find a roost.

Shade wasted no time. Into the trees he plunged, not caring how much noise he made now.

"Griffin!" he bellowed. "Griffin!"

He was astonished to see that the forest was streaming with other Silverwings, and his spirits soared.

"Hey!" he called out. "I'm looking for someone! Can you help me?"

Not one of them stopped. And it wasn't because they couldn't hear him. He caught several of them making quick backward glances, and then beating their wings even faster, as if fleeing a deadly predator. They evaporated through the branches so quickly he couldn't keep up.

"Wait!" he called out in frustration. "I'm looking for someone! Griffin Silverwing!"

"You were calling that name when I first saw you."

Shade jolted round to see Murk fly down through the foliage towards him. He'd thought Murk had sailed off to the rendezvous point to wait. How long had he been trailing him? No wonder he wasn't having any luck talking to the other bats.

"You're scaring them all off!" Shade said sharply.

"Perhaps it's your glow they're frightened of," Murk retorted.

"A glow is one thing, a cannibal bat is a whole new level of terror."

"Did you lose Griffin in your travels?"

Shade said nothing, having no desire to share anything about his son with Murk. He hated the fact this creature even knew his son's name. And he certainly didn't want Murk to know Griffin was alive.

"Look," said Shade, flustered, "maybe it's best if you just wait for us at the rendezvous."

"Did you want to talk to these bats?"

"That was my plan, yes."

Murk grunted impatiently, then flew past Shade into a clearing, circling at treetop level.

"Hear me!" Murk blared. "You know my kind, you know that we live here in the billions. Shade Silverwing would like to speak with you. Answer his questions! Or I will send an army of Vampyrum who will enslave each and every one of you, and take you to a place of suffering too great to imagine! Speak now!"

Murk flew up to a tree and roosted, gazing malevolently over the clearing. Shade circled in amazement, astounded at what Murk had just done.

Whispers flitted through the trees. Wings creaked in agitation. Then from the cover of a large pine came the uncertain voice of a Silverwing female.

"I am Corona, elder here. I will speak to you."

Shade could scarcely believe his good fortune. "I'm looking for a newborn," he said eagerly. "Griffin Silverwing. Is he here?"

There was a brief pause and then, "We have seen a newborn, though he never told us his name. He was like you though. With a glow to him."

A glow. A life.

"Where is he?"

"No longer here."

"How long ago did he leave?" Shade asked, dismayed.

"Not long at all. Perhaps a full rotation of the stars."

"Did he say where he was he going?"

"He spoke with the Pilgrims, and left for the Tree they talk of." Here her words took on a scornful tone.

"He went alone?"

"No. He convinced another bat to go with him. Another newborn called Luna. Foolish child."

Luna. Why was that name familiar? Then he remembered it was Griffin's friend from Tree Haven. The one injured in the fire, he realized with a cold jolt. She must have died and come here. He felt relief though that his son was not alone. That was good news. It would keep his spirits up, and they would help each other. One of them must have the map.

"Was he well, the boy?" Shade demanded. "Not injured?"

A dreadful silence seeped out from the trees. Shade's heart contracted in fear. What were they hiding?

"Tell him what he asks!" roared Murk from his branch.

"Yes," stammered Corona. "He was fine."

"Tell the truth," barked Murk, "or I will be back to confront you with your lies!"

"Some were suspicious of his glow, and wanted him gone. They tried to drive him off."

Shade's heartbeat pounded in his ears so he could barely hear. Rage threatened to choke his voice.

"You attacked him?"

"He wasn't hurt. They simply wanted to scare him away."

"Because he *glowed*?"

"Because he wanted to poison this colony with lies! Telling us we were dead, that we should go to the Tree. But I promise you, the newborn was not harmed. I have answered your questions. I'd ask you to be on your way now."

With a rush of wings, the bats were gone.

Shade circled, relief sapping his anger. Griffin was alive, and now Shade knew where he was going. He would catch up with him. If there was time, they could escape through the tunnel in the stone sky. If not, they would have to take their chances in the Tree.

"So. Your son is already on his way," Murk said, flying over.

"Yes," Shade said, then frowned, a peal of alarm sounding through his head. He looked at Murk. "I never said he was my son."

Murk gave a hoarse laugh. "You didn't need to. I too had children once."

"Oh," Shade said, unable to meet Murk's eye, unable to thank him. Never had he imagined he'd get help from a cannibal. Still he was suspicious, but his suspicion was barbed with guilt. Perhaps, here in the Underworld, it *was* possible for Silverwings and Vampyrum to live in a kind of amnesty; yet he didn't know if he could ever stop thinking about them as vile enemies.

Shade called out across the treetops for Java and Nemo. He told them his happy news as they made their way to the rendezvous together. The tree – some weird hybrid Shade had never encountered, half oak, half cedar – was near the crater's rim. From the top branches, Shade looked out at more interminable badlands. Yorick was already there waiting for them.

"You're late, all of you," he snapped by way of greeting. "I was just about to strike out on my own."

"Spare us," said Nemo. "You're about as likely to strike out on your own as get struck by a shooting star."

"Shade's son was here," Java told Yorick with a smile.

"He's gone on to the Tree ahead of us," Shade added. "Any chance of catching up with them?

"Let's not get ahead of ourselves, shall we?" said Yorick. "I've got to plot our next route, and my wing is still killing me by the way, not that anyone has ever shown the slightest bit of concern."

"We've put up with you, haven't we?" Nemo remarked. "Not many would, I reckon."

Yorick didn't reply to this, only lifted from the tree and circled, taking his bearings. Shade waited impatiently.

"It's all wrong," Yorick muttered, his voice rising. "The wretched Pilgrim must have made a mistake. There should be a clear furrow in the earth for us to follow, but it's not here."

Shade looked down at the spider's web of cracks in the mud plain; certainly there wasn't any one gouge that cut a straight path.

"It's like the landscape has changed completely!" wailed Yorick.

"Frieda told us the map could change," Java said. "I remember that."

"That's why we were to hurry!" Yorick moaned, shooting a resentful look at Shade and Murk. "And not waste time on *distractions*. Remember? She warned us all. Now look at the mess we're in!"

Shade flew up from the tree. "Sing me the map," he told Yorick, and regretted the harshness of his tone immediately.

"Certainly not," said Yorick. "The map is mine and mine alone."

"Don't be ridiculous. It's for everyone who needs to get to the Tree."

"I won't tell you, and you can't make me," Yorick said petulantly.

"Sing it to him," said Nemo. "Maybe he'll have some luck with it."

"I won't!"

"Why not?" demanded Shade. "You want to get to the Tree, don't you?"

"Of course but—"

"What is it you're afraid of, Yorick?" asked Java in her mellifluous voice.

"If I sing it to you all, how do I know you won't fly on without me? It's not like you need a crippled bat slowing you down."

He looked so crestfallen and pathetic that Shade instantly felt sorry for him.

"Of course we wouldn't do that," said Shade. "I just thought I could help. I'm good with maps, too."

But Yorick, despite the reassurances pouring from Java and Nemo, was still unwilling to sing the map.

Shade looked out to the horizon desperately.

"Look," he said with sudden realization, "my son must have got a map just recently, right? So all we have to do is follow him."

"Granted, but how?" Yorick demanded, as if Shade had gone crazy.

"If he was nearby, I'll be able to hear his echoes."

"You can do this?" Java asked, incredulous. "With your ears?"

Shade closed his eyes and listened, shutting out the other sounds, swimming back through time. He heard the trace of an echo image ahead of him and flew after it over the desert. Closer, he saw that it was a Silverwing newborn, a female – and off to her left was a second vaporous flash of wings. Griffin.

Shade listened as their echo residues wisped towards the horizon, then opened his eyes, and superimposed their sonic trajectory against the landscape, plotting their course.

"I've got it!" he called out to the others. "We'll follow them."

Yorick looked unconvinced, muttering glumly under his breath.

"You're assuming, of course, that they're going in the right direction."

"It's the best we've got," said Shade, intent on following his son, wherever it might lead.

"Good, then," said Murk. "Let's go."

"I need to know our course!" said Yorick petulantly. Shade paused, circled back to him, and showed him their destination on the horizon.

"This way!" said Yorick, and pulled ahead. Reluctantly, Shade let Yorick take the lead. They flew. After a few hundred wingbeats, Shade listened again for Griffin's echo traces. Still on course. He was about to open his eyes when his echovision caught a faint trace of something else, a more recent noise, but on the same course as his son.

Shade pulled away from the others for a moment, hoping for a clearer image. As he'd thought, it was the blurry silhouette of another bat. He listened harder, urging the silver image to crystallize in his mind's eye.

A wing, a face.

Goth.

Griffin was dreaming of bugs. Too many bugs. His sugar maple was covered with tent caterpillars and he could see the leaves being devoured before his eyes. The caterpillars swarmed over the branches and trunk, burrowing into it, eating the tree into a skeleton of itself. And there was nothing he could do. Too many caterpillars, how was he expected to eat them all? Why weren't any of the others helping him? At least Luna should be helping him. Suddenly the bugs weren't just on the tree, they were on him, all over him, thickly coating his fur, and he couldn't shake them off fast enough, and they were eating *him* now, boring into him.

Luna, he was shouting. *Luna, Luna, Luna!*

"Luna!"

He wrenched open his eyes. She was watching him.

"Did I shout your name?" he asked.

"Yes. What's wrong?"

"I . . . I had a . . . hey, am I still alive?" he blurted in panic.

"You're still very sparkly," she said with a grin. "I take that as a yes."

"Just a bad dream," he said uncertainly. "Sorry if I woke you."

"I wasn't sleeping."

He frowned. "Not at all?"

"I guess we don't need sleep any more," she said a bit wistfully.

"You were just hanging there the whole time?" Her face looked a bit pinched, and he wondered if the pain was still there.

"I was thinking," she said. "Remembering bits of things."

"That's good," said Griffin, hoping she wouldn't ever remember how he'd dropped the fire stick on her.

He noticed that the earth was finally still, gelled into a plain of hardened mud.

"You rested enough to get going?" Luna asked. She seemed as eager as he was to get out of here.

"Yeah. We just need to set our new course." He flexed and was ready to fly to the hole when Luna cried out. He looked over and saw her dangling in mid-air, an inch below the branch, thrashing indignantly.

"Something's got my leg!" she shouted, swinging wildly.

Astonished, Griffin stared for a moment before he understood. He started laughing. "It's just a little shoot from the cactus. It got kind of tangled around your left ankle." Luna jerked her leg hard, but the tendril held tight.

"Griffin, get it off me, will you?"

"Hang on. I'll just bite it off." He swung his upper body on to the branch and held tight with his thumb claws. He crawled towards the base of the tendril and put his jaws around it. The moment he started to bite, the tendril flinched against his teeth, and Griffin pulled back with a yelp.

"What? What's going on?" Luna demanded beneath him.

Griffin stared at the tendril. It was *growing*, slithering like a snake up Luna's leg.

She giggled in alarm. "Um, Griff, it's crawling up me!" She beat her wings hard, trying to pull free. Useless. With her free foot she slashed at the shoot, but it just tightened and twined itself even higher towards her hips.

"OK," Griffin said. "It's OK. Just a slithering tendril kind of situation here. I'm going to . . . um . . . try again."

He clenched his eyes shut and bit, the fleshy tendril writhing in his jaws like a living thing. His teeth went all the way through. There was a sharp hiss, like a shocked intake of breath. In revulsion Griffin spat it out immediately. The severed shoot fell earthwards, withering off Luna's ankle, dissolving into thin air.

"Fly clear!" he shouted.

"Can't!"

Wildly he looked around and saw that a second shoot had sprung from the branch and coiled around Luna's leg. He fearfully checked over his own body – he was clear – then stretched forward to bite off this new shoot. Suddenly, all along its length, wicked little thorns were pricking up.

"Griffin, there's something coming!"

He jerked around, thinking: *not someone, something*. His eyes swept the sky and picked out the silhouette, flapping towards them over the desert plain. It was still quite far away, but just from its size and the jagged cut of its wings, he knew it was not a Silverwing. Every second he stared it was getting bigger. He didn't know why the sight of it made his body turn liquidy with fear. The creature was alone, but aimed straight at the cactus, and there was something brutal about the bundled intensity of its hunched shoulders, the ferocious slash of its wings, which made Griffin think: *Coming for us*.

"Come on, Griff," shouted Luna, dangling helplessly, "get this thing *off* me!"

"Working on it!"

He turned back to the thorny shoot and found a bare patch. Even as he clamped down, from the corner of his eye he saw two new tendrils spring from the branch. Quick as he could, he severed the tendril in his mouth, but the others had already coiled themselves around Luna's wings.

"Griffin!"

He cast a frenzied glance skywards and –

The bat's huge wings blocked out the stars as it plunged. Griffin stared, transfixed with horror. Three-foot wingspan, a big-chested body, a long skull whose snout flared upwards into a spike. Its jaws, opening.

I know what that is.

Vampyrum Spectrum.

The cannibal bat made a quick circle of the cactus, studying the thorny weave of branches, plotting the best approach. Griffin let go with his thumb claws and hung by his feet, watching, wanting to fly. Maybe it was just terror. Maybe it was Luna, tangled and helpless beside him. But he could not fly.

The Vampyrum swung in, disappeared for a second beneath the lower branches – and then came straight up at them. Griffin heard screaming, didn't know if it was his own or not. He saw Luna flailing her wings. He saw the Vampyrum and its eyes locking on to him. What Griffin did next was pure instinct. He'd never fought another bat in his life. He pulled his wings tight across his chest, and lashed out with both of them, putting his whole might behind the blow. He heard and felt the concussion through his entire body, waited for his wings to crumple, waited for the numbing final impact of hard body and jaws.

It didn't happen.

He could scarcely believe his senses as he felt the Vampyrum being driven away from him. The cannibal bat staggered back through the air, and hard against a branch. Thorns pierced its wings and it roared. And even as it tried to wrench itself free, the cactus sent out quick tendrils around its legs and shoulders.

Griffin wasted not a second. With three brutal bites, he severed the last tendrils around Luna, and she lurched free. Shaking terribly, Griffin flipped himself off the branch and unfurled his wings, wincing at the sharp lightning bolt of pain through his bruised forearms.

"The map!" he cried in dismay. The Vampyrum was flailing directly in front of the oval hole that was to guide them on their voyage. Griffin didn't dare go any closer. They'd just have to guess.

Before he could stop her, though, Luna flew for the hole, passing a mere wingbeat from Goth's snapping jaws. She took a quick look through, then veered up and away.

"Just like the owl game," she panted.

"You get it?" he said, catching up.

"Not great, but it'll have to do."

They flew hard over the desert plain, wanting to put as much distance as possible between themselves and the thrashing monster impaled on the cactus.

"What could have been easier, Goth?"

Zotz's laughter was a tremor, rumbling the cactus on which he was pierced.

"I led you to the newborn," Zotz said. "I delayed him by melting the earth and destroying his trail."

"I don't understand," said Goth, burning with shame and fury. "I was upon him and he struck me, and—"

"Could it be that he was stronger than you?"

"Impossible," said Goth. "A bat of his kind, a newborn . . ."

"You are forgetting one important thing. You are dead. He is alive."

Goth said nothing.

"Arrogance, Goth. You assume too much."

Shaking, Goth bit back his temper. That such a pathetic little creature could best him was more than he could bear. And the added humiliation of being impaled on thorns, while Zotz rebuked him by wrapping him up in these tendrils.

"My failure is despicable," said Goth evenly, "but I wonder, my Lord, that you did not ensnare the newborn in the same way as me."

"Have you not understood me, Goth?" came Zotz's sharp reply, so deep in his ear that he winced. "I can not touch the living. I can not harm them. I can not kill them. That is your task – and a simple one I had thought."

"I did not know I would be so weakened."

"Know this, then. Without food, without water, the newborn's strength decreases second by second. Yours grows. As you become acclimatized to my world you will regain all your strength. But wait too long and the newborn will die, and his life will be lost."

"I understand, Lord Zotz."

The tendrils which entangled him suddenly fell away like dead twigs. The thorns melted from his wings, and Goth pushed away from the branch, flying clear.

"You've lost surprise now. He knows you will come again."

"You will have his life forthwith," Goth promised.

"And let this sharpen your resolve," whispered the air around Goth's face. "The newborn you seek is the child of Shade Silverwing. Now hurry."

THE CAVE OF MOURNERS

"I can't believe the way you slugged that thing," Luna said when they finally slowed down, confident the Vampyrum wasn't in pursuit. "I thought you were a goner, Griff, but you just smashed it off. How'd you do that?"

"I don't know." He'd been wondering the same thing. He was a fraction the size of the cannibal bat. He should've been massacred. "Some kind of fluke, I guess."

Luna was looking at him in amazement and a kind of grudging admiration. "Were you this strong back home?"

"No, I wasn't," Griffin said, astonished. He didn't see how he could be strong right now either. He felt lousy, hunger gnawing at his stomach, and he knew he would be trembling if all his limbs and muscles weren't already busy with the labour of flight. Most of all he yearned for water, just a spray of it, cool and wet, down his sore throat.

"Well, down here, you're strong," Luna said with conviction. "Which is a good thing for us."

"Yeah, I'm fabulous in the land of the dead," Griffin mumbled sarcastically. But for a moment he was pleased.

The way Luna looked at him was like being illuminated by the full glow of the moon. He'd impressed her. Strong. Maybe if he was strong he could be braver. What he'd done to that Vampyrum was hardly brave though. He was just plain petrified, and he'd lashed out in self-defence. Like anyone would have done. Any pleasure he felt at the idea of being strong was quickly evaporating. He wasn't sure he wanted to be the strongest, the one who had to do things.

"Thanks," Luna said. "For not taking off on me."

"Oh," he said, surprised, remembering how much he'd wanted to.

"I don't know if I could've done it," Luna said, "hold my ground with that thing flying for me. What was it anyway?"

"Vampyrum Spectrum. They're cannibals from the southern jungles. I guess you don't remember all those stories we used to tell."

She shook her head.

"We used to play games about them. You liked being one of the cannibals."

"I did?" Luna asked, amazed, but she was smiling too.

"Yeah. You got to chase everyone and pretend to eat them. You thought it was fun."

"Well," she said, "it couldn't have been as much fun as this. First we get the evil cactus and . . . what did you call it? A slithering tendril kind of situation? Then, just when we thought it couldn't get much more hilarious, the giant flesh-eating bat shows up!"

Shade laughed so hard he got a cramp in his side. He hadn't realized how tightly he'd been holding himself, one big knot of muscle and sinew and worry. He looked back over his shoulder.

"You think it'll follow us?"

"No chance. He's going to stay a million wingbeats away from you!"

Griffin smiled, wishing he could feel so sure.

"It's weird," he said, "the way it came for me. Looking straight at me. Never you. It was like it was hunting just for me. Like it knew where I was."

"I think you're being a little paranoid."

"Paranoid? Let's see. We're in the land of the dead, the ground boils, a cactus starts wrapping you up like a cocoon, and a cannibal bat tries to eat me. Yep, I'd say I'm pretty paranoid!"

"How could it be looking for you?" Luna said. "That's crazy."

"My glow! Maybe he could tell I was alive!" He looked around warily, feeling like a giant firefly, blazing a trail for every predator in the Underworld. "What if he's following me? We can't stop again, Luna. We won't be able to sleep any more."

"I wasn't sleeping," she reminded him.

"Me then. How am I supposed to sleep? I mean, where's safe? And if I can't rest, I'm going to get really tired and weak, and if I'm weak how am I gonna—"

"Griff, it's OK," she said firmly. "You can rest. You can sleep. I'll keep watch."

"What if things start moving or *growing*—"

"I'll pay more attention next time. Promise. Hey, how come those tendrils never tangled *you* up?"

Griffin frowned. He hadn't thought of that. "I don't know. This place is freaking me out, though."

"We'll be gone soon, no problem."

"OK, good. Thanks." He forced a deep breath. He was so glad Luna was here. "You're sure this is the right course?" he asked suddenly. The mud-cracked plains stretched to all horizons with no distinguishing features – nothing that triggered his memory of Frieda's map.

"I think so," Luna said.

"*Think* so?"

She winced suddenly, glancing at the angry scars on her wings. "I took as good a look as I could, with that thing flapping around," she said sharply. "Didn't notice you doing it."

"Sorry." After a moment he asked, "Is it bad, the pain?"

"Sure not getting any better." Her face was pinched and her wing strokes, he noticed, were not as smooth or powerful as before.

Griffin said nothing more, ashamed. But it didn't stop him worrying about their direction. He was angry at himself too. Back at the cactus he should've taken his bearings before he'd slept; why hadn't he just done it?

Wings creaking quietly through the eternal night, they flew on.

"It's changing up ahead," said Luna.

Griffin had noticed too. Near the horizon, the monotonous plains ended in a ragged coastline. Beyond stretched a great body of water, undulating gently, sparkling in the starlight. The simple sight of all that water somehow lifted his spirits, though he didn't remember any water on Frieda's map. The sea undulated and, farther out, rolled up into hills which folded over one another before melting away. It was all strange and strikingly beautiful. But—

"It's not water," Griffin said with a sinking heart.

A few hundred wingbeats on, and he saw that it was in fact an ocean of pale sand, lapping and slapping, roiling in ferocious currents. The sand would suddenly pile up into mountains, hold for a few seconds, only to dissolve with a thunderous rumble. Griffin put some more altitude between himself and the sand. He saw how quickly it could rise up into a dizzying peak, and he didn't want to get engulfed by it. All the heaving and rolling below was sending up turbulence, and he and Luna went bobbing along overhead, the air so thick it almost felt like they were rowing through water. Griffin tried not to look down; the pitching landscape only made him dizzy.

"This normal?" Luna asked.

"Nope."

"Just making sure."

Was this the right route? Griffin knew that if they were going astray, it would be harder to find their way back with every wingbeat. He checked over his shoulder for the Vampyrum, then, with Luna, laboured on through the sky. They crested a mountain range of sand that crashed towards them like a tidal wave, its sandy froth nearly washing over them. On the other side they found themselves over a more serene stretch. The change was abrupt, and welcome. Fighting the turbulence, trying to stay on course, had tired Griffin out. A thousand wingbeats distant, jutting up from the sand was a low hill.

With a melting sense of relief, Griffin recognized it.

"Now that," he said delighted, "was on Frieda's map! We're on the right course!" He beamed at Luna. "You did it!"

Etched against the night he could see the serrated shudder of bats' wings, but could tell, even from this distance, there were no Vampyrum amongst them. The bats were scattered across the sky, approaching the hill in little knots.

"Must be other Pilgrims," Luna said.

Griffin noticed that the bats all seemed to be heading for the far side of the hill, where they dipped down out of view.

"What's so interesting over there?" Luna said.

"A cave," Griffin muttered, as Frieda's sound map flared before his mind's eye. He remembered how he was whipped past. "Luna, we're not supposed to stop here."

"Why not?"

He wanted to stay high, but passing overhead he caught a glimpse of the cave's entrance. It was vast, like the mouth of an enormous beached sea creature, gasping its final breaths. All around it sand lapped gently, but did not spill inside. Tendrils of mysterious misty light seeped out. Half a dozen Graywings streaked past Griffin and Luna from above, wings beating impatiently for the cave.

"Hey, what's down there?" Luna called after them.

"The way home!" one of the Graywings chattered excitedly. "Come on!"

"Hurry!" another bat shouted, looking back over her wing. "They say you can get your life back!"

Luna turned to Griffin expectantly.

"Frieda didn't say anything about this," Griffin muttered. "The Tree's the only way out."

"Yeah, like the last tree was such a good time," said Luna.

"That was a *cactus*, actually. Frieda said we shouldn't stop . . ." But his eyes kept getting drawn back to the silky light undulating from the cave mouth.

"I want to go," said Luna.

"No," said Griffin firmly. "It's not on the map."

"You're just saying that because you're scared."

"Correct."

"What's the worst that can happen?" she said with a grin. "I'm already dead."

"Hilarious, Luna, really funny."

"Aren't you just a bit curious?"

"Luna . . ."

"Come *on*, Griffin." She was already flying down towards the cave without him. He hesitated a moment, then went after her.

"We're close," Shade said.

He barely had to listen backwards through time to catch Griffin's echo traces. Now they were crystalline, fresh, maybe not even a thousand wingbeats old. Shade allowed himself to feel hopeful, despite the lingering image of Goth he'd heard earlier. Maybe it wasn't even Goth, he kept telling himself. Why couldn't it have been another Vampyrum? Maybe even a kind of rogue echo thrown off from Murk? But this was just trying to make himself feel better. It was Goth. Shade knew it. Normally the idea of Goth being dead would have filled him with relief. Down here it was the opposite. He could only hope that Goth's presence near his son was a complete coincidence, a crossing of paths separated by plenty of time. Shade beat his wings harder.

Below him, the sea of sand heaved and sprayed.

"When you find your son," Java said, "how will you get home?"

Shade looked across the stone sky of the Underworld, hardly daring to believe his good fortune. During the flight, he'd been watching anxiously, hoping his circle of stars would emerge over the earth's rim. And now there it was. The exit. Within hours, if all went well, he'd be heading for it with Griffin. The climb up and out wouldn't be easy, but he would help his son. They would make it out together, back inside Tree Haven, before the entrance was blocked.

"The same crack we both came through," Shade told Java eagerly. "I know where it is, and it'll take us right back—" He flinched. He'd forgotten himself. Stupidly talking about the Upper World and how to get there. Worriedly he glanced at Murk, hoping the Vampyrum hadn't heard.

Murk was looking directly at him.

"I already know," said the Vampyrum. "It's not the first time I've seen that glow around the living. And you don't need to worry: I won't try to follow you back to the Upper World." He looked at Yorick and Java and Nemo. "And if any of you were thinking the same, I can spare you the labour and disappointment. It can't be done."

"How do you know?" Shade asked.

"Because I myself tried it. Long ago. I found a crack in the heavens and crawled up. How long it took, I couldn't say. It felt like forever, fighting a screaming wind, and the pull of the Underworld. But I reached the surface. And out I flew."

Shade's fur lifted in alarm. "But—"

"And then dissolved," finished Murk. "In the world of the living I became nothing but an echo, a little wisp of vapour, and I could not fly clear of the crack's pull. It was as if I had no solid body. The moment I saw the world – and I can tell you, all of it blazed with the same light that surrounds you, Silverwing – I imploded. I was sucked back into the fissure, and down and down into the Underworld's sky. And only then did I once again have a form. Without life in them, these dead bodies are useless up there. Save yourselves the agony of seeing the Upper

World, only for a moment, and then having it ripped away from you."

Shade said nothing, thinking of the hissing crack near Stonehold, imagining Murk scrabbling at its rim, desperately trying to return to the surface. It was a pathetic image, but most of all he felt relieved that dead Vampyrum were forbidden re-entry into the Upper World. He hoped Murk was telling the truth.

Shade turned to Java. It seemed unfair that after all their help he was about to abandon them on this dismal journey. Across the Underworld to a Tree that might or might not exist.

"I'm sorry," he said.

"Don't be," she told him. "We will be sorry to see you go. But go without any pity for us. We have the Tree."

Shade nodded, and flew off for a moment to check Griffin's trail again. Still right on course, and he was about to open his eyes when a flare in his echo vision chilled his heart. It was Goth again, the image recent and clearly etched. And he was on the same course as Griffin's.

Bright vapour veiled the cave mouth, making it impossible to see inside. Griffin shot out sound, but his echo vision was just a silvery smear.

"Let me talk you out of this," he said to Luna, circling.

"Just a peek, Griff." Something about those words made him even more uneasy.

"I'm having troubling thoughts," he told her. "A worst case scenario kind of thing. I mean, this is an easy one, Luna. Frieda told us we're supposed to ignore this and fly past. And look at this thing. The cave could slam shut like a set of jaws. The entire hill could sink into the sand and take us with it. Trapped inside. For ever. That would not surprise me in a place like this. In fact, it would be pretty typical."

"Please," she said sweetly.

"You're making me feel mean."

"That's good."

"It's hard to say no to a dead person."

"You'd feel pretty cruel, wouldn't you? *I'd* feel cruel."

"Luna, I haven't seen anyone come out."

She cocked her head, ears pricked. "I'm not hearing any crying or screaming. Maybe they're just having a good time."

As if to bolster her argument, Griffin heard from inside a kind of melodious thrum, some laughter, the rustle of excited voices.

"See?" Luna said.

"This really isn't a good idea."

"Well, I'm going in. Wait out here if you want."

She flew for the entrance, and was quickly swallowed up in the luminous fog. Griffin waited a second, heart pounding, then went after her. He couldn't let her go in there alone. And, frankly, he didn't want to be out *here* alone. The light enveloped him like a warm mist, and immediately he felt calmer. There was something so soothing about it, and he flew on, blind, until he cleared the mist and found himself within an enormous cavern, its walls and ceiling awash with flickering light. Millions of bats roosted here, staring intently at the cave floor.

Griffin looked. It was an immense lake of sound and light, pulsing gently. From its surface lifted skinny tendrils of luminosity as well as thick radiant columns, towering up to the ceiling. Hanging in the air, misty gossamer sheets chimed softly, marbled with light.

Up ahead he saw Luna and flapped to catch up.

"What is all this?" he asked in a hushed voice, gazing down.

She just shook her head. Together they circled the cavern, looking for somewhere to roost. It wasn't easy, but eventually they found a spot and hung side by side. He didn't want to stay long. He glanced at all the bats densely clustered around them. Occasionally some of them would laugh or make a happy exclamation, or mutter cheerfully – to themselves or each other he didn't know. Mostly the bats were incredibly still and silent, hardly a wing twitching, just staring at the pool of light. It was very pretty down there, but Griffin didn't entirely understand their rapt attention.

"Oh," he heard Luna breathe.

He looked over and saw her staring down, the marvellous light reflected in her eyes.

"What?" he asked. "What is it?"

"Can't you see it, Griff?"

"Yeah, I see the light."

"No," she whispered. "*Home*."

He peered back down, squinting. "Um, no, I'm not getting that. I see some nice fluffy shapes – that one looks kind of like a bear maybe – but it's a bit like looking at clouds. All lit up by the moon on a windy night. Scudding along. Changing all the time. But I'm not seeing anything really . . ."

Maybe he had a bad spot. Back home he was always getting the bad spot, couldn't see, couldn't hear. He should move, but Luna seemed happy with her roost, and anyway he didn't want to get separated from her in this crowd.

"What exactly do you see?" he asked in frustration.

"Tree Haven," Luna whispered with a contented sigh, her eyes not straying from the lake of light. "The sun's just gone down and we're all heading out to hunt." A smile swept her face. "And there's that tree you're always feeding at, Griff. The sugar maple with all the tent caterpillars. I can't believe you eat so many of those . . ."

He smiled too, and for just a second, it was as if the vaporous light below shaped itself into an image of his beloved forest: trees, and bats flooding the skies. Then it dissolved. Just light.

"Oh, Griffin," Luna murmured, "this is really good. I'm so glad we came to see all this. It's exactly the way you told it to me. But it's so much better than just remembering. And the pain's gone. My wings don't hurt any more."

"That's great," he said, confused.

Her face was so tranquil and happy he felt a sharp thrust of guilt. He'd taken everything away from her; how could he ask her to hurry up and get out of here?

"Hey, look, there's Falstaff and Skye and Rowan," Luna said now. "Hey, guys." She laughed, then nodded her head, listening to a conversation Griffin couldn't hear. He stared down hard at the sea of light, and felt a creeping of unease beneath his fur.

"Luna," he said, "I'm not getting any of this."

"Just look," she said absently, her gaze fixed on the lake, unwavering. "You'll see it. It's clear as anything. It's like . . ." her voice was so soft he could barely hear now, "I'm already there . . ."

He looked at her, alarmed. Whatever she was seeing, she must know it was just pictures, some kind of echo mirage.

He jostled her. "Luna?"

"Shhh."

He glanced around at the countless other bats. Surely

they weren't all seeing the same thing. Yet they all gazed with the same desperate longing, looks that could only be directed at the things they loved. Perhaps this swirling pool of light and sound showed everyone what they most wanted to see.

Except him.

Alive, he thought. *It's because you're alive.*

Maybe here, only the dead could see things. Their past, their homes, the things they'd lost for ever.

Goth slunk closer, belly to the ceiling, working his way around the clusters of roosting bats. They scarcely seemed to notice him, so intent were they on the lights below. Earlier he had made the mistake of looking too, and was transfixed by the image of the royal pyramid in the jungle, and all the Vampyrum circling him and calling out his name, "King Goth, King Goth!" It had taken all his might to tear away his gaze, and now he focused only on one thing:

The Silverwing newborn, aglow.

He was close, so close that Goth was starting to salivate, except he had no saliva. But the sensation was the same, that almost painful tingling in the hinges of his jaws, and the involuntary grinding of his teeth.

So this was Shade Silverwing's son. Not as runty as his father, but with ridiculous swaths of bright fur across his shoulders and back. Goth continued to approach from behind. The newborn wouldn't even know what hit him. Within seconds, Goth would have his jaws around his throat, clenching, and all that radiant life would come spilling out and—

Be inhaled by Zotz.

Not him, but Zotz.

Goth faltered, not knowing if he could bear it. To kill the newborn, to see its life sucked away and squandered when it could have given him life instead. It was greedy of his god, cruel, to do this to him. But there was nothing he could do. He must obey Zotz. Unless . . .

What if he took the newborn's life? Took it quickly and became alive again. Zotz could do nothing. Zotz had no power over the living; he would be unable to punish Goth. Goth felt himself tremble at the idea. To defy one's god was a terrible thing. Even if it was for Zotz's own good. At first, Cama Zotz would be furious, but once Goth returned to the Upper World, and began to gather new followers, to work towards liberating their god from the Underworld, surely Zotz would forgive him – and see that Goth's actions had been noble and right.

He wanted life. How could he wait when it was right before him?

Only wingbeats away.

"Griffin! Griffin Silverwing!"

His ears twitched higher at the sound of his name – and there was something strangely familiar in the voice itself, though he was sure he'd never heard it. Who else knew his name down here? Luna, silent beside him, and Frieda. But it certainly wasn't her voice.

"Griffin!"

The call was so urgent, so beseeching that he almost replied, but hesitated, thinking of the Vampyrum.

"It's your father! Griffin! Where are you?"

Griffin's skin prickled as the words echoed faintly through the cave. His father? It couldn't be true. His father was back at Stonehold with the other males; he wouldn't even know about the earthquake at Tree Haven.

"Luna?" Griffin whispered. "Are you hearing this?" But she didn't reply; she was still staring down, oblivious.

Griffin gazed all around, seeing nothing. Must be hearing things himself, now. Then, from the misty sheets of light, a Silverwing male emerged, soaring across the cavern. He was still quite far away, flying towards the ceiling to look at all the roosting bats, calling out Griffin's name again and again.

Searching for me.

Griffin remembered to breathe. It was just a mirage. Just seeing what he wanted, like Luna. He watched as the Silverwing male drew closer, closer, then veered away to look in another direction. Going away from him. Griffin's heart clenched. He couldn't stop himself. He dropped from his roost, and fluttered cautiously after, still not calling out. Just looking.

After a minute, the Silverwing male banked suddenly and saw him. He stared at Griffin, missed a wing stroke, and then streaked towards him with such speed that Griffin braked sharply, pulling away in a wary circle.

"Griffin, what's wrong?"

Griffin kept his distance. "Are you real?"

"I'm your father!"

Griffin glanced at all the mesmerized bats roosting from the ceiling. "Everyone's seeing things here. Maybe I'm seeing things, too. And how would I know what you look like anyway? I've never met you."

"Well . . . that's true." He seemed flustered. "But your mother must've told you about me!"

Circling, not letting himself get too close, Griffin looked for signs of himself in this older bat. He'd seen his own reflection in the stream, in droplets of water, and he had a vague idea what he looked like. But he wasn't sure he saw any hint of it in this other bat – or mirage, he still wasn't sure which.

"I thought Shade was bigger," Griffin said suspiciously. He knew his father was a runt, but in his own mind, he was always a formidable presence, almost a giant. This bat before him could have been anyone.

"No, this is the right size for me," the older Silverwing said with a chuckle.

"Prove it's you!" Griffin demanded.

"Who else would come down here to rescue you!"

"There's some pretty weird stuff down here," Griffin insisted. "If it's really you, you'll know everything about Shade."

"All right. Ask me a question, then!"

"OK, let me think. In the Human City, Shade got chased by pigeons. How many pigeons were there?"

"It was . . . um, six, I think."

"I heard it was nine!"

"Well, it happened a long time ago, but I'm pretty sure it was just six."

"All the other newborns said it was nine," Griffin insisted stubbornly.

"I was there!"

"*Were* you?" Griffin said. "I *wonder*. How about this. In the southern jungle, what was the first kind of creature Shade fought with?"

"Would you stop talking about me like I'm not here!"

"So you don't know the answer?" Griffin said.

"A giant bug, about a foot long, with jagged pincers."

"OK, that's right," said Griffin. "I'll give you that one. But how many bugs were there?"

"Just one."

"Wrong! There were five! And Shade killed all of them with Chinook's help."

"No. There was just one," the other bat said with a sigh.

"If you're Shade, how come you don't know? *I* know. *I* know all the stories – they're practically all the newborns talk about. Shade this, Shade that."

"And it was actually Chinook who killed the bug, not me. These stories get exaggerated."

"Tell me how Shade met Marina," Griffin said doggedly.

"And I thought I was suspicious!"

"Down here you can never be too careful," said Griffin. "Go on."

"I met her on an island, after I was blasted out to sea in the storm. Your mom was roosting right beside me on a branch, all wrapped up in her wings, and I didn't even notice her because she looked exactly like a bright autumn leaf."

Griffin couldn't help smiling. "That's right." He frowned. "But anyone could know that story."

"Griffin!"

"Last question. What were you going to call me if I was a female?"

"Well, I'd wanted to call you Aurora . . ."

Griffin stiffened.

". . . but your mother had her heart set on Celeste. So it was going to be Celeste."

Griffin felt his entire body unclench. Cautiously he drew closer and, for the first time since arriving in this place, his nostrils filled with the scent of another living creature. His heart was beating so quickly it was hard to breathe. He grabbed hold of his father in mid-air and just for a moment buried his face in the fur of his neck. It was the smell of family, the smell of himself. A wonderful warmth – not the terrible seeping chill of the dead – caressed him, and through it he felt the strong beat of his father's heart, and felt his father's wing thrown across his shoulder and he thought: *Yes. Home.* He didn't want to let go. He was crying with relief and happiness. He was all right now. His father was here. The hero Shade Silverwing. Nothing could harm him.

"Oh," he said. "This is good. This is really, really good."

"I was worried I wouldn't find you," his father said. "Worried I'd never know you."

They found space to roost together on the wall. His father chuckled.

" *'Prove it's you'*," Shade said, imitating his son. "Your mother will love that."

Griffin just smiled, basking in the warmth of his father's body against him. For the first time in ages, his mind was unrippled as a glassy summer pond. It was all too brief.

"We've got to go," Shade said. "The tunnel you fell down, it's right overhead now. We can climb back out."

"You think we can make it?" He remembered how hard it had been just to reach the stone sky. "And there's that wind."

"We'll be back in Tree Haven with your mother before the next nightfall."

Griffin nodded gladly, then stopped. "Luna," he said.

"Your friend. I know what happened."

Griffin looked away, ashamed. "I can't leave her."

"She can't come with us, Griffin."

"Why not?"

"The moment she reached the surface she'd dissolve and get sucked back down. It would be too cruel. She has to go to the Tree."

"But I just can't let her go on all by herself."

"She won't have to. I've met a group of Pilgrims. I trust them. She can carry on with them. See, that's one of them . . . Java."

Griffin followed his father's gaze and jerked in surprise. Circling near the mouth of the cave was the biggest winged creature he'd ever seen.

"*That's* a bat?"

"A Foxwing. Huge, isn't she?"

"Huge," he muttered.

"Luna can reach the Tree with them."

Griffin said nothing. It felt like he was abandoning her.

"She'll be fine, Griffin," his father said. "There's nothing else we can do."

"Frieda said I could get out through the Tree, too."

"You met her?" Shade asked in surprise.

Griffin nodded, pleased he'd impressed his father. "She's the one who gave me the map and explained everything. She remembered you and Mom."

Shade smiled. "I wish I'd seen her."

"She told me the Tree was the only way out."

"I trust Frieda," Shade said, "but the crack is right above us now, and I know exactly where it goes. I still think it makes most sense for us. But we should get going. The stars move fast here and—" He was about to say something more, but seemed to change his mind. "Say goodbye to Luna."

Griffin just nodded. He wasn't about to argue with his father. Of course he knew best. He was a hero, everything he did worked out.

"I just want to make sure she makes it to the Tree, that's all," he said. "Frieda said there're bats who might never get there . . ."

He looked around at the thousands of bats roosting from the ceiling. How long had they been here? Right beside him hung a Brightwing female, her unblinking eyes aglow with the mysterious light. Then he noticed her claws. There was something wrong with them. They were all scaly, as if the stone from the ceiling had seeped down over her talons and started up both ankles. His eyes skittered further along. Almost all the claws he saw were coated with stone, and on some of the bats the stone had reached as far as their abdomens and folded wings. No wonder they were so still!

"Dad . . ." he said with mounting alarm. "Look at them!"

Instantly he lifted his own claws, left then right, to make sure nothing was sticking to them. He checked his father's, and they too seemed to be free. In horror Griffin caught sight of a nearby male whose entire body was crusted over. He looked dead, like something mummified, but then Griffin saw his bright eyes and gasped when they blinked.

With a brittle clicking sound, the petrified bat cracked away from the roof, and plummeted like a stone. The bat made no effort to open his wings – how could he? – and disappeared into the swirling mist. There was no splash of water, no thud of impact on stone. The bat was gone.

"Luna," Griffin said in a strangled voice. He dropped from his roost. He couldn't believe he'd left her alone. Abandoned her. He was such a bad friend. What if she'd already scaled over?

"Where is she?" his father asked at his wingtip.

Millions of bats here, like a carpet of dark moss, and he'd forgotten where he and Luna had been roosting. Another bat fell from the ceiling and whistled past his wingtip.

"Luna!" he called out. "Luna!"

No answer, nothing.

"I think she was over here," he gasped. In his frenzy the bats were all starting to look the same.

"I see her," said his father calmly.

And there she was, her body and claws still clear of the dreadful creeping stone. She didn't stir as Griffin landed beside her.

"Luna, my dad's here."

"That's great, Griff." Her voice was drowsy.

"We should get going, don't you think?"

"Thanks for helping me get back here," she said. "Thank you so much."

"No, it's not true, Luna," he told her worriedly. "You're not back. This isn't the way back."

"Sure it is, Griff."

"We've got to go!"

"You go on ahead. I'm just fine here. I don't want to leave her."

"Who?"

"My mother." Luna sighed contentedly, and her face had that look newborns got when being groomed. Total comfort, total happiness. How could he take that away from her again? But how could he possibly leave her in this place?

"Luna," he pleaded, "you've got to get to the Tree."

"I want this," she said simply.

Griffin turned to his father, who was circling below them. "What do we do?"

"We'd better just grab her and—"

Griffin saw his father's look of shock the same moment he felt Luna falling past him. Wings furled tight, she plummeted.

"Dad!"

"I'll get her! You stay here!"

Shade threw himself into a nosedive and streaked after Luna. Griffin couldn't bear it. The sight of them both getting farther and farther away – and him doing nothing. He dropped too. To overtake Luna his father had opened his wings, was actually beating them to speed his vertical plunge. Griffin was afraid of the speed, kept braking as he crashed through layer after layer of misty light. He was terrified the ground would loom up suddenly and they would all be shattered against it.

He plunged through a final sheet of light and below him saw a great pool of perfect blackness, so much like a starless night sky he almost flipped over in confusion. *Not blackness*, he thought. *Darkness*. Its surface shimmered like some kind of thick fluid. A few echoey ripples flitted across it, and it was strangely beautiful. Luna was still dropping headfirst towards it, but he saw his father now pulling alongside her. They were not more than ten wingbeats from the pool and Griffin watched with amazement as his father dipped beneath her and slowly braked, pulling up out of his dive, and lifting Luna with him on his back.

"I've got you," he heard his father say.

Luna was so still, wings wrapped tight, and she wasn't even trying to hold on. Rocking from side to side, she wasn't at all secure, and Griffin was worried she might roll off, even though his father was flying as level as he could.

Griffin beat hard to catch up.

"I told you to stay back," his father said.

"I wanted to help."

Without warning, the jagged shadow of a huge winged creature strafed him and slammed into his father, knocking him over on to his back. Luna came flying off, straight for Griffin, and hit him hard, sending him into a tailspin.

"Dad!" he shouted.

Tumbling backwards, wings buckled, his eyes caught only snatches of things: Luna plunging alongside him; his father, falling too, a Vampyrum clutching at his belly, driving him down.

The dark pool, soaring up to meet him.

THE RIVER

Shade instantly recognized the winged fiend riding atop him. Its face was seared for ever into his memory, as inescapable as a recurring nightmare. Goth's body seemed slightly wizened, his grip not quite as piercing as Shade recalled, but there was nothing diminished about the savagery blazing from his eyes. The cannibal's flesh was scaringly cold. Quickly Shade furled his right wing, and punched out his left. The air caught hard beneath it and slammed him around – and Goth with him. Now Shade was on top, and Goth underneath – and coming up fast, the vast pool of darkness.

Goth snapped at him, and Shade tried to push him off and away, but the cannibal's rear claws were locked in his flesh and fur, and one of his thumbs had pierced his wing.

Shade gulped air, ready to batter Goth with a sonic blast, but before he could open his mouth, Goth had his free thumb claw flexed around his muzzle, clamping it painfully shut. He was mute, half blind. Goth's writhing head lunged forward suddenly and Shade recoiled, teeth grazing his throat.

Can't – you – just – die? Shade raged inwardly, trying to wrench himself free.

Something hit Goth. Shade didn't even see it coming,

but felt the impact through the cannibal's body as his claws ripped loose. He was suddenly free. Braking, Shade opened his wounded mouth, singing out sound, and the world came back into silver focus. He saw Goth spin down, and hit the pool. A small geyser of darkness shot up, a fierce ripple raced away from the impact, and Goth was gone, instantly swept beneath the surface.

Shade glanced up to see Murk flying towards him.

"*You* hit him?" Shade gasped.

Murk nodded.

"Thank you." Twice now the cannibal had helped him. Anxiously he searched for Griffin. Luna was nowhere to be seen, and he feared the worst for her if she hadn't opened her wings. But where was his son?

"I saw them both fall into the pool," Murk said quietly.

Shade dived low over the surface, but all he saw was his own dark reflection.

He was about to dive in when he heard Murk cry out his name. He jerked his head up to see a skinny object plummeting for him. A petrified bat, whistling down from the ceiling like a stalactite. He didn't even have time to move, just tense as it hit him.

Helplessly Murk watched as Shade's lifeless body plunged into the black pool and was swallowed up.

It was as if all light and sound had been abruptly sucked from the universe.

From above, the pool of darkness had looked still as ice, but it had seized Griffin hard and swept him right under. He'd expected a choking rush of water down his mouth, but there was no water at all, just viscous, silent darkness instantly enveloping him.

He couldn't hear the creak of his own wings, nor the

panicked rasp of his breath. Nothing. He sang out, but whatever this stuff was, it ate sound. In his mind's eye, he saw only an eternity of blackness, not so much as a silver spark or shimmer. For the first time in his life he was truly blind. He could see no part of himself. All he could do was *feel* himself, his heart thumping against his ribs, wings flapping, trying to lift himself free of this terrible sludge.

"Luna, are you there?"

He felt his mouth moving, the muscles vibrating at the back of his throat, but he was mute.

They had been tumbling together, had hit the pool at the same time, so she had to be close by. With his wings he reached out, desperately hoping he'd nudge her body.

"Luna!" he shouted silently. "Luna!"

He had to get out; he couldn't endure much more of this blind nothingness. Wherever this deathly river flowed, he was sure it wasn't pleasant. Or maybe it had no end. Maybe this was all there was, for ever and ever. He thought of all those petrified bats, minds empty. Drifting dead.

Flailing out, he touched something with his wingtip and lurched closer. Luna, it must be Luna. He nudged up against it, and felt the cold hard scrape of stone against his fur. With revulsion he knew it was a crusted-over bat. It was almost worse not seeing it. He pushed away hurriedly with his legs, his whole body shivering with disgust.

How was he ever going to find Luna like this?

For a weird moment, he wasn't sure he was even moving at all, simply floating in a terrible black abyss.

Was he even *here* at all?

Do you feel your heartbeat? Hear yourself thinking? Then you're still here.

His left wing grazed something cold, but soft this time.

Clumsily he steered closer. For a terrible moment he wondered if this might be the cannibal bat, and he was drawing near only to be eaten alive, silently, invisibly. He tapped cautiously with his wingtip: a furred flank, the edge of a furled wing. Didn't feel too big.

"Luna?" he called out, hoping his need would transmit itself through touch.

No reply.

He was next to her now – at least he hoped it was her. He sank his rear claws into her fur, and with his teeth grabbed her by the scruff of the neck, and beat his wings hard, pulling up. Was this really up?

Help me, Luna, he thought, *please help*. He had no idea if she was flapping too, but somehow, he felt they were rising. He pulled, smashed his wings down again and again until his heart was racing too fast for his breath and he felt his chest would burst.

Up.

And then out, the sudden noise of his own breath so loud it made him look around in terror. The darkness was pouring off him like water and he was in open air again. Beneath him, her own wings beating in tandem, was Luna. He let go and together they soared above the strange river, and the high canyon walls which encased it. In the starlight the river's surface was almost translucent, and he could see the skinny shapes of countless petrified bats pulsing past in the current. He turned away with a shudder.

"Why did you pull me out?"

Startled by the anger in Luna's voice, he didn't know what to say for a moment. "Well, I . . . wanted to save you."

"*Save*," she muttered bitterly.

Griffin was bewildered. "You wanted to stay in that weird river of . . . of nothing?"

"It wasn't nothing! It had everything I wanted! It had my home and my family and . . . *everything*. And there was no pain, and now it's back!"

She started to cry, hopelessly, and he flew towards her. But when he gently touched her wingtip, she pulled away and trailed behind him. He let her alone. He felt confused and useless. He hated making her sad, and hated the greater suffering he'd caused her since the accident, her normally buoyant personality all pinched by sadness and the burning pain in her wings. He'd done that to her. So now he would get her out of here – that's what he could do. He would do things *right*.

After a while he circled back and flew alongside her. She'd stopped crying.

"I'm sorry," he said. "I know you wanted to stay, but it was all mirages and lies."

Luna said nothing, staring down at the river morosely. "It's fine for you. You get to go back home."

"You'll get to go some place good too, though."

"Nothing was better than the way things were back home. I was happy there. Now I'm dead and I can't ever get it back. I'll never see Tree Haven again, or my mother . . . it's not fair!"

"I know."

"Anyway," she said after a pause, "it's not your fault." *It is*, he thought.

"You should've just left me, Griff. At least I would've *thought* I was back home. And isn't that just as good in the end? As long as you *think* it?"

He didn't know what to say to that.

She looked over at him sharply, remembering

something. "Was your father there? Was *that* real?"

Griffin nodded miserably. "He came down to look for me. He was going to take me home."

His sob came out like a bark, something held back too long. Luna flew closer and patted him as they circled. It took him a while to stop crying, and then he told Luna about how his father had found him, tried to save her from falling into the darkness, and then how the Vampyrum had attacked him.

"It had my father in its claws, and that was the last thing I saw."

"You father can take care of himself," Luna said promptly. "All those stories you told me about him. There's nothing he can't do. And remember the slap you gave that one at the cactus? You're just a newborn! Imagine what your father can do!"

Griffin nodded, feeling a bit better.

For the first time he made a careful sweep of his surroundings. Flanked by more desert, the river canyon ran to both horizons. There was no sign of the cave: the current must have shuttled them a great distance in a very short time – or maybe they were in it for a long time, who knew? Several hundred wingbeats downstream, a pair of strange stone spikes curved up from the canyon walls like massive horns, almost touching at the tips. Griffin stared at them a long time before recognizing what they were.

"That's the next landmark," he said in surprise. "We fly between the points and that sets us on our last course. That is so lucky. If we'd come out of the river later or earlier, we might've missed it."

He took a deep breath, unable to feel much pleasure at this good fortune. Every joint in his body ached now, and he felt feverish, his muscles gelid with fatigue.

"I don't know what to do," he said. "Way I see it, we've got three choices. We could travel back to the cave and try to find my father. We could wait here, and hope he finds us. Or we could just keep going."

"Go back to the cave and find your father."

"OK. Good." She made it sound so simple. But almost right away his mind started working.

"What if my father's been killed, and it's just the Vampyrum back there, waiting for us?"

Luna grunted as if she hadn't thought of that. "Your father's fine," she said.

"So maybe he thinks *we* drowned or something, and he's given up on me and gone home alone." Just speaking the thought was enough to make his heart break into a gallop. It was worse now, being alone, after having seen his father, and thinking escape was so near.

"And we don't even know how far away that cave is," Griffin went on, worries coming like a torrent now. "The river's pretty fast, it might have taken us really far and if we go back, and my dad's not even there and we've just wasted all that time and I might not . . . well, make it out in time. Before I die."

Luna sighed impatiently. "These are all maybes. Why waste time with all the maybes?"

"Because you can't make a decision if you don't know all the maybes!" Griffin told her, exasperated. "Otherwise it's not a decision. It's a *guess!*"

"OK, so you make the decision!"

Griffin felt his mind clouding with panic, suffocating him.

"I can't," he wheezed. "I can't decide. I don't feel good, Luna."

"Roost," she said. "Stop flying in circles."

"Don't want to," he croaked. "I'm afraid."

"Of what?"

"Everything. Afraid if I stop moving, I'll stop breathing. Afraid of dying . . ."

"It's OK, Griff," she said kindly. "You're not gonna die. It's all right. Hey, look, dying's not so bad anyway. Look at me. Don't I seem cheerful?"

He laughed, and felt a bit of anxiety evaporate from his mind.

"You're the nicest dead bat I've ever met," he said.

Luna sniffed. "How many dead bats do you know?"

"You're the nicest bat I know, dead or alive."

"That's better."

Griffin shut his eyes tight, tried to make some sense of his swirling thoughts. "All those stories about him – my father, I mean. How he was in the jungle with just a few dozen northern bats, and there were millions of cannibals, and he could have just flown home, but he stayed and rescued his father from the pyramid. He did that for *his* father."

"He was older," Luna pointed out.

"Not by much. I want to get to the Tree and get out, but I can't just go and leave him alone down here. He came down here because of me – this is all my fault."

"It's not your fault you got sucked down here," Luna said. "It was a freak accident."

"We've got to go back, you're right," he said after a moment. "He won't know what's happened to me, otherwise. He might waste all his time looking for me . . ."

Luna nodded.

"You don't have to come," he told her hurriedly.

"I've got nothing better to do."

"You should go on to the Tree."

"Well, the Tree's not going anywhere. And to be perfectly honest, I don't much want to be alone down here."

"Me neither," Griffin grinned, relieved.

But his heart was heavy as he turned away from the giant stone horns. He wasn't even sure he was doing the right thing – but at least he was doing *something*. With Luna at his wingtip he followed the dreadful black river upstream, back towards the cave. His father was alive: he forced himself to assume that. He'd have defeated the Vampyrum somehow, and would be looking for him. Maybe even right now he was on his way.

He noticed he was having trouble keeping up with Luna.

"You all right?" she asked, slowing.

"Just tired."

And hungry. Before, he'd sometimes been able to forget, but now hunger was always with him, clawing at his stomach, sending a spidery, crampy pain across his belly and up into his chest. He felt all jittery, pressure at both his temples crumpling his vision into a tunnel. His tongue was dry and sluggish, like something that didn't belong in his mouth.

They flew on. It was all he could do to lift his wings yet again, stay in motion. Below them the river flowed black, reflecting the false starlight.

"No," he heard Luna breathe beside him.

Then he saw it too, a pair of enormously long wings in the distance, carrying a giant bat towards them.

"It's that Vampyrum," she hissed.

Griffin stared. What did this mean? Had this thing killed his father?

"We've got to get out of here, Griff," said Luna, already

scanning the landscape for an escape route.

"No," he said, squinting, "wait."

This huge creature wasn't alone. Alongside it he could just now make out two other bats, smaller. And the big bat was almost *too* big. Much bigger than the Vampyrum. This one's wings must be almost five feet across.

"That one was with my father!" he said excitedly. "In the cave. I saw her! She's a Foxwing!"

"You're sure?" Luna said uncertainly.

"Her name's Java. She's a Pilgrim." He squinted at the smaller bats again, beating their way towards him.

A Silverwing!

There was definitely a Silverwing among them!

"Hey!" Griffin cried out, surging ahead with a pulse of newfound energy. "Dad!" Then his wingbeats faltered. Even from this distance he could tell: the profile, the strange limping gait – this wasn't his father. Just another dead bat.

"Griffin!" he heard Java call out.

And it was then he really did see the Vampyrum. It must have been flying directly behind Java, cloaked by the billowy sweep of her massive wings.

"Behind you!" Griffin bellowed. "Look out!"

Java whirled, accidentally smacking the cannibal in the head.

"Hey!" barked the Vampyrum.

"Oh, sorry," said Java. She turned back to Griffin. "That's just Murk," she called out. "It's all right. He's with us."

"He is?"

Griffin held back, taking another look at Murk, and caught an unsettling flash of chiselled black teeth. He definitely wasn't the same cannibal from the cactus. Still, how could they trust him? His father hadn't mentioned anything about a Vampyrum Pilgrim! But his father had trusted Java, so he too would have to trust her.

"Where's my father?" Griffin asked.

The Foxwing's hesitation made him feel sick.

"I saw him fight with the other Vampyrum," Java said. "Murk knocked him into the black pool. Your father was all right at first. But then something fell from the ceiling, and hit him, hard, very hard I think, and he went into the pool." Java's eyes were huge. "He did not come up. I watched for him, a long time, but he did not come up."

"Well, he might've come out along the river," said Griffin, fighting for control of his voice.

"We've been flying over the river," said Java, "and seen no sign of him."

"I got out," Griffin said. "If I can get out, he can. I mean, he's way stronger than me, and I was pulling Luna, too!"

"Your father was not conscious when he fell," Murk said. "His body was limp. He may already have been dead."

"Was he still glowing?" Luna demanded. "You know, that light in his fur? If he died, it would come away from his body."

Murk squinted, trying to remember. "So much light was swirling there above the pool, I couldn't tell."

"We were on our way back to find him," Griffin said.

"Travel with us now," said Java. "To the Tree."

Despairingly Griffin looked down the stretch of black canyon. "But what if he comes out somewhere, and keeps looking for me?"

"Your father can track you with sound," Java said. "He would want you to go to the Tree. Not waste time searching for him."

Would he? Griffin wondered. He'd gone back for Cassiel, his own father. Why wouldn't he expect the same of his son? And what would he tell his mother, if he ever did get home? *I left my father. I got out myself, but left him there.*

"You must come with us," said the misshapen Silverwing impatiently. "There's nothing more to be done about it."

Griffin stared at this grumpy bat with dislike.

"Please," said Java softly, "both of you, come with us. We will watch for your father along the river. But there is no point going back to the cave or lingering here. None at all."

"She's right, Griff," said Luna.

"I guess," was all he could say.

Luna nudged him gently, turning him round in the direction of the Tree.

PART THREE

THE FALLS

Dead.

What else could this be, Shade thought, all this silence? All this darkness. It was so total he felt short of breath – was there air here? His only sensation was that of floating, somehow moving without any effort. He forced himself to be still, until he felt his limbs, his wings, and deep within himself the beating of his heart. A heartbeat meant alive. So did the pain all across his shoulders and left flank. Memory came with it. Something must have hit him . . . one of those petrified bats from the cave. He must've been knocked unconscious, and now he was just waking up.

In the pool.

He coughed in panic, silently thrashing his wings, then realized he was not in the least wet. Not immersed in water at all. He paused, but it wasn't a sound he heard, it was a vibration, a vague shimmering in every part of his body. It intensified. He was trembling. The current was obvious now and it was very difficult to row against it. He was being sucked somewhere, and he did not want to go. He flapped, flying blind, trying to gain altitude. No sound or light to guide him, only a frail instinct of which way was up.

His head broke the surface, and he was nearly blinded by starlight. The dark river was sticky, did not want to release him. It clung as he pulled, clutching at his ankles and tail. Suddenly he was free, soaring over this strange river which—

Was no longer a river.

In a split second, it had tipped over a broad cliff and was now pouring down into a narrow chasm, down and down, all the more dreadful because it made not the slightest noise as it fell.

That could have been me, Shade thought numbly. *A few more seconds was all it would have taken.*

Then he thought: Griffin. He circled as close to the cataract as he dared – he did not want to be swept into its pull. Not even the blazing starlight could illuminate its full depth, and when Shade sang out sound, no echoes came back. His entire being quailed at the thought of going lower. Down there was a place no rescue was possible. For a long time he circled hopelessly, unable to wrench his gaze away.

He lifted his eyes to the stone sky. His circle of stars was still there. His route home. This would almost surely be his last chance to take it before it was blocked off at Tree Haven.

Griffin and Luna might have pulled themselves free of the river. He would fly back over it, scouring the sky for their echo signals. If he lost his escape route, he would try for the Tree. He cursed himself for not forcing Yorick to sing the map to him. Stupid, prissy old bat.

He fervently hoped that if Griffin was alive he'd carry on to the Tree, not go back to the cave. His son wasn't foolhardy enough to go back, was he? Shade turned, and flapped upstream, scanning the sky for the sound of any winged creature.

If his son was alive, Shade would find him.

Goth heaved himself from the darkness, choking with rage.

He cast around wildly, but the cave was gone, as were the bats. Below him, a black, silent river ran between steep canyon walls. Spreading out all around, more interminable desert. He had no idea where he was, but he was too consumed with anger to care much.

He'd had his claws into Shade Silverwing until that other bat had knocked him off – a Vampyrum, one of his own kind! He should have had Shade's life by now.

The earth rumbled ominously, and Zotz spoke.

"You were to attack the newborn, not Shade Silverwing."

"Why did you not tell me he was here?" said Goth, unable to hide his indignation.

"His presence has nothing to do with the task I set you."

"No, my Lord, but—"

Dust rose from the desert. "But what, Goth?"

"I merely thought that if I first took Shade's life, I would be all the stronger to catch the newborn, and sacrifice him to you, my Lord."

"I wonder, Goth, if your desire for life is more important to you than me?"

"No, my Lord!" Goth said, shouting to cloak his guilt. Could Zotz know that, before Shade had appeared, his plan had been to steal the newborn's life? "I very nearly had the newborn, but his father called to him. I knew that if I attacked the son, I would also be fighting the father. So I decided to kill Shade first."

A long silence settled over the desert, but Goth felt Zotz's presence all around him, studying him, boring into him with invisible eyes. Could Zotz know of his temptation in the cave? He tried to keep his breathing calm.

"Follow the river to the horns," said Zotz, his voice swirling around Goth like a tornado. "Fly between the tips. The newborn is travelling with a group of Pilgrims. They will soon reach the Tree."

"And Shade Silverwing?"

"He is not your concern, Goth. First the newborn."

"Yes, my Lord."

"Do not fail me a third time."

At the stone horns, Griffin hesitated. Below, the river gouged its eerie liquid path across the Underworld. He looked to the horizons, still hoping.

"Call out to your father," Java told him. "Leave your trace. If he's alive, he will hear your echoes when he passes."

"Dad!" Griffin shouted with all his might. "It's me, Griffin!"

He saw Yorick wince at all this noise, look around fretfully.

"We're going to the Tree!"

His throat hurt, and he had no more words inside him. How long would his echoes live down here, before the Underworld sucked them away? Like it sucked away everything else, including his life. He thought of those terrible, petrified bats in the cave, imagined the blow they'd deliver if they hit you. He squeezed his eyes shut, gave his head a fierce shake, trying to jar loose the image of his father, unconscious, drifting for ever down that river.

"Where does it go?" he asked, but no one knew.

"That's one river I'll be glad to part company with," Nemo said, shuddering. "Bodies of water have a way of whispering to you, and this one has nothing good to say."

Griffin had learned the names of the Pilgrims, and already was most attached to Java. It was hard not to be won over by those huge, soulful eyes, her expressive face, and gentle voice. When he had questions she was the one he asked; he stuck close to her. Yorick seemed grumpy, and Nemo had those claws, which he found unsettling, though Griffin did like his eyes and his friendly way of winking. Murk he stayed clear of altogether. Just looking at him made his stomach clench.

"You ready, Griffin?" Java said, looking at him sympathetically. "On to the Tree?"

He nodded. With Luna at his wingtip, he followed Yorick between the tips of the horns.

"Your dad'll find you," Luna told him quietly.

Griffin tried to smile, but his mouth and face felt taut, as if his skin might crack like splintered ice. He looked back, opened his mouth to spray out sound and check for his father, but stopped – he couldn't bear the disappointment again.

His hunger was gone now. Mostly he was glad, but he couldn't help worrying if this was an ominous sign, as if his body was starting to give up on him. His thirst was not so easily vanquished. He saw water everywhere, little oases sparkling in the hard rock, glimmering on the arid horizon. He hadn't had a pee for a long time either. That was a bad sign, he was sure of it.

Labouring through the air, he wondered how something that had once seemed so effortless, as easy as breathing, could now be such a torment. *Home*, he thought, *I want to be home*.

"I'm sorry," he said when he couldn't endure the pain coursing through his exhausted body any longer. "I've got to take a little break. Just a couple of minutes. I'm really sorry."

He avoided glancing at Yorick, but heard his grunt of impatience.

Java turned her large eyes on Griffin. "Hop on," she said. "That way we won't have to stop."

"Really?" he asked, gazing longingly at her soft, broad back. There was more than enough room for him up there.

"Just hold on tight. Try not to pinch me with your claws, mind."

She dipped below him, and held her wings straight out, gliding for a moment while he flapped into position, braked and dropped clumsily on to her back. Between her wings, he sank down on all fours, clenching her long fur. Before, he'd found the chill of the dead unsettling; now the cool of her body was soothing against his fevered face and chest.

"Am I heavy?" he asked.

"Not at all. Just rest now, child."

"Thank you very much. Just for a minute."

When he woke up, he saw that the landscape had changed. The sandy desert plains had given way to arid hills, and shallow valleys, not much vegetation, and no sign of bats. He wrinkled his nostrils, trying to identify the smell that lingered there. Something unfamiliar, but unmistakably from the real world. It had a freshness and vitality which reminded him of the wind, with a salty edge to it. A pulse of expectation went through him. Still, he didn't mention it, in case it turned out to be just a residue from a dream.

"How long have I slept?" he asked Java.

"Not so long," she said. "To tell you the truth, I don't much bother keeping track of time any more down here."

He felt spoiled and a bit embarrassed letting Java do the flying for him, but it was so wonderful to rest, and he wasn't quite ready to launch himself back into the air.

"Feeling better?" Luna called out, coming in close, then darting away so she wouldn't get clobbered by Java's mighty wings.

"If you want to talk, best you hop up, too," the Foxwing told her. "I don't want to knock you out."

So Luna came in from behind, and tumbled down on Java's back beside Griffin.

"Never offered me a ride," Yorick grumbled, "and, not that anyone cared to notice, my wings are obviously disabled."

"Not your mouth though," said Nemo. "Which is a pity."

Griffin couldn't help giggling as he and Luna hunkered down together. In any other time and place, this would have been the most fabulous fun, sailing through the air on the back of this splendid creature. Even now he couldn't deny the giddy pleasure of it. It felt so strange to be flying without doing any work.

"How are your wings?" he asked Luna.

"Worse," she said, "but I'm OK."

"How can you be so brave?"

"You're in pain too," she pointed out. "I don't hear you complaining."

"Yeah, but I'm the one who needs rest. Doesn't rest help you at all?"

"I don't think it makes a difference. Anyway, Yorick said it's not so far now. All we have to do is keep on course, and we'll end up right at the Tree. Do you think it's like Tree Haven?"

Griffin remembered the image from his sound map. "It's not like a normal tree," he said. "It's really big." He didn't want to tell her how it looked like pure flame; he didn't want to frighten her, or get her thinking about the last fire she'd seen.

"But after we go *inside*," Luna said quietly. "What happens then?"

"I don't know."

"You of all people should have an idea!" Luna said with a grin. "I never knew anyone who talked more about dying."

"You remember that stuff?"

"Yeah," she said, surprised, "I guess I do. You were always scared of things."

"Nothing's changed, I can tell you."

Back at Tree Haven he used to worry constantly about getting hurt or killed. And in the colony there was often talk of death. Newborns who weren't strong enough to live. Careless bats who got eaten by skunks, or racoons or wildcats. And the migration was dangerous too, everyone knew that. There would be plenty of bats who wouldn't make it. Death was everywhere, lurking around ever leaf and pebble practically. But even he had never really imagined what it would be like in the afterlife.

"Our mothers said Nocturna would take care of us when we died," Griffin said.

"Somewhere nice, though," Luna added. "It was always supposed to be somewhere nice. Come on, Griff, imagine it for me. You were always good at imagining things. No one's better at words than you."

Words. For a moment he was at a loss. But for Luna's sake, he shut his eyes, tried to concentrate.

"It would be a forest," Griffin told her, trying to sound confident.

Luna gave a satisfied grunt: good start. Her eyes were closed, brow creased, and he was reminded of how she looked after they'd brought her back to Tree Haven. Her burns looked worse now somehow, like they'd be hot just to touch. She was in great pain, he could tell, trying hard to float free from it. Words were something he could give her.

"Always summer and never winter," he continued. "Lots of bugs, fresh water, no beasts or birds to bother us. No gypsy moth caterpillars to eat the leaves," he added, remembering his favourite sugar maple.

Luna gave a quiet chuckle. "I like the other animals, though," she said, "to look at. It makes it more interesting."

"OK, then there should be animals, you're right. But they don't need to eat you any more. Maybe they don't need to eat at all."

He hesitated. It was sounding a bit too much like down here. No need to eat. Nothing to hunt you. It confused him for a moment. This couldn't be a kind of paradise, could it? No, the thought was too creepy.

"A sun," he went on with more passion, getting warmed up. This wasn't really so different from his usual worst-case-scenario imaginings – just in a happier direction. "There would have to be light, and maybe lots of moons for the night, different shaped ones so you could look up into the sky and see round ones and crescent ones and star-shaped ones all at once."

"I like that," Luna murmured. "What else?"

"Everyone around you," Griffin said. "Everyone you love, everyone who loves you."

"That's good. What if they're still alive?"

"Maybe that doesn't matter."

"You can't be both places at once," she said reasonably.

"Well, maybe once you go through the Tree, time's different, and it goes by so quickly it's like you hardly have to wait at all."

"Hmmm."

"Look, I'm doing my best here," Griffin said.

"No, it's really good," she said. "I can see it in my head now. Friends, too. Skye and Rowan, and Falstaff."

"Well, OK, if you really want those little hairballs hanging around," Griffin said. "Frankly, I always found them a bit irritating."

"Maybe they'll be more interesting dead," Luna said.

"Probably. I like dead bats. Some of my best friends are dead, you know."

She was giggling, just the way she used to, and it made Griffin's heart swell.

"And you'll be there with me, too," she said firmly.

Griffin said nothing, pleased she was singling him out, even if he did feel terribly unworthy of her affection.

"And we can do things together," she went on. "We can go anywhere, big journeys all over this big new world."

"Well, I'm really more a roost-at-home sort of bat," he said, "but, sure, why not. If it makes you happy."

She was silent for a moment. She winced, then: "What if it's not like that?"

"No, no, it'll be great."

"What if it's *worse* than this place?"

"Um, no. It couldn't be. Not possible."

"What if I'm all alone, and have to wait a long time for anyone I know to show up? You're just a newborn, and my parents could live another thirty years. I don't want to be all by myself."

"You're starting to sound like me," Griffin said. "Worrying's *my* thing. And frankly, I'm better at it. You and your *little* worries – I laugh at them!"

Luna gave a low chuckle.

"I know what awaits me," said Nemo, pulling alongside, "if you don't mind me horning in on your chatter. A big stretch of river, as broad as you could hope for, and enough fish to make the water boil."

Yorick looked back over his wing, "You're assuming, my soggy friend, that we will be eating in this next world."

"To be sure, my boy! What greater pleasure is there than to eat well! And not the fake food they supplied for us here, but real food. Trout, salmon, bass!"

"Interesting," said Yorick with a dismissive smirk. "A most inspiring view of the afterlife."

"So what's it you're after, then?" Nemo said. "Do tell us."

"It's obvious, isn't it?" Yorick said. "I want to be whole again. I've endured centuries with this crippled wing, and the pain it brings – I know you scoff at my suffering, *Oh there goes Yorick again about his wing*, yawn! But all I want is a world without the constant nag of it. I could quite happily spend eternity staring at wood lice so long as I could do it without pain."

"Fair enough, then," said Nemo, not sarcastically but with genuine respect. "Let's hope in the next world, you'll get fixed up."

"All I ask is a little fairness," Yorick continued. "This place is completely unfair. Let me offer up an example. In the Upper World Nemo got eaten. Chewed up. *Digested.* Unpleasant, I admit. But down here in the Underworld, he got his body back whole. He shouldn't look like anything at all but a pile of bones and gristle."

"I've got to look like *something*," protested Nemo.

"Fine. But me, I only got smashed into a tree, died on impact, and look at me! Look at this wing and shoulder. Still crooked, still throbbing. And poor Luna, she's even worse off. Badly burned and still suffering, anyone can see that! Where's the fairness? Where's the *logic* of it?"

Nemo shook his head. "You've got a good point, my boy. All I can say is thank goodness I'm on the lucky end. And thank goodness we'll soon all be free of this vexing place." After a moment he turned to Murk. "Can't help inquiring about you. What's your new world like? You're hoping there's lots of juicy little bats waiting for you, I wouldn't doubt."

"Perhaps there are different places for different bats," said Murk, with a hint of a smile. At least Griffin assumed it was a smile: he still wasn't used to the dark flash of those teeth.

"Be a bit much if we have to worry about getting eaten, even in this new life," muttered Yorick.

"And you?" Luna asked Java. "Are there orchards in your afterlife?"

"Maybe so, but I was hoping for something completely new."

"Really?" Griffin asked, curious.

"Well, doesn't it seem a touch repetitive? To get the same thing all over again?"

"No! I want the same thing," Luna said stoutly. "I want it to be *exactly* the way things were at Tree Haven. I can't imagine anything better."

"You are young, and should have had more, to be sure," said Java. "But I was lucky enough to live a full life, and now am curious to see another face of the world, for I am hopeful there are many."

Griffin saw Murk nod. "Yes, that is my craving as well."

"And it will be something wonderful," said Java, with such serenity that Griffin felt his mood lighten. But Luna, he saw, made no comment, staring straight ahead. She was trembling.

"You all right?" he asked, moving closer.

"Just all this stuff about it being different," she whispered, as the others went on talking. "Don't know if I want anything else different. I'm not even used to being dead yet in the first place. You don't know what it's like, Griffin."

"I know."

"I don't *want* this."

"You always got through things all right," said Griffin. "You always did. Owls and high winds and lightning. Whenever I was scared, you weren't. There's nothing you're afraid of."

"This," she said.

He didn't like the fact she was afraid. He counted on her to be fearless, to help dilute his own perpetual fear. He could almost feel her anxiety leaking into his already wasted muscles, and he experienced a sting of resentment. How was he supposed to keep it all together by himself?

"What in Nocturna's name is that?" Yorick asked, squinting into the distance.

Griffin pushed up on Java's back. Dead ahead he made out a shadowy grey cliff towering up so high it dissolved into the blackness of the sky, blotting out the stars. But its base looked far from solid, and couldn't be rock because it kept shifting in and out of focus, fading and then coalescing darker. He sniffed: the same scent he'd caught earlier, only amplified. And now he noticed the change in the air too. His eyes, when he blinked, no longer felt as if there was sand lodged behind his lids. Even his parched mouth and raw throat were eased.

"It's rain," said Nemo in amazement. "Listen."

Flaring his ears, Griffin heard a faraway clatter of droplets, and beyond that, a low growing rumble which suggested something bigger and more powerful.

"Bit of a downpour by the sound of it," Nemo remarked cheerfully.

"This wasn't on the map," said Yorick, peeved. "We weren't told about this."

"Passed overhead not long ago," said Nemo. "Down there, look, the ground's still wet."

Water. Without thinking, Griffin leaped off Java's back, nearly getting swatted by her left wing, and dropped earthward in a jerky spiral. Nemo was right. The ground, normally cracked and dry, was softened to mud, glistening in some places where the rainwater had pooled.

"Griffin!" Luna called after him. "Wait up!"

He couldn't wait. He wanted water in his mouth, down his throat. He skimmed the ground, watching the water being loudly sucked into the parched soil. Before his eyes, puddles turned into mud, mud turned back into arid dirt. Griffin flew on, only half aware that Luna was now alongside him, and the other Pilgrims were overhead protectively. Spotting another pool, Griffin sailed on, tumbling head over tail in a clumsy landing. This time he was fast enough to plunge his face into the water and inhale. It was real! He felt his tongue softening even as he spluttered and choked more icy water down his throat, not even tasting it. When the pool was sucked empty by the earth and himself, Griffin lifted his head, panting. He ran his tongue around the inside of his mouth, finally tasting the water. Not like the stream back home. This had a strong salty flavour, and it left him a little queasy, yet still thirsting for more, just for the searing liquid cold of it. As he launched himself back into the air, the water sloshed heavily in his stomach.

"Was that good?" Luna asked him.

He nodded. Probably he shouldn't have had so much. But salty water was better than nothing, wasn't it?

"Sorry," he said to the others. "I really needed that."

Together they flew on towards the shadowy cliff of rain. Its low rumble grew, the air shuddering around them. A fine mist pearled Griffin's fur, and a wind kicked at the underside of his wings. Suddenly they were in the rain proper. Griffin felt exultant as it struck his fur, this cold, but welcome reminder of the world of the living. He weaved through the raindrops with Luna, opening his mouth and catching them on his tongue, drinking in mid-air. Luna laughed – a sound he hadn't heard down here nearly enough – and for just a moment, Griffin almost forgot where they were.

Before them the rain intensified into a looming grey wall. It wasn't falling in single drops any more, but in thick, drenching splashes that made Griffin dip down whenever he was struck. All around him the other Pilgrims were making slow progress, trying to steer their way through the deluge.

"I don't like this," said Yorick above the roar of the rain. "We should go around or wait this out!"

"This is nothing," said Nemo. "Look up ahead!"

Griffin blinked, finally understanding. No more than

fifty wingbeats away was a colossal waterfall spilling down from the sky, thousands of wingbeats across. The water sparkled and danced in the starlight. Griffin and the other Pilgrims pulled back, circling.

"Where's it all coming from?" Java wondered.

"A hole!" Griffin shouted. "A hole in the sky! It must come from the Upper World!"

From deep beneath the great lakes, from deep beneath the oceans, the water must be trickling and leaking through the soil and stone, down and down, and finally plunging through some gash in the Underworld's stone sky. Just the idea of it awoke in Griffin a fierce yearning. To fly high, to find that crack, to somehow force his way into it, and swim up. He'd never make it of course. Not without air, not against the colossal weight of all that water.

He could smell the falls. He'd never thought of water having a smell, but here in this odourless world it was almost overwhelming – it brought with it the fragrance of the soil through which it must have sifted, the rock it flowed over, the smell of fish, salt, seaweed. Who knew where all the water had come from, but every drop was packed with tantalizing fragrance. Maybe some of this water had once flowed through the stream near Tree Haven.

"We'll have to go around," Yorick said.

"What if we lose our course?" Java pointed out.

"I say straight through!" Nemo said. "Bit of water never did anyone any harm."

"Except for drowning," muttered Yorick.

"No chance of that," said Nemo. "Look, there's great gaps. I'll see us through, dry as a whale's elbow!"

As Griffin stared at the waterfall, listening, he saw that

Nemo was right: it wasn't really a solid wall at all. It was made up of countless individual streams of plunging water, forming undulating sheets, and spiralled columns. If you watched hard enough you could see the chinks in between them all. The face of the waterfall changed constantly. Whole segments would suddenly dry up, leaving a vertical channel of open air, with only a fine drizzle to remind you of the thunderous torrent that had just fallen there. Elsewhere, without warning, other gaps would snap shut with a thunderclap. Griffin forced a swallow down his throat.

"You're sure about this?" Java asked Nemo.

"Just stay close and we'll nip right through. Won't take a second."

Yorick insisted on being right behind Nemo – as leader, naturally. Java made sure Luna and Griffin went next, and she and Murk brought up the rear

"Don't forget, your path has to be wide enough for me!" the Foxwing called out to Nemo, and he gave her a reassuring backwards flick of his wing.

"Follow me!" he cried.

Griffin soared towards the waterfall. The bellow of it was overwhelming. The salty water felt heavy in his stomach. He *absolutely* did not want to do this. Closer now, and every sinew told him to pull up and away. He clamped down hard on his fear, and concentrated on Luna's wings, letting them be his guide. They were heading right for solid water, and then Nemo swerved and sliced through an opening, and was gone, and before Griffin could even pull in a big breath he too was inside the waterfall.

If he thought it was loud outside, here it was like something that lived within your skull. All around him soared great roaring pillars of water. It was almost completely dark, the starlight blotted out, except for the occasional shaft which broke through and refracted brilliantly through the layers of water and heavy mist.

They flew at a dizzying speed, veering and diving and climbing through the ever-changing innards of the waterfall. Nemo seemed to have an almost supernatural understanding of all this water, knew how to see around it and even through it, to guess when it was about to dry up, and when it was going to plunge down.

"Almost there!" he heard Nemo call out from up ahead, and then Luna braked so sharply Griffin nearly slammed into her.

"What's wrong?" he gulped. Then he saw. They'd hit a dead-end. Nemo and Yorick circled tightly, the fisher bat peering intently at an unbroken wall of water.

"Not too much of a problem," Nemo muttered. "Up we go."

With that, he launched himself into a near vertical climb. Gasping, Griffin followed, Java and Murk close behind him. Higher and higher they went. Surely they couldn't keep going up for ever! They'd hit the stone sky.

Suddenly Luna levelled off in front of him.

"Be quick here!" he heard Nemo calling out. "We've got clear passage but it's not going to last."

Before them, Griffin saw two dizzyingly high walls of water forming a narrow canyon, only these walls were moving, slowly but steadily coming together with an animal roar. At the canyon's end – and it looked a long way away – Griffin saw stars. Sky. The end of the waterfall.

"Fly hard!" Nemo called, already streaking on ahead.

Luna went too, but Griffin faltered for a moment. He forced himself to talk.

"The walls are closing, sort of a crushing water kind of situation, but the rate seems constant, and I can probably make it if I flap hard and it shouldn't be a problem if I leave—"

"Right now!" Murk urged, nudging him as he pulled alongside.

"Come on, Griffin," said Java, "I'll keep pace with you."

Griffin pumped as fast as he could, streaking through the steep canyon. It couldn't have been more than seven feet across, and closing. He concentrated on Luna and Yorick and Nemo up ahead, and beyond them the stars glinting in the open sky. Get there. He blinked as the spray thickened suddenly, and glanced over at the watery walls. They were converging faster, and he wasn't even halfway yet. Six feet across now.

"Quick as you can, Griffin," Java told him.

"Go on ahead!" he told her. "Your wings!" Their span was five feet, and before long the walls would be clutching at the tips.

"I'll keep pace with him," Murk told Java. "You go on."

Griffin wasn't crazy about being left alone with Murk, but there was no time for argument now. Java nodded, and streaked over Griffin, pulling for the end of the canyon, mist spinning off her massive wings.

The walls were so narrow now that Griffin and Murk could no longer fly side by side. The Vampyrum pulled into the lead, looking back frequently over his wing to check on Griffin. The walls weren't so much closing in now as collapsing, sending ever larger spills of water down their sides, swelling outwards.

Up ahead, Griffin saw Nemo streak clear, then Yorick and Luna, and then Java, tilting wildly so the walls wouldn't crush her wings. The noise of the falls was deafening.

"I'm OK!" Griffin yelled when Murk looked back. "Go! You go ahead!" The walls were closing in on the Vampyrum's three-foot wingspan, and he had no choice but to pull ahead, leaving Griffin alone.

"I'm OK," Griffin said to himself now, eyes narrowed against the maelstrom of spray. He had to pull his wings in tight and it made him a bit tippy, but he was almost there. He saw everyone circling in the clear, waiting for him, the stars so bright.

"Hey!" he called out. "Made it!"

The walls toppled, catching his left wing and dragging him back inside the waterfall. He plunged like a hailstone, drenched, the water battering every inch of his body, pounding at his skull until he was afraid he'd pass out but –

Miraculously, he was clear.

He was trapped inside the falls, circling frantically within a narrow shaft of air, water seething all around him. He looked up, hoping to see Java or Murk. How far had he been driven down? He called out, but his voice echoed dully and was instantly spirited away. He couldn't stay still. The entire waterfall was moving slowly but steadily on its course across the Underworld, and he had to move with it. His stomach clenched and he thought he was going to be sick.

"Hey!" he called again, veering away from a twisting spigot of water. "Java! Luna!"

He fluttered along through the watery maze, spraying sound straight up, making sure nothing was about to crash down on him. His ears pricked. Muffled voices wafted from all sides.

"Griffin . . . Griffin . . . Griffin . . ."

Thank you, he thought, limp with relief. They were looking for him.

"I'm here!" he called out. "Over here!"

Jaws plunged through a wall of mist, carrying with them a body and a ferocious set of wings. The Vampyrum's rear claws sank into his back with a scalding coldness. Griffin flailed at the cannibal, but this time his blows had no power. His wings crumpled as if they'd struck granite. Not strong any more.

The Vampyrum bit.

Griffin felt the teeth plunge through the flesh and muscle of his shoulder, and he screamed. Not simply from the pain, but the knowledge that this creature's fangs were gouging deep into him, taking away part of his life.

"Zotz!" the Vampyrum roared. There was blood on his teeth. *My blood*, Griffin thought, staring in stunned horror. From his wounded shoulder suddenly sprang a coil of sound and light: his life, unwinding from his body.

"Hear me, my Lord!" bellowed the Vampyrum. "I have your sacrifice!"

At once Griffin felt a presence swirling around him, slow and powerful, pawing at him, lapping hungrily. Griffin could not fill his lungs to scream.

"This life," shouted the Vampyrum to the unseen monster, "I release for you!"

He reared back, jaws open for the fatal bite, when Griffin saw a wisp of his glowing life touch the Vampyrum's face. His nostrils flared greedily and a tendril of the light was sucked in. Griffin heard the Vampyrum growl with pleasure, and at that moment, the creature's grasp loosened for a split second.

Griffin thrashed, ripping free and skidding against a plunging wall of water. His collision unleashed a small tidal wave against the Vampyrum, knocking him backwards. Whimpering, Griffin darted headlong down one crushingly narrow corridor after another, hoping the cannibal bat would be too big to get through. Strangely, there was no pain in his shoulder and he glanced over hopefully. His vision swam with nausea. A blazing aura surrounded the ugly wound, blood trailing off the tips of his fur, spinning brightly into the water and blinking out like drowned fireflies.

Dead-end. He whirled round, and saw the cannibal flying straight for him. A sheet of water plunged down between them, sealing Griffin within a hollow shaft. But through the undulating fissures in the wall, he could still make out the dark shadows of the cannibal bat, circling, waiting.

"I can see you!" he heard it yell. "I can see your glow! And I'm going to wrench it from you and offer it up to my god!"

Nearly choking with fear, Griffin looked for escape. He could barely circle without his wings grazing the surging water that encased him. Slowly he started to spiral upwards, not making much progress, telling himself he was putting distance between himself and the cannibal.

"I'm still with you," came its voice beyond the water, right near his ear. He sprawled back in alarm. If only the wall behind him would dissolve so he could get away! He climbed higher and to his horror, the slab of water between himself and the cannibal was beginning to thin, slivers opening all along its face. Behind him, too, the water was weakening, though not nearly enough for him to risk darting through.

Rain startled him, and he looked up and saw, directly

overhead, a deluge plummeting towards him, carrying the weight of all the earth's oceans. Wildly he looked at the water around him, still thinning, but not fast enough. Through the cracks he saw the dark flash of the Vampyrum's fur. The torrent overhead howled down, seconds away.

All at once the walls of water encircling him dried up. The Vampyrum angled himself, lifted his wings, and with a single powerful stroke, launched himself straight at Griffin's throat. Griffin recoiled, flapping himself backwards, feet pummelling air and—

The waterfall from the stone sky hit the Vampyrum with a sickening crack, and he disappeared, driven down by its catastrophic force.

"Griffin!"

He said nothing, afraid to speak now, in case some new terror was stalking him.

"Griffin!"

He flinched as a small bat swooped towards him. Luna. She sucked air sharply through her teeth. "Your shoulder," she said.

Numbly he stared at the wound, still glowing, leaking blood. He wasn't thinking very well. Luna said something about everyone looking for him, and how they had to get out of here, and he followed her like an obedient newborn through the waterfall.

After a minute he realized the general roar was definitely behind them now, and the water fell less thickly, and soon it was heavy rain, then a drizzle, then just mist, or maybe that was his own bleary eyesight. The pain had started in earnest now, inhabiting his whole left shoulder and wing, pounding in time with his heart.

"You OK? Griff?" Luna was saying to him, maybe for

the second time. She seemed to be talking very loudly.

"Where are the others?" he asked, looking around. In the distance he saw the massive wall of water spilling from the heavens, moving away from them now.

"We'll find them," Luna said.

As Luna called out for Java and Nemo and Yorick, Griffin stared at the strange new landscape spread before him. Gouged from the crumpled plains were a network of shallow valleys whose walls glowed with bands of phosphorescent stone. From the valley floor rose countless stone towers, some tapering to a single sharp spire, others craggy and misshapen, some flat-topped. All of them were notched with many small entrances.

"Griff," Luna was saying, "we've got to go look for them, OK?"

"I've got to land." His stomach clenched and he vomited. "Oh no," he said, starting to cry. All his water.

"Don't worry about it," said Luna. "You're just tired. Let's have a rest. Looks like there's plenty of places down there."

Griffin angled down into one of the valleys, aiming for a conical stone tower with a broad ledge cut into the side. He came in too heavily and fell on his wounded shoulder with a cry of pain. It was still bleeding freely, and he watched as a fat drop of blood hit the stone and sizzled before being sucked up. Griffin clenched his teeth to stop them chattering. *Stop bleeding*, he told himself.

"The elders will know what to do," he mumbled.

"What?" said Luna.

"They know how to do things with leaves and berries and stuff," Griffin said, wondering why Luna kept wobbling in and out of focus. The glowing walls of the valley were moving, accelerating past him with terrific speed.

"They should've saved you, too," Griffin told Luna thickly. "I thought they were going to. Guess they didn't have enough berries and stuff."

"Griffin?" Luna was saying to him insistently. "You OK?"

"Yeah," he said. "Just stay still."

Then the world undulated and crumpled up.

THE VALLEY

The soaring walls were carved with so many niches and ledges that at first Griffin thought he was inside a tree. Holes overhead let in shafts of brilliant starlight. Bats roosted everywhere, talking and grooming themselves, just like Tree Haven at sunrise.

He was on all fours, lying on a bed of smooth stones. Just lifting his head was exhausting. Cold lapped through him. Pressed close to his side, Luna watched him.

"Hey," she said. "You picked a good place to pass out. Turns out there's a big colony down here. They seem pretty friendly. They helped me carry you inside one of the towers. Even got these stones for you so you'd be more comfortable. I think they're a little freaked out by your glowing."

Griffin saw that most of the bats – every species under the moon it seemed – were staring at him, whispering amongst themselves.

"I think they've sent for their elder," Luna said.

"What about Java?"

Luna just shook her head. "They'll be looking for us. Java wouldn't go on without us. How do you feel?"

"Weak." He lifted his wing and was punished with a slash of pain through his shoulder and chest. The wound was still bleeding, thought not quite as freely, and the surrounding area was raised and scorched-looking. "I don't think I can fly like this."

"You just need some more rest."

"Ah, so this is the glowing newborn." The voice came from overhead as three bats fluttered into the tower and roosted on the wall overlooking Griffin and Luna.

"My name's Dante," said a male with a broad collar of bright fur around his shoulders and chest. "I'm one of the elders here." When he flared his large pale ears, the starlight backlit the tracery of fine veins in their skin, making them flash silver. His nose was a shape Griffin hadn't seen before, a bit bulbous, but he was surprised at Dante's fur. It was sort of like his, alternating streaks of bright and dark all across the back and chest. Dante's quick eyes darted over every inch of him, and he gave a little shake of his head.

"I wish I had something to heal your wound, but this world, as you know, is not concerned with the living."

"You know, then," said Griffin, surprised. He'd worried they would be like the Oasis bats, still convinced they were alive, and that he was some kind of demonic ghoul.

Dante smiled, amused. "Oh yes. We all know where we are and *what* we are. But it's not often we see one of the living. Occasionally there is an earthquake in the Upper World, and some unlucky bat gets dragged down a fissure and dumped here."

"That's what happened to me, exactly!" said Griffin.

"And me too," Dante told him. "Over a thousand years ago."

Griffin stared in confusion. "And—"

"Yes, I died down here."

"But why haven't you gone to the Tree?"

"I decided to stay."

"Here?" Griffin said, unable to keep the squeak of amazement from his voice. He looked at all the bats roosting on the stone walls of the tower: hundreds, presumably more in the other roosts. They were *choosing* to stay in the Underworld?

Dante laughed. "I take it you find this an unappealing idea."

"But the Tree . . ." He looked in confusion at Luna. Was it possible that Dante didn't understand the Tree was a portal to a new world?

"We know that many of the dead choose to enter the Tree," said Dante, "and we wish them well. But we prefer to make our home here."

"But I thought we were all meant to go," Luna said. "That's what Frieda said."

"Yes, we know Frieda well, and before her, the hundreds of other elder Pilgrims who have spread their message across the Underworld."

"You don't believe her?" Griffin asked, icy doubt beginning to creep through him.

Dante looked away thoughtfully. "This will sound terrible to you. From our highest tower in the valley I can see the Tree's glow and believe me I have stared at it, and thought about it a great deal in the centuries I have been here. We have seen countless bats stream across the sky towards it, and talked to many, said goodbye to most, and welcomed a few to remain with us. Facts are all I trust. And it's a fact that once a bat enters the Tree, he does not come out again."

"Because they go to the new world," said Luna impatiently.

"Perhaps. But how do you know? You might *believe*. But you do not *know*."

Griffin shifted uncomfortably, his shoulder and wing pounding. Dante was right. Not even Frieda could tell him what awaited them on the other side of the Tree.

"We all grew up thinking Nocturna was looking over us," said Dante. "We never saw her, she never spoke to us. We assumed she was good and kind and cared for our well-being, but who is to know? And if she even exists, who knows what she meant for us in our deaths? Perhaps what awaits us beyond the Tree is worse than this place."

"Couldn't be!" said Griffin.

Dante tilted his head thoughtfully. "You may be right. Perhaps the Tree contains a world fabulous beyond our comprehension. But it may also be a place of total death that puts an end to all movement, all thought, all consciousness."

Griffin shuddered, thinking of the terrible river of silence.

"What the Tree holds is a question we can never answer," Dante said. "Whereas we know *exactly* what we have here. And we are happy with it."

"You are?" Luna said.

"When I first died, I felt much the same as you. But I spent years travelling this world and there is beauty in it. Perhaps not the same kind as we once knew. But it is still a place of wonders. The seas of sand, the waterfall you must have passed through to reach our valley, the dazzling play of starlight, the glow of these rock formations we chose to roost within. But these are not the main reasons we stay. All of us here have one thing in common: we are content in our deaths."

Griffin looked at Luna, uncomprehending. How could anyone be happy being dead? It was the worst thing imaginable.

"Strange as it may seem," Dante said, "with death also comes the death of fear. Fear is the greatest tyrant of all in our lives. It makes us greedy, selfish, violent. Here, we don't have to worry about food, or the elements, or predators."

"What about the Vampyrum?" Luna asked.

"They never bother us here. The waterfall's passage encircles us, and seems to protect us. Or perhaps we've just been happily forgotten. We're left to ourselves entirely, and we want for nothing. Best of all we have each other for companionship, and we have an eternity to talk and think about the universe."

"But not be a part of it," said Luna coldly.

"How is what we have here any less part of the universe than the Upper World, or any possible world to come? Life and freedom are in the mind. Where else do things exist?"

"I want to smell things and eat things and see real things," muttered Luna angrily.

"Here we get to be our truest selves," Dante told her.

"I'm nothing like my real self here," Luna said.

"That's because you haven't accepted what you are. In time you will, and then know perfect peace."

Griffin said nothing, but he was listening intently. He felt so tired of this journey, of always being afraid. Afraid of dying. Afraid of everything. What a relief it would be to just stop being afraid. To free his mind of all those mights and coulds and woulds which beat down at him like a perpetual hail. He looked around the inside of the stone tower, and saw bats roosting happily together in little groups: males and females and newborns, just like families.

"Dying here is nothing to be afraid of," Dante was saying to him. "A blink of the eyes. No pain. And then an eternity of peace."

"He's going to be fine," Luna said tersely. "He just needs some more sleep."

"His wounds won't heal," Dante replied. "Mine didn't."

"He'll be *fine*," she insisted.

Dante gave a gracious nod. "You are welcome to stay as long as you need."

"Won't be long," Luna muttered.

Griffin felt numbingly tired, and the cold of his wound seemed to have gone deeper into his body. Pain with every heartbeat. Another drop of blood slid from his fur and hit the stone ledge, sparking light before it disappeared with a hiss. With a quiet dreadful certainty he knew he would die if he didn't escape soon. But was the Tree really an escape after all?

All he wanted right now was the oblivion of sleep.

He opened his eyes with a start and saw Luna beside him.

"Am I—"

"Don't worry," she said, and looked genuinely relieved. "You're still alive. But we should get going now."

"Can't I just sleep a bit more?"

"You've already been asleep a while." Luna looked away, sighed, then said, "Griff, you don't look so good."

"This is supposed to surprise me?"

"Your glow."

"What about it?"

"It's fading. When you were sleeping, it was almost . . . maybe it was just me, but it would lift off your body a little bit, like it did when the bats attacked you."

"Oh," he said numbly.

"Come on, Griff, up you get!"

The Tree. Just another journey. And what if it led nowhere at all, or somewhere worse. He remembered the monstrous burning image from Frieda's map. Go inside and maybe they'd just be turned to ashes. He looked at all the other bats, contentedly roosting within their stone tree, grooming one another, talking. They could talk for ever here. He liked talking. He was good at it. Luna said so. He'd fit right in.

"Do you think my father's even alive?" he asked her.

"If he is, he'll make it out. If he's dead, there's nothing we can do about it. Either way he'd want you to get out."

But Griffin knew there was something more holding him back.

"Maybe I should stay with you," he said desperately.

"What d'you mean? I'm not staying here!"

"It just doesn't seem fair if I get to go home, and you don't."

"Come on, Griff, that's silly!"

"How about this?" he said, the words spilling out almost faster than his thoughts. "I die here, then we'll go together, OK? Into the Tree. We'll end up in exactly the same place. You won't be alone. It's only fair!"

"What's all this stuff about *fair*?"

" 'Cause it's my fault you're dead!" he blurted. He couldn't hold it back from her any longer. It was choking him, like something caught in his throat. In his heart.

"What're you talking about?" she said quietly.

"I dropped fire on you."

"But you said—"

"No. We were stealing fire. My idea, so I could impress everyone, and I was carrying a burning stick from the Humans' fire in my claws. But it burned down faster than I thought, and I was worried I was going to get scorched, and I dropped it. I dropped it right on top of you, and you caught fire."

Luna said nothing, staring past him.

"Luna?" Griffin said miserably. It wasn't just the guilt, the deception, that had made him tell. It was something selfish too. He wanted to confess, to be free of it; he wanted her to tell him it was OK.

"So you didn't know I was underneath you," she said dully.

"I can't remember," he said, feeling desperately unhappy, "I don't know."

"You just felt it burning your claws, so you dropped it." She was so calm and understanding. He'd hoped it would be this way. She would understand and tell him not to worry about it.

"It just happened. I didn't even think about it. I just opened my claws and it fell."

"You didn't have time to check underneath."

"No."

"You couldn't have taken a split second just to look?"

Griffin stared at her, not breathing.

"You couldn't have just *flicked* it off to the side so it wouldn't hit me?"

"I . . . I guess I could've . . ." he stammered. "I didn't think . . ."

She laughed, but it wasn't a nice laugh, not the kind she always made back home. "This is so *unfair*! I got killed because you were too gutless to look or hold on a second longer!"

"I'm sorry. I know. It was terrible." He'd wanted to make it disappear somehow. But there was no getting away from himself, from what he was and always would be: a coward. How could he have expected her to forgive him?

"Lightning would have been OK," she said, "and getting hit by a burning branch, that was a good story, Griffin. But some stupid accident like *this*? And *I'm* the one who dies! And you're alive! And you don't even *want* to be alive! You just want to stay here with these other dead bats!" She was shouting even louder now, flanks heaving, and for the first time in his life, Griffin felt afraid of her.

"I'm sorry," he said again.

She whirled on him. "You don't want it? Give it to me!"

"What?"

"Your life! It's mine anyway. I want it back!"

"Luna—"

She pounced, batting him with her wings. " 'Cause of you, I'll never see my mother again, I'll never get to be alive ever again!"

He couldn't bring himself to fight back; it felt wrong. She was so angry and he deserved it, and he just tensed up into a ball, flattened his ears, wings wrapped around himself, taking her blows.

"You and your stupid glow!" she was shouting. "I want that glow!"

He felt her teeth yanking at the fur between his shoulders, then bite deeper. He thought of his aura, lifting from his body, and fear pumped through him.

"Luna! Stop it, Luna, you're hurting me!"

"It's not fair!" she wailed, thrashing at him again and again. "You think dying solves your problems? That's just *giving up*!"

"Like you in the cave!" Griffin shouted back. "Remember? You wanted to give up, too!"

One of her claws gouged his wounded shoulder, sending a terrifying jolt of pain through his whole being. Without thinking, he thrust open his wings and bared his teeth, hissing. She scrambled back a few wingspans, staring, panting. She looked as though she'd just woken from a nightmare.

"Oh," she breathed. "Oh, Griffin . . . I'm sorry." Her face crumpled.

"It's OK."

"No." She was wagging her head in horror. "That was disgusting. I can't believe I . . . just like those bats back in Oasis."

"No. You just panicked, that's all," said Griffin. "Anyone would have done the same."

"Did I hurt you?"

"Scared me."

For a long time they said nothing, catching their breath.

"But I'm sort of glad you did it," Griffin admitted.

"Why?"

"For showing me I want to live," he said. "I don't want to die here."

Dante led them to the tallest stone tower in the valley, its peak thrusting above the luminous crumpled hills. Every wing stroke hurt, and it took Griffin two tries to roost from the ledge at the tower's summit.

They couldn't see the Tree itself, just an angry glow pulsing above the horizon. Occasionally a band of intense

Firewing   255

flame, thick as a rainbow, would arch through the sky. Griffin flinched and looked at Luna, but her face was stony, unreadable.

"That is your Tree," Dante said. "Not far, perhaps ten thousand wingbeats."

"Thank you," said Griffin, wondering if he would be able to make it.

"Good luck," Dante said. "I hope it is all you wish for."

Half-buried in mud, Goth woke. Opening his eyes was all he was able to do. The impact of the waterfall, and his collision with the ground, had broken every dead bone in his body. He felt nothing.

For a third time he had failed to kill the newborn, and it was almost impossible for his mind to grasp this. He bellowed despair through his shattered jaws and splintered teeth. He had failed, and he would not be given another chance. All that awaited him now was an eternity of suffering in the acid whirlpool within Cama Zotz. If only he could drag himself from this mud so he could accept his fate with dignity.

A wind stirred around him.

"Goth . . ."

He shut his eyes and waited.

"Do you really think me so merciless?" said Zotz. "I am not without pity. You have suffered in the service of your god, and that is not something I choose to punish."

Goth heard a snap, and suddenly felt his spine again, sensation pouring along it like a flooded river, coursing through the rest of his thawing body. His mangled limbs sang with pain, but one by one he felt his bones fusing together, the long fingers of his wings, his hips, his ribs, his jaws, knitting and healing.

He pulled himself from the mud, flexed his wings.

"Come," said Cama Zotz, "there is work yet to be done."

And Goth felt himself lifted high on a powerful current, and propelled effortlessly across the skies of the Underworld.

THE SPIRE

Hewn from the face of the cliff, the cathedral looked unreal, a mirage projected by Shade's fevered brain. He tried to blink it away, but it remained. Two massive twin towers flanked the entrance, and further back along the high vaulted roof, a central spire soared into the air, crowned by a cross. It was a sight so familiar he gave a hoarse chuckle of pleasure. In the northern city of the Humans, not so far from Tree Haven, was an almost identical cathedral, and in its spire he'd found refuge as a lost newborn.

He'd been flying hard for hours now without a rest, over a strange crumpled landscape of luminous hills and shallow valleys. Earlier, near the shores of the dark river, at the two stone horns, he'd picked up his son's echo image – and his beseeching voice calling to him. At the sight and sound of his son, he'd muttered thank you, over and over again. And to his relief, he had also picked up traces of Luna and Java and the other Pilgrims. It made his mind easier to think they had found each other and were travelling together for the Tree.

Now the cathedral lay directly in his path, and he found himself flapping eagerly towards it. Then he braked. There was something ominous about the sight of this very

Human structure in a place without Humans. Who had carved it from the rock face, chiselled its mighty towers? Against the stone he caught a wrinkle of movement, and saw a small bat scuttling across the spire's base, and through an opening beneath one of the gargoyles. Tipping himself into a slow dive, he pumped his wings, gaining speed. He did not want his son in there.

"Griffin!" he shouted, but his son didn't hear him. He had already disappeared inside.

Shade made a quick circle of the spire – a stone gargoyle crouched motionless at each corner of the base – before coming in to land. He braked, flipped upside down, and grabbed hold of a bony protrusion of stone. Fearfully he gazed up at the gargoyle peering down at him, and his breath jolted. The gargoyle was a Foxwing, and looked disconcertingly like a giant twin of Java. The expression on the frozen face was one of horror. Shade turned away, and clambered through the same small opening his son had taken.

"Griffin!"

No answer. Why wasn't he answering? Inside, the spire was completely dark, windowless. Shade lit it with sound, sweeping for his son. In the centre was a tight weave of wooden beams, huge bulbs of metal suspended on ropes. It was eerie how similar it was to Zephyr's spire in the Upper World. Shade half expected to see the old albino bat, smiling benevolently down at him.

"Here I am!"

Hanging from a beam high above him was Griffin, all alone. Shade moaned in relief, flying towards him. He didn't want to waste any time.

"Griffin, we need to get out of here. Where are the others?"

"Outside. Didn't you see them?"

"No."

"You must've. The gargoyles."

His son was smiling in a way that unnerved Shade. The smile didn't fit his face, seemed too large, all lopsided. Shade's skin crawled as he remembered the Foxwing gargoyle. And the other three? Yorick... Nemo... Murk... all turned to stone?

"Griffin, what's going on?" He had almost reached his son, ready to roost beside him.

His son's body ruptured, fur and flesh exploding into tiny motes of sound and light. At the same time a new, bigger body swelled through the remains of the old, a powerful chest crackling out through Griffin's small ribs, huge wings unfurling to a three-foot span. Shade reared back in mid-air. Through his son's face thrust a terrible new face with a long snout, spiked nose, and a crest of bristly fur atop the skull.

Goth shook free the residue of Griffin's skin, and leered down. Shade knew what he'd just seen was a sonic illusion, and yet the image of his son being torn asunder was so terrible that his eyes and ears skittered desperately around the spire, looking for the remnants – as if he might, if quick enough, gather and mend all those tiny pieces.

He was still stunned when Goth struck, slamming him down to the floor, pinning him on his back. Somehow Goth was heavier now, Shade could tell that at once. How could the dead get heavier and stronger?

"Where is he?" he shouted up at Goth. "Where's my son?"

"Limping his way towards the Tree. With the other newborn."

Get out. Get to him. Spraying out desperate volleys of echoes, Shade saw that there was only a single exit from the spire, the same tunnel he'd come through. With a great inhalation of breath, he aimed at Goth's chest and let fly a bellow. The blow jerked Goth several inches up into the air, long enough for Shade to flip on to his belly and launch himself. He streaked towards the tunnel exit, pulling in his wings so he could sail right through it.

Like an eyelid snapping shut, the opening sealed itself, and Shade hit the stone, crumpling. Goth's laughter reverberated painfully in his skull. Again he took to the air, not wanting to be an inert target. He was sealed with Goth inside this spire, though he knew they were not entirely alone. He sensed another presence, slithering invisibly through the air, through the stone around him. It could only be Cama Zotz who had cloaked Goth in his son's form, sealed the opening with such ease. Frantically Shade soared around the spire, searching for exits, searching for Goth. The ceiling began to glow with sonic pictographs: a feathered serpent, a jaguar, a pair of eyes without pupils.

From above, Goth streaked down at him with deadly intent, and Shade peeled off to the right, veering through a skinny gap between wooden beams. That was something he still had, his smallness. He clung beneath a plank, trying to suck air into his nostrils silently, hearing the clatter of Goth's wings as he wheeled.

"I was worried I had lost my chance to feast on you, Shade!"

Shade said nothing, trying to think. His only way out was blocked. He'd been lured here for one brutally simple purpose, to be killed. He pressed himself harder against the wood to stop himself shaking. It wasn't just *him* shaking; the wood beneath his claws shivered as if it were a living thing, newly aware of his presence. In alarm, Shade scuttled further along. But everything he touched now seemed bizarrely malleable, like some kind of spongy vegetation.

"But you mustn't think this is simply vengeance," Goth shouted overhead. "Certainly I'll enjoy eating you. You've been no end of misery to me. But that's the least of it. It's not really personal at all."

Personal to me, Shade thought as he scrambled along. *Getting eaten is very personal.*

"You're just unlucky enough to be alive in the world of the dead," Goth was saying now: "And I need your life to get back to the Upper World so I can serve my god."

Shade wondered how he could possibly survive this.

"You can't hide for ever!" Goth called out. "I never thought you were a coward!"

The beam to which Shade clung suddenly became animate, and an eye and mouth opened in the wood, bulging towards him. With a grunt of surprise, Shade sprang free, and was out in the open again. He felt Goth's barrage of sound pass over his body, and knew he'd been sighted.

"*I'm* not the coward!" Shade yelled furiously. "Isn't this easy for you, being helped by your god? Cloaked by him. Having him trap me here!"

"Ah. But you have *life* in you! And your own tricks to play. Don't think I've forgotten. Your tricks robbed me of *my* life and victory, and my god of his dominion over the Upper World!"

Shade sprayed a veil of sound around himself, deflecting Goth's echoes, and making himself temporarily invisible. He couldn't keep it up for long, the effort was incredibly draining, and he remembered how Zotz had once stripped his invisibility from him like a snakeskin. At any moment he could be exposed.

Shade flew straight for Goth and felt his fear harden into a grim, terrible resolve. He was being forced to fight. There was no other escape. He sensed a pulse of bloodthirsty anticipation in the air, as if Zotz were watching with greedy interest. What chance did he have against a creature who was already dead?

Almost there. Goth's head was whipping from side to side, spraying sound. He must have heard Shade's wingbeats, for he tensed, flaring his wings protectively. Shade rolled past, and landed on Goth's back, digging in with all claws. Roaring with surprise and pain Goth bucked. Shade held tight. He dragged himself forward. He might not be able to kill this creature, but he could blind it.

He opened his jaws and sank his teeth around the base of Goth's right ear. No ears, no sound sight. Blind. He'd never done this before, never set out to deliberately maim a living creature, but this was survival now. He took another chomp from the cannibal's ear. There was no blood, and no taste, just a cold, leathery texture of this dead flesh in his mouth. It made him retch, but he would not, could not, stop.

"Enough!"

The voice erupted within the spire, its force sucking the air from Shade's nostrils, and plucking him off Goth's back. He tumbled down and hit the floor hard. Before he could flex his legs and wings to take flight again, the stone around him flinched and rippled, and a gaunt, reptilian head thrust up, long jaws snapping. Shade recoiled and turned, but a second enormous head burst from the floor to confront him. Again he swerved, and again another identical head swelled from the stone wall to leer down at him. Any move Shade made to fly was quickly blocked by one of these three giant heads, swaying over him on their snaky necks.

Shade had only to glance at the black, unblinking eyes to know these grotesque white skulls were some form of Cama Zotz, bizarrely emanating from the stone itself. He tensed, waiting for the hissing jaws to tear him to shreds.

"You are impressive, little bat," said one of Zotz's heads.

"Quite a warrior," said another.

"Making up in resourcefulness what you lack in strength and size," the third head hissed.

With every word Zotz spoke came the distant but unmistakable sound of bats screaming, and it set Shade's fur alight with horror. Only death awaited him now, he was sure of it, and he just hoped it would come quickly.

Goth suddenly flew past one of Zotz's heads and settled on the floor near Shade.

"It will give me great pleasure to soar back into the Upper World with your life," Goth told him, rearing back, aiming for his neck.

"No!"

The voice was not Shade's, though it was the same word shrieking in his own mind. It was the voice of Cama Zotz.

"He is not for you, Goth!" hissed one of the god's heads. "You have not earned him. This little bat has bested you."

Shade saw Goth's nostrils flare at this criticism.

"Then let me sacrifice him for you, my Lord."

"I intend his life for another."

"Who?" Goth demanded, obviously forgetting himself. But when Zotz's jaws moved ominously towards him, the

Vampyrum bowed his head and murmured, "It is only that I am surprised, my Lord, by this change in your masterful plan."

Shade watched, even through his own terror, amazed at the sight of Goth fearfully humbling himself. Two of Zotz's heads were turned towards the Vampyrum now, and Shade stealthily shifted his gaze to the third head, hoping that maybe, in this moment of distraction, he might make a break for it. But Zotz's third head was directly behind him, only inches away, watching with unblinking eyes.

"There is no escape for you, Silverwing," Zotz whispered, even as another of his heads spoke to Goth.

"As you have failed, Goth, my plans have changed. I intend Shade Silverwing's life for my Chief Builder. You became acquainted with her at the mines, I believe. Her name is Phoenix."

"She is to have this one's life – for herself?" Goth said, and Shade could hear the consternation and reproach in his voice.

"That is correct, Goth. I needed you to lure Shade Silverwing to me. Phoenix is travelling here now, to claim his life. She has served me well."

"Have I not also served you well, my Lord?"

"Indeed you have. It was your plan which has now inspired mine."

"But now it is Phoenix who will return to the Upper World."

Zotz's heads smiled in unison, laughed through pointed teeth.

"Phoenix is your equal in every way – perhaps even more relentless. She will accompany you to the Upper

World. Should you not have a mate? A means to breed and repopulate the Upper World with my followers?"

Goth bowed his head. "I understand now, Lord Zotz. Thank you. But how am I to rise?"

All three of Zotz's heads turned to Shade as they spoke. "The newborn."

"No!" cried Shade. "Take me!"

"Soon enough," Zotz said. "This is your final test, Goth. The newborn's life is yours. Go now. I will provide a favourable wind for you. And a disguise."

As Shade watched with his echo vision, Goth began to shimmer. His body wizened, his wings shrank, his face collapsed in on itself and began to reform into a smoother, smaller face. A few seconds more and Goth looked exactly like Shade.

"No . . ." Shade breathed.

"Your son will see you again," Goth told him.

"Take me instead!" Shade shouted. His only thought was that the longer Goth remained here, the longer Griffin might have to reach the Tree and make his escape.

"Come on, Goth, how can you turn away from this chance? Isn't this what you always wanted? The little runt who outsmarted you every time, you gutless idiot! Here's your chance!"

Shade saw his mirror image hesitate, flanks heaving hungrily.

"No," Goth said. "It will give me greater pleasure to cause you a greater pain."

"Go," Zotz commanded, and in the spire's roof, a hole opened, admitting a blaze of starlight. Goth flew for it. Shade launched himself in pursuit, but one of Zotz's heads plunged down at him, hissing and snapping, and he had to bank sharply, nearly stalling in mid-air. Circling, he saw Goth, his diabolical double, disappear through the hole in the ceiling. Then the opening sealed itself.

Sobbing, Shade careened around the spire, searching for another way out, a chink in the stone, a rotten plank. Griffin would think it was him. He would see him coming, and be so happy, and perhaps he would fly to meet him. And then . . . Shade grunted at the image before his mind's eye. That was the worst: that his son's last moment of life would be confusion, unable to comprehend why his own father was betraying him.

"Your son will soon be dead," Zotz told him, his gaunt heads looming closer. "And so too will you. This is no tragedy. Death comes to all creatures. And all bats must come to my kingdom. You and your son will see each other again."

The words were spoken seemingly without malice, and Shade, the fur of his face matted with tears, couldn't help feeling a rush of gratitude for this promise of reunion with his son. He stared at the three-headed Cama Zotz, unsettled. He would almost have preferred cruel mockery. He detested compassion from this god who had imprisoned him, and was waiting with him here until his murder.

"And then what?" Shade said. "We'll be enslaved in your mines, I suppose."

"For that, you must blame your own god's tyranny."

"Nocturna?" he said, startled not so much by what Zotz had said, but by the simple fact he had mentioned her at all. "She *exists*?"

"She was my twin," Zotz said. "We were meant to rule equally, Nocturna the world of the living, me the world of the dead. I was content with my role, for I knew the world of the dead would very quickly become the larger and greater kingdom. I ruled well, and loved all my subjects. I gave them an endless night which they could inhabit. I gave them homes like those they were used to. I gave them places where they could remember their past lives eternally. I *eased their pain* – took it away altogether so they could forget and know bliss!"

Shade thought of the vast cave where the bats fossilized and plunged into that terrible river of oblivion. Was that bliss to them?

"But after a time, despite my efforts, some of the dead grew restless. They missed the Upper World. I asked Nocturna if the dead might return; and I could rise and govern my subjects in both worlds. We held a council here in my kingdom. Heartlessly Nocturna refused to let the dead – or me – return to the Upper World. She said it was not the way of things."

Shade felt an uncomfortable pang of sympathy. Wasn't that his own singular wish in this place: escape? Anyone trapped down here for centuries would be driven practically insane with the urge to return to the living world.

"And so," Zotz said, "I killed Nocturna."

Shade exhaled raggedly, not knowing whether to believe this. In his heart he'd always harboured a gloomy and guilty instinct that Nocturna had never existed. She was a mistake, just another legend the elders had confused. But now he felt a pulse of jubilation to be proven wrong, even though Zotz claimed he had murdered her. Maybe this explained her mysterious absence from Shade's world, the fact that she was never seen, never heard, while Zotz was able to sweep over the earth, and guide and strengthen his followers.

"When?" Shade said. "When did this happen?"

"Thousands of years ago. She was vicious in her refusal to liberate me or the dead. So I wrapped myself around her, and choked the life from her, and she died. Her body fluttered like a leaf to the ground. But it was in her death that she committed her greatest act of treachery. From the spot where she lay, a Tree grew."

Shade's heart quickened.

"The Tree grew tall and strong," hissed Zotz, "until its branches touched the stone heavens. She'd left this living thing behind in my kingdom. Without my consent. It would not die or wither. I could not touch it. I could not even go near it. But the dead who entered the Tree were liberated from my kingdom. Pilgrims began to travel the Underworld and preach that the Tree was a portal to a new world, a world Nocturna had created for them after her death."

"So she lives?" Shade demanded.

"Somehow she managed to release herself back into the Upper World. But you will *never* see her," Zotz said, a note of contempt seeping into his voice. "She exists only in little things. Leaves and dust, dewdrops and pebbles. She has no larger body to inhabit. She spreads herself thinly across the entire world. She does not act. She merely *watches*. And she will contentedly watch both you and your son die. She will not stop it. Your fate has been decided by Nocturna, not me. It is she who has made it necessary for you to die, so Goth and Phoenix might have your lives. Just as it is she who has made the mines necessary by forbidding me any other means of return to the Upper World. Once we were equals. Now I must restore the balance."

"How?" Shade asked. How was it even now he wanted to know things? He and his son were at risk of death, yet he could not shut down his mind, or quell the hope that if he heard more, learned more, he might be able to escape.

"I am not as greedy as Nocturna," Zotz said. "I do not want to destroy or steal her world from her. I merely want to make our two worlds one. I want to break down the barriers and reunite the living and the dead. Is that not just?"

"I don't know," said Shade honestly. What would Nocturna say? But she never spoke anyway, not to him.

Zotz loomed closer with all three enormous heads, nudging Shade's face and inhaling mightily. Shade winced in revulsion.

"Life," Zotz intoned. "That's all I need to rise. Not just one though. A hundred, in the space of a total eclipse. You must remember, little bat, you were the one who prevented my liberation in the jungle. The tunnel I'm digging here will suck all those lives down to me. But I hope that I do no have to wait so long. When Goth and Phoenix return to the Upper World, they will breed, make followers, and instruct them. And once I have a hundred hearts sacrificed to me I will have the power to break through this stone sky, break through to the Upper World, and kill the sun. And then I will bring the dead with me. Billions upon billions of loyal Vampyrum. Nocturna will no longer be able to thwart me."

"But without the sun," Shade croaked, "everything will die. Trees, plants, Humans, animals. All of us."

"Correct," said Zotz calmly. "All will be equal in the kingdom of the dead."

"Then everything will be just like your kingdom now. What would the difference be?"

"The difference is this: I would reign."

"And Nocturna?"

"You think your god is so superior to me. Does she excel at looking after her creatures? I have saved my faithful from death, healed their wings, guided them, spoken to them, shown my *face* to them! What has yours done for you!"

Shade said nothing, afraid of the doubt and despair coursing through him. How would he ever know what Nocturna had done for him? He had been fortunate: he had escaped fatal danger many times; and yet he had experienced terrible things too. Was Nocturna responsible for the good, but not the bad? Or simply nothing at all.

"And how would you reign?" Shade couldn't stop himself asking, tongue heavy.

Zotz smiled, silent for a moment.

"There are many injustices to be corrected. The Humans, who turned away from worshipping me, who have gone on to persecute bats, like yourself. They will be punished. All creatures who have ever been our enemies, the beasts, the owls especially, they too will be made to atone."

"But we're at peace with the owls," Shade said, startled.

"For now," Zotz replied. "Peace is unpredictable. It is best to ensure peace by annihilating all possibility of war." The reptilian flesh of Zotz's three heads wrinkled in amusement. "You think me ruthless. You think me bloodthirsty. I simply do what must be done. Perhaps you are not so different."

Shade laughed hoarsely.

"Why do you laugh?" Zotz asked sharply. "Have you not killed your own kind?"

"No!" said Shade.

"You are wrong! How many Vampyrum lived in my temple in the jungle?"

"I don't know . . ." Shade said, confused.

"Millions!" Zotz roared.

"I did not kill them," Shade said feverishly.

"You dropped the Human's explosive disc on the temple."

"No, one of your followers did! I stopped it."

"Yes. Just long enough for your friends to escape."

Shade remembered the effort of keeping the heavy disc aloft with just sound, the cannibal bat hurling himself against it, the strain nearly rupturing his mind.

"I couldn't hold it any longer!" Shade protested.

"Perhaps you didn't think those million lives were important? That they were all monsters and didn't deserve a second thought? Or did you enjoy the delirious power of killing your enemies, wiping out an entire species?"

"What could I have done?" Shade demanded.

"You could have caught it, you could at least have deflected its path."

Could I? Shade's mind worked furiously. A million lives. Could he have used sound to shunt the disc hard enough to miss the pyramid? Maybe, maybe. But he'd been desperate for time. Exhausted and weak. The cannibals had tried to kill him, his father, a hundred victims waiting to be sacrificed. Should he even feel guilty? Then he thought of Murk, and felt a flicker of shame.

"You too are a killer in your own way," Zotz's heads insisted. "Does that make you good or evil?"

"It was self-preservation," he said weakly.

"Yes. You admit it at least. You have killed. And you would again, just as you would have killed Goth now if needed. Survival. Something we all have in common, even a god. That is why we strive. That is why I will no longer let Nocturna persecute me. I will overthrow her if necessary. That upsets you. But ask yourself: who loves their creatures more, me or Nocturna?"

"Nocturna made everything," said Shade.

"She helped set creation in motion," Zotz corrected him. "But that is all. Her role is finished. She *is* creation. But me, I am the stronger. I have killed her. And I have laboured harder. I have made this place into something from nothing. I have sung this world into being, every mote of it, every second of it. For my own creatures, the Vampyrum, I have made a city and jungle beautiful beyond anything they had in the Upper World. Temples and plazas and rainforest which I made for them block by block, vine by vine. For the other dead I have spun their desires. Yes, I want them to stay here in my kingdom. I give them a place of rest, instead of breeding discontent and confusion like the Pilgrims, setting them on another anxious journey, trying to fathom Nocturna's plan! I have made this place for them with nothing but sound!"

"Sound," Shade breathed.

"Yes," said Zotz, heads rearing back proudly. "Before me, this place was merely a void. And I have filled it for my subjects. I *am* the Underworld."

Shade looked about in amazement.

Just sound.

The stone, the wood, the metal. The entire spire which imprisoned him.

Nothing but sound?

It was almost too much to comprehend. Sound which was so dense, so convincing that it took shape before his mind's eye, perfectly solid objects, real as anything he'd ever known. How could this be just sound?

"It is persuasive, is it not?" Zotz said. "It is flawless."

"Yes," Shade muttered, but to himself he said, *Look harder*.

Very slightly he changed the pitch of his sonic spray, sharpening it, forming it into a spike. He aimed at the stone wall, bored into it with sound, and saw the blocks shimmer ever so slightly, like water touched by a breeze. For the first time in hours, he felt hope. Sweat itching the fur of his brow, he bored deeper and harder, sonically chiselling away the mortar around a large block. With a grating scratch, the stone tilted and then fell away.

Startled, Shade opened his eyes and stared. Part of the wall was gone, admitting a flood of starlight. He saw Zotz's heads rear up on their snaky necks and dart down to the damaged wall, peering in consternation.

Shade flew for the hole. Zotz whirled, three heads, all jaws wide, blocking his path. Shade was going too quickly to stop. He winced, anticipating the collision with lashing tongues and teeth. But the second before contact, Zotz pulled his heads sharply away, and Shade streaked through the hole into open sky.

Starlight rained down on him. He climbed, not understanding what had happened, how he had escaped. It was almost as if Zotz was afraid to touch him. A god, afraid of him? Far in the distance, Shade could make out a hot glow on the curved horizon, licks of fire dancing into the air. At first he thought it was the sun, rising finally, but then he saw that the light tapered into the shape of branches. The Tree.

Before he could even angle his tail and wings to set course, a terrible rumbling drew his gaze down. The cathedral's twin towers flexed and unfurled into massive wings. From the body of the cathedral grew a narrow neck which bulged into an elongated white skull. Cama Zotz in all his might. There was something indescribably ancient about him: his skin like eroded stone and petrified bark, his skull assembled from the oldest bones of the world.

Zotz's massive head lifted swiftly through the air, arching over Shade and twisting to face him, wingbeats away. Shade braked, dipped, tried to avoid Zotz's shrieking jaws, but they kept pace with him, stopping him from flying towards the Tree.

Shade remembered how the god had recoiled from him inside the spire. Still, to intentionally hurl himself at this thing was unthinkable. But—

If everything's sound, Shade thought desperately, *maybe he is too.*

Plunging into a dive, Shade aimed himself at the base of Zotz's throat. Wincing with intense concentration, he sang at the god's flesh, probing, testing if it were real. No, just sound! This gargantuan thing was not the god himself, but some sonic apparition Zotz spun, like the Underworld itself. With a bark, he drove a sonic wedge into Zotz's neck, trying to cut through the tissue. Deep, deeper. Shade slammed against the neck, dug in with his claws, still singing sound.

Zotz's flesh began to spark and melt wherever it came into contact with Shade's body. It was as if Shade were acid to this sonic creature. Zotz thrashed, trying to shake him off, and Shade felt like he was caught in a typhoon. He was still cutting, not quite finished, but his claws tore loose and he went tumbling back through the air. Spinning, he saw Zotz's head whistling straight for him, eyes and jaws wide. Shade veered, and Zotz plunged past, head and neck severed from his colossal body.

Even as it fell, Zotz's head was dissolving like dandelion spore caught by the wind, a billion glimmers of sound raining down towards the winged body of the cathedral, now twitching senselessly.

Go get Griffin.

But as he turned, Shade saw the four stone gargoyles on the corners of the spire. He faltered. Were the Pilgrims really in there? Quickly he flew to the Foxwing's statue and roosted. He sang sound against the rock, felt his way into it, deeper, and then delivered a savage sonic blow. The rock cracked, and the gargoyle's shell split in two. Out tumbled Java, spluttering, her fur covered with dust. Shade didn't hesitate. He went to Yorick's gargoyle and then Nemo's, cracking the giant stone skins that had been cast around them. At Murk's, he hesitated.

"Leave him!" shouted Yorick. "Let him stay with the rest of his accursed kind."

Nemo offered no objection. Not even Java spoke.

Shade took a breath. Let free one more of these creatures into the world? Why should he? But with one final volley of sound he blasted at the stone. It cracked into a hundred fissures and fell away like eggshell. Murk leapt free.

"Thank you," said the Vampyrum shakily.

"You killed Zotz," Java said to Shade in awe. "I saw it."

"Can't kill a god," panted Shade. "He'll be back. I have to get Griffin."

"We're going with you," said Java.

Shade swirled round and pointed himself at the Tree's fierce glow on the horizon. He would fly faster than he'd ever flown before, and he would reach his son in time.

THE TREE

They heard the Tree before they saw it, a high, keening song that sent a strange vibration through every sinew of Griffin's body. It was the sound of wind shrieking through branches, rain battering leaves, the dawn chorus of a thousand birds – something primal and urgent. It might have been frightening had it not been fiercely beautiful at the same time, like the sound of the whole world combined and amplified. It was a homing signal, undeniably beckoning.

"It's the same," Luna said beside him.

Griffin nodded, knowing what she meant. It was a more intense version of the sound his own glow made whenever it separated from his body. The sound of life.

The Tree itself was still blocked from view by endless ranges of high hills. Always they could see its glow in the distant sky, and occasionally they'd catch a glimpse of fiery tendrils licking up towards the stars.

The song drew them on. Griffin's flying was slow and laboured now. He was losing strength in his right wing, and had to compensate with his left, lurching through the sky and squandering his vanishing energy just to sail on a straight course. Luna was even worse off, wincing with every stroke, breath ragged. The wounds on her wings looked as if they'd been scorched anew.

"You OK?" he asked her.

She nodded, too tired to voice a reply.

"We're almost there," he croaked. He'd been saying that for the last couple of hours, trying to keep her spirits up, but was beginning to wonder if they would ever really reach the Tree, or if it was some kind of tortuous mirage: not what you thought, and never even there. Was it just him or was it getting hotter, and was the air thicker here, harder to flap through?

Up and up he struggled along the slope of yet another steep hill, over the crest, and there he faltered, banking into a tight spiral, squinting against the sudden glare of sound and heat.

The Tree was even more enormous than Griffin had imagined. From Frieda's sound map it had looked huge, and he had visualized the tallest fir in the northern forest. But this Tree towered up from the deep valley floor, its trunk as thick as a hundred trees, stretching over a thousand feet into the air. Its network of undulating branches soared higher than the gaunt mountains which enclosed the valley, and spanned the sky. Every inch of the Tree's surface was coated in flame, lapping hungrily at the air. There was no smoke though. The fire wasn't consuming the Tree; the fire *was* the Tree.

"Doesn't look too welcoming, does it?" Griffin said, attempting a laugh.

Luna said nothing. She was circling alongside him, the light from the Tree flashing in her eyes with each turn.

Griffin looked up along the colossal trunk.

"There!" he said. "That's the way inside!"

Halfway up was a knothole. It must have been a huge opening, but in relation to the Tree it looked no bigger than the secret entrance to his nursery roost, just wide enough for Silverwings. The opening shimmered darkly, and he caught the flicker of stars before they faded into the liquidy blackness again. All around the knothole, fire roared.

"Ready?" he said.

Luna could only stare.

Griffin frowned. "Luna?"

"It hurts," she said, "the scars."

Her wings were twitching so badly she staggered through the air.

"I remember now," she said. "The fire. The way it burned me. It really, really hurt, Griffin. I'm not going in there!"

He looked at the wall of liquid flame, and the small black opening in its middle, and felt himself quail. What if Dante were right: merely a place of final death? But Frieda had said the opposite. The sound of the Tree was the sound of his own life. It had to be the way.

"I can't," Luna choked.

"It's OK," he told her gently.

"It's *hot*, can't you feel it? It's gonna burn us up!"

Her terror was so palpable it was like a third winged creature flapping around them.

"It's not going to burn us up," he promised. "It's where we're supposed to go."

"*You* go, then!"

"Listen," he said, forcing her to look straight into his eyes. "What's the worst that can happen?"

She gave a startled snort. "We fly close and get incinerated. We die, not like I am now, but even worse. So dead we can't see or hear or talk. Just feel pain. For ever and ever."

"That's bad," he agreed. "But you know what? I don't

think it's going to be like that. I bet it'll be . . . the *best* that could happen." He didn't know how he was able to say this, or even if he believed it. But he believed he *had* to say it, to *speak* it aloud and hope the words themselves would set something in motion. "Don't look at it," he told her. "Just close your eyes."

"I see it in my head anyway."

"Close your ears too, then. Pin them flat. Just keep your wingtip touching mine and I'll lead you there, OK?"

After a moment she nodded. "I'll try. Just do it for me, OK, Griff? Get me there."

He felt pain and weakness sweeping through his body. But very little fear, he realized with a start. Luna was so much more frightened than him, that somehow his own fear had dwindled, neglected and forgotten as he'd tried to comfort her.

"It's not so far now," he told her.

Leading Luna with his wingtip, nudging her along when she faltered, he lumbered down into the deep valley towards the Tree.

A fierce headwind kicked up, and Shade was barely able to avoid being blown backwards. Java and the others fared no better. The air whistled in his ears, carrying with it a trace of mocking laughter. Zotz, wasting his time, making him too late. Desperately Shade climbed and dipped, trying to find a less turbulent passage – and couldn't help thinking of Marina, how she'd shown him how to find favourable slipstreams as they flew from her island back to the mainland. A lifetime ago. But now, wherever Shade tried, the wind was relentless.

But it wasn't wind at all, he realized suddenly. Just waves of sound whipped up by Zotz. If he could crack sonic stone, the neck of a god, surely he could tunnel through the wind.

"Get behind me!" he shouted to the others. "And stay in a single line."

He listened to the wind, watched it in his mind's eye, and then spun out a sharp wedge of sound before him. The leading edge pierced the gale, sent it spraying over and under him, creating a tunnel of placid air. Shade surged ahead on the resulting slipstream, ploughing the wind away from him as he flew.

A whoop of glee rose up from Java. "Whatever you did, I like it!"

Shade blasted over the landscape, towards a range of hills backlit by the intense glow of the Tree. Not much further, he told himself, hardly any distance at all, a few thousands more wingbeats

He *felt* the rumbling as much as heard it, and looked down to see the earth roiling up into a huge wave, keeping pace with them as they sailed overhead. A crested skull broke the surface, cutting a massive furrow of stone and mud.

"Is that him?" shrieked Yorick from behind.

Yep, Shade thought, but all his energy was still funnelled into pushing sound. Below, Zotz was outstripping them, moving past them into the range of hills, where his massive bulk suddenly disappeared. For a moment all was still. The tremor in the air subsided. Shade counted seconds. They were nearing the foothills now, and angling their path for the summit.

Beneath Shade and the four Pilgrims, the hills trembled, swelled, then began heaving themselves up into mountains. They rose with unreal speed, thrusting from the bones of the earth in a geyser of rubble and dust. A hundred wingbeats ahead of them, a sheer cliff face reared up, blocking their path.

"No!" Shade shouted, as he caught sight of Java, nosing upwards to gain altitude. "It'll take too long to go over!"

"What then?"

"Straight through."

"How?" cried Yorick in disbelief.

"You're sure?" Java asked uncertainly.

"Yes!" Shade swallowed. He wasn't sure at all. He stared at the rock face they were streaking towards. It looked so real, so dense.

Just sound. Only sound. Bend it. Ten more wingbeats would slam him into its surface. He drilled into the rock with sound, and plunged ahead. The noise was deafening as he bored his way through the mountain, the tunnel walls hurtling past all around them, solid as real stone. Inches before his nose, the rock melted against his sonic barrage.

Behind him, he could hear Yorick bellowing in terror. Shade's throat was so raw he tasted blood, but anger held his exhaustion at bay. He would not be held back; he would push and push until they came out the other side. And near the Tree, Zotz would have no power.

His ears popped as they blasted through into open air.

Before them was the Tree.

Griffin took a wide berth around the trunk, waiting until he could approach the knothole in a direct line. He didn't like the idea of skirting past all that blazing bark, didn't want to feel the heat, or get caught in one of those erratic spurts of flame. Also, he didn't want Luna any more scared than she already was.

There. Dead ahead was the knothole, and he was sure he could feel a slipstream, drawing him in.

"We're going now," he told Luna.

"Don't tell me anything else, OK." Her eyes were still tightly shut. "Let's just do it."

"Once we go in—" he began, and didn't know how to finish. He didn't know what would happen or where they would go, but he suspected it would be to different places.

She edged closer, pressed her cool cheek against his.

"Thanks, Griffin. For bringing me all this way."

"I think you brought me, mostly."

"I'm going to see you again. Remember, all the people I love will be there. You said that."

"Yeah," he said. "That's right."

"Maybe not right away, but soon."

"Griffin!"

With a shock of delight he turned and saw his father, flying towards him.

"Dad!" He led Luna in a slow curve towards his father. "This is so *good*," he said. "It's so good you're alive! And here!"

"My son," said his father, and then his fur seemed to shimmer and slip, peeling away from his body, even as it enlarged monstrously.

"Dad?" Griffin screamed.

And then his father, who was not his father, was upon him.

"No!" Shade bellowed from above, flapping so hard he felt his wings would wrench his chest apart. He saw Goth, his sonic disguise rupturing, sailing towards his son, calling out his name, and Griffin was going to him.

"Griffin, don't!" Shade bellowed, but it was too late.

Goth had his son in his talons, jaws clamping into him, wrenching. Luna was veering wildly around Goth, striking at the cannibal bat, but the Vampyrum paid no attention, so intent was he on his murderous work.

"Goth!" Shade roared as he pelted downwards. He had never felt such fury in his life. He was screaming and did not know what he was screaming; the world was nothing but insane noise, threatening to implode his skull. He needed to be faster. Two words only in his head:

Let me.

Dazzling light suddenly swirled out from his son's body with a pure, transfixing wail. Shade gasped as it coursed across Griffin's fur, his limp wings, his pinched face, and then begin to rise off him like a luminous plume of smoke – and Shade knew it was over. Goth reared back, and his son's body fluttered earthwards like a tattered leaf, leaving the intense beautiful bundle of light and sound swirling in the air.

His son's life.

What Shade saw next was the most terrible thing he had ever witnessed – more terrible even than the actual murder. Knocking Luna aside, Goth swirled around the pulsating mist of sound and light, gathered it in his wings, and hungrily shoved his snout right into it.

"No!" Shade cried, rage pouring from his eyes and throat like lava.

Goth opened his jaws, and his chest swelled massively as he sucked the light and sound into himself. Inhaling Griffin's life. In went the light. In went the sound. Into Goth's body.

"Done!" Goth roared when he had gorged on the last flicker.

"We will catch him!" Java shouted off Shade's left

wingtip, but Goth looked up and saw them all plunging towards him. He had a life in him now, but it was the life of a weakened newborn, and Goth must have known it would not be enough to triumph in battle now. He whirled towards the inferno of the Tree and streaked for the knothole.

Shade angled himself to cut Goth off. He would catch him and take him by the neck and wrench Griffin's stolen life out of him, tooth and claw. He swung down behind Goth, not ten wingbeats away, and felt a powerful current pulling him headlong towards the knothole.

"Goth!" he shouted.

With one final stroke, Goth accelerated towards the Tree at a speed that no creature could naturally achieve. To Shade's eyes and echo vision, he became a blur as he blasted through the knothole and instantly disappeared. Gone. Shade braked sharply, fighting the Tree's current with all his might, and pulling away just in time. The flames scorched his belly and the underside of his wings.

He circled, muttering to himself, staring at the knothole, not quite believing he'd lost Goth. Then he turned and flew back to the place where he had seen Griffin's body fall.

Griffin opened his eyes to find his father beside him, face pressed against him.

"You're glowing," Griffin told him groggily.

His father nodded, and Griffin felt the strange warmth of his tears.

"What's the matter?" he asked, confused, and then he saw Luna off to his right, and four other familiar bats whose names he couldn't recall just yet.

"I'm sorry," said his father. "I wasn't fast enough."

Griffin looked at the massive fiery column of the Tree, towering overhead. They weren't far from its base, the earth mounded high around the trunk, some of its fiery roots arching up through the soil. He could feel its heat. He saw the knothole, remembered how close he had been to entering – and now felt the first tectonic stirring of panic within him. He forced himself to listen, and sensed no beating of his heart. His heartbeat stolen by Goth.

He was dead.

Pain awoke in his neck and chest and he winced, looking at his wounds. He would not be going home now. His mind kept shunting the thought aside, not wanting it to get too close, not wanting to understand its full, terrible shape.

"Dad?" he said in alarm. "What's going to happen?"

"It's all right," his father said. "Everything's going to be all right. We'll get you home. Wait here."

Griffin nodded, then a chill seized the place where his heart used to beat. He hooked a wing around his father.

"Dad, don't do it, OK?"

"It's all right, Griffin." Gently Shade pulled away.

"Don't go." Griffin was shaking, his voice weak and desperate. "I wanted to go home with you."

"Do what I tell you now," his father said to him firmly. "Wait here and be ready."

Still Griffin clung to him, wings tight around his chest, but Shade shook him off a second time, and flew before his son could clutch hold. Too weak to take flight himself, Griffin watched helplessly as his father flew away from him, higher and higher until he was just a dark wrinkle silhouetted against the flaming canopy of the Tree.

* * *

Shade flew higher still, counting his wingbeats, wondering how much altitude he'd need. Finally he levelled off. This was good. This would be enough. He looked down, plotted his trajectory and then took a huge breath, held it, listened to himself, tried to feel every part of himself, as if to store it away in some place he could always find it.

I'm sorry, Marina.

He folded his wings against his body, and pitched forward into a freefall.

Griffin saw his father plummeting, like a star flung from the heavens. The impact was almost silent, a soft final thud, but in Griffin's head it exploded like thunder, and it left him gulping in shock. With Luna's help he dragged himself over and looked at his father, broken on the ground, wings tangled, the bones of his wrists and fingers jutting through the membrane. There was blood around his nose and ears, matted in the fur of his face.

"Oh no," Griffin moaned, shambling closer. "No, no . . ." until the words became the sound of one long, wordless moan.

There were little embers of light flaring in the tips of his father's fur, and then, it was as if he'd been ignited. With an ecstatic burst of music, light welled up from his father's body, swaddling him in a cocoon before separating itself from his flesh, and coalescing into a swirling pillar. The sound and sight of it was so impossibly beautiful Griffin laughed through his tears. His father's life. What could be more alive than that symphonic blaze?

But slowly it began to lift, drifting towards the Tree, ushered by the knothole's powerful current.

Griffin saw Yorick flutter tentatively towards the dazzling swirl, sniffing, a look almost of hunger on his face. At once Murk was beside him, wings flared in warning.

"No," the cannibal bat said to Yorick, and the misshapen Silverwing looked ashamed and nodded, dropping quickly away.

"Griffin," Luna was saying beside him, "you know what your father wanted you to do."

He swallowed, knowing, but still shaking his head.

"Take it!" said Luna. "He did it for you. That's yours."

Griffin looked at her. "Yours too."

"There's not enough."

Griffin looked at all that light and music his father had left behind.

"There's enough," he told her.

They flew up to the light together, Griffin groaning with the weight of his new dead body. But the sight of his father's life hovering there gave him the strength he needed. He made it, and opened his mouth and breathed it in – the sound and the light – and he felt it filling him and he smelled all the things he loved – the balsam, the pitch, the earth, his mother and father's fur – and his lungs swelled inside him until he was coughing and choking, and his heart gave a lurch and broke into a startled gallop and suddenly all the sound was gone, and the light too. His father's life coursing through him.

Panting, he looked at Luna in surprise. She stared back, breath held expectantly.

"Am I?" she whispered.

"Both nice and sparkly!" Nemo shouted out happily from below.

Together Griffin and Luna swirled to the ground and he nuzzled against her and smelled the warm scent of her fur, felt the excited beat of her heart.

"I'm alive!" Luna shouted. "I knew it! I could just feel it! It feels different, doesn't it, right away?" She fell silent. "Thanks, Griffin."

"I didn't do anything. It was my dad." He pulled himself over to his father's body, still warm. "How long until he wakes up?"

"You didn't take long," Luna said. "Just a few minutes really."

"We've got time," Nemo said. "Doesn't seem like Zotz can harm us near the Tree."

Griffin followed Nemo's gaze to the mountains ranged around the valley. Their stone bulk throbbed angrily, as though something wanted to break free from them, but couldn't. He settled down to wait. Gradually he felt his father's body cool, and it seemed so still that he began to despair it could ever become animate again. How could this cold shell ever contain any part of his father?

Shade's wings twitched and Griffin yelped.

"Dad?"

Slowly his father's eyes opened. For a long time he stared at Griffin, saying nothing.

"It's me, Dad. Griffin."

His father nodded. "Good," he said, looking at him and Luna. Griffin could see, in his father's weary eyes, the reflection of the glow that clung to them. "Both of you. That's good."

He stirred, trying to gather together his broken wings. "Heavy," he said. "Everything feels incredibly heavy."

"Only for a little bit," Griffin told him, wanting to be useful, wanting to fix things somehow, even though he knew this was something he could never fix. His father's gaze strayed to the four Pilgrims with whom he'd travelled across the Underworld.

"You should get going."

"We'll go together," said Java. "I can lift you to the Tree."

"Thank you," Shade told them. "For helping me find my son."

Griffin helped shift his father on to Java's back, and climbed on beside him with Luna. The Foxwing lifted off with a grunt.

Up they rose towards the knothole. Griffin lay nestled close to his father, not knowing what to say. Within minutes they'd be there.

"When—" he began, but his voice collapsed on itself and he couldn't continue. He coughed, fought the tight grip around his throat.

"Everything will be fine," said his father. "You and I can never really leave each other. One way or another we'll always be together."

Griffin nodded, feeling no consolation.

"You've had quite an adventure," his father said with a grin. "I'm starting to wonder if this wasn't some way to outdo me."

Griffin couldn't even laugh. "Mom's going to be so angry with me."

"Of course she won't."

"It's my fault. All of it. If I hadn't hurt Luna, if I hadn't got dragged down here and made you come after me so that now—"

"Griffin. It was an accident. You did the best you could, and you brought Luna with you, and you made it to the Tree. Without my help."

"But I wasn't brave!" he blurted out. He didn't know why this was so important right now, but it was. "I'm not like you. I'm a coward."

"No," said his father.

"I was always scared. *Always*."

"That's right," his father told him. "Being scared but doing it anyway. *That's* brave."

Griffin stared in surprise and his father pressed his cheek against his son's. "I'm very proud of you," he said into Griffin's ear.

"Ready?" Java asked, looking back over her shoulder at them.

"Ready," said Luna.

Shade nodded.

"I guess," said Griffin.

The others went first, Yorick, then Nemo, then Murk, hurtling straight for the knothole and disappearing so quickly it was hard to believe they'd ever been there. Griffin held on tighter as Java too was gripped by the cyclone current and pulled in fast. He saw the blackness of the knothole racing towards him, shimmer and then –

It was difficult to keep things straight.

Speed was what he was most aware of, the teeth-rattling, eye-jarring speed as they were hurled up through the blazing trunk of the Tree. His sight, his echo vision, was a shuddering mess and he could catch only smears of things. Java, he noticed, wasn't even really flapping any more; in fact she had folded her wings in against her body. The speed made him want to scream; he wanted it to stop. He wanted *off*. They were flying straight up and with his thumbs and claws and everything else he was clinging to his father, and Luna and Java all at once. The cool of his father's fur, the warmth of Luna's. They would be dashed to pieces, burned, whirled into dust!

Ahead of them, he saw a circular portal of flames, and beyond that a great network of flaming passageways, and he realized these must be the Tree's maze of branches spreading across the sky.

"Dad," he said through his wobbling mouth. "Dad?"

"I'm here," came his father's reply, close to his ear.

They shot up into the tangle of branches and something tugged hard at Griffin and he was jarred from Java's back. He felt his father's fur slip through his thumbs. Griffin looked, and his father was gone.

"Dad!"

He tried to slow down, to see where he had gone, but there was no stopping, no changing course. He was being propelled by some hurricane force and it was all he could do to hold his own body together.

"Luna!" he wailed, for he could not see her either.

He was being hurtled down one branch after another, shunted, smacked, twisted until he simply closed his eyes, flattened his ears so he couldn't see, couldn't hear. He tried to hold on tight to himself, afraid that he would die, afraid that he would never get—

HOME

Home.

Goth circled above the jungle canopy, gazing down at the ruins of the royal pyramid. In the many months since his death, the rainforest had reclaimed the heap of scorched and shattered stone, enveloping it with giant ferns and creepers and mist and leaves so that he had almost flown past. This place had once been the sacred temple of Cama Zotz and home to millions of Vampyrum Spectrum.

Keep going, a voice whispered within him, and he flew on, south, deeper into the jungle. He stopped only to drink from a stream and feed on a nest of macaw hatchlings, and he felt his strength swelling through him. When he'd first burst out into the Upper World, he was weak as a wounded newborn. But the mere sight of familiar constellations and homeland had invigorated him.

He flew all through the night, and just as dawn was breaking saw a gap in the misty canopy. He plunged into the forest and there, veiled by jungle, was another pyramid. He had to hack his way through a wall of vegetation to find an opening in the upper temple. The inside was a nest of cobwebs, and he slashed his way through and roosted on the wall. Casting out sound he saw, barely recognizable through dust, carved markings: the jaguar, the feathered serpent, the eyes watching him from the corners of the ceiling.

He directed his echo vision lower and there, lying at the chamber's bottom, was an enormous stone disk. Eagerly, he dropped down to it, brushing away the dried cocoons, insect husks and years of animal droppings until the hieroglyphs flared in his mind's eye. Round and round the disc's surface the images ran, spiralling in towards the centre. Stars, moon, other symbols he didn't understand. But he would.

He would study the heavens so he could predict the next total eclipse. He would wait for Phoenix to emerge from the Underworld and mate with her to create a new royal family. And together they would finally raise Zotz from the Underworld.

Creaking wings overhead made him jerk around.

"Who's there?" he roared.

Clinging to a corner of the ceiling was a small group of Vampyrum, watching him fearfully. Goth smiled.

"Do you know what this place is?" he asked them.

"No," said a young male.

"This is a temple of Cama Zotz, and this Stone contains the future. Did you know that?"

They shook their heads, bewildered.

"Then listen to me," said Goth, "and I will tell you about your god, and all the things to come."

Goth spoke through the day, feeling stronger by the second.

He was alive.

Zotz was watching over him.

His life had just begun.

* * *

Griffin felt wetness against his fur and opened his eyes to find himself flapping through mist. He banked and suddenly he was out of it, beneath a clear sky jangling with stars and a full moon. The moon! He licked his mouth and tasted the water beaded in his hair: not salty this time, just right. It seemed to awaken all his senses: how thirsty he was, how tired, and how hungry.

He circled, looking all around for Luna, and then exhaled with relief when she streamed out from the same bank of mist. They flew as close together as their wingbeats would allow, and looked at the silver forest below them. The scent of it was almost too much for Griffin's nostrils. He was sure he could smell every single tree and flower and animal within a thousand wingbeats.

"Look," said Luna. "We're home."

Below them was his favourite sugar maple, rising up from its little hill on the valley floor.

"Still lots of caterpillars for you," said Luna.

Griffin grinned. He would eat later. Right now all he wanted was to see his mother, and he felt in Luna the same pulse of impatience and excitement to be truly home. In the distance he could see the peak of Tree Haven, and heard other bats in the forest, hunting. He only wished his father were making this journey with them.

With Luna at his side, he beat his wings hard for home.

Shade came out over the forest.

He had no body, no shape that he could discern.

He was just *here*.

And *here* was anywhere he wanted, just by wishing it. He glided low over the treetops and skimmed a maple leaf – not above it, or below it or near it, but *inside* it. With elation he felt his whole being enter the leaf and course through its tissue, through the tiny tributaries which carried water and food, and then down the fibrous twig which held it, and into the strong tendons of a larger branch and then down the wise old muscle and bones of the trunk itself – and finally Shade knew what it felt like to be a tree. He slipped out through the bark back into the forest.

This was great!

He shimmered through the wings of a firefly, danced through some sleeping wildflowers, submerged himself briefly in the stream and came back up, giddy with happiness. When he passed through all these things, it wasn't like he was visiting, it was like he was, for that moment, the thing itself, all his senses guided through it. And it seemed he could pick and choose, which suited him just fine because as much as he'd liked the wildflower, he thought it might be a bit dull to *be* a flower for ever.

The forest hummed and pulsed all around him – and he felt more alive and connected to it than he could ever remember. He became aware of the living creatures out below the full moon. He couldn't quite bring himself to pass through the skunk – he'd do that later when he had more practice – but worked up the courage to fly through an owl, and felt its superb power and skill.

It was not merely the living he felt either. Within every fibre of the forest, he was aware of the others, those who had died and passed through the Tree. He could not see them or hear them or speak to them, but he sensed they were all around him – in the leaves and dust, dewdrops and pebbles – and knew they were equally content.

When he saw the Silverwings, he felt a quick pang of longing. They were streaking through the forest, hunting, and they looked so superb he wished momentarily he could have a living body again. He passed through one, and felt the familiar glee of flight, the anticipation of the hunt for insects. They were all chittering rapidly to one another, and he listened, though he had no need of their words to understand their excitement, and their destination.

Shade too felt a quickening within him, and soared on ahead of the bats, and saw before him Tree Haven. He circled once, just to admire it, and watch all the newborns and mothers racing back to the roost, even though it was far from sunrise. Shade slipped inside and there, in the central hollow of the trunk, was a great gathering of the entire colony, the walls and ceilings all crowded with Silverwings. The elders were roosting in the middle, and beside them were Roma and her child Luna and . . .

He felt himself expand with joy when he saw Marina with Griffin, talking and enfolding each other in their wings. Shade streamed towards them and embraced them both, flowing through Marina and Griffin, his mate and his son, and being closer to them than they could possibly comprehend. He felt all the things in their hearts, and became a part of them, and so the homecoming was his as well.

SILVERWING

Kenneth Oppel

Shade – the runt of the bat colony – is determined to prove himself on the long and dangerous migration south to Hibernaculum. But he is bolder than he is strong, and when he strays from his mother and is lost in a storm, he is on his own.

He knows he must rejoin his colony, and so begins an epic journey – from the pigeon stronghold in the city's spires to the rat kingdom in the caverns of the ground. He meets Marina, a Brightwing; Zephyr, a mysterious albino who can see into the future and the past; and Goth, a formidable giant jungle bat. But who can he trust – and where will his journey end?

'*Silverwing* is top-notch fantasy adventure writing. Go for it.' *The Daily Telegraph*